GAMES FOR COUPLES

Science Traveler Series

Book 9

GAMES FOR COUPLES

Science Traveler Series

Book 9

J.L. Greger

Bug Press

Bernalillo, New Mexico

Games for Couples

Bug Press
An imprint of IngramSpark
Bernalillo, New Mexico 87004
http: //www.jlgreger.com
Copyright ©2021 by J. L. Greger
Cover design by Barbara Hodges for Got You Covered Bookcover
Design©2021
ISBN (paperback): 9781735421407
ISBN (EPUB): 9781735421414
Library of Congress Catalogue Number: 2021911083

DEDICATION

To Bug, my loyal and understanding companion.

To all of the women scared by sexual harassment in the workplace.

ACKNOWLEDGMENTS

I want to thank John Byram for editing this manuscript. I also want to thank Barbara Hodges for her patience and creativity when designing covers for my books.

I want to honor the food scientists I've known. I never understood why food science wasn't a more popular college major because it applies science to intriguing practical problems.

CHAPTER 1: Sara Almquist near Albuquerque on Thursday

"Cultured meat will meet the world's need for high quality protein in an ecologically sound manner. And Miracle Foods has the best cultured meat products." Mendel Lopez, the CEO of Miracle Foods, gave a forced, thin smile. "Dr. Almquist, may I call you Sara? Let me show you our prospectus." His associate Jim Jackson said nothing but grinned enthusiastically.

When the men had entered my house, I'd noticed both were several inches taller than me at five-eight and not much heavier. As I studied them sitting at my dining room table, I realized both were attractive in contrasting ways. Mendel had a wiry, almost hard look with frizzled gray hair, wore a perfectly tailored navy suit, and seemed to be in a hurry. He was probably in his fifties. His associate Jim Jackson frequently brushed his slightly too long brown hair from his youthful face or tugged at his brown tie as he silently eyed his boss.

Yesterday, Jim had spoken with a slow drawl as he explained how Miracle Foods, a start-up company based in Fort Collins, Colorado, was in a tight race to produce and market cultured meat products. He piqued my interest when he said, "I was told you were a tenured professor in epidemiology at Michigan State, but lately you've had experience with our kinda problem. I reckon someone is tryin' to kill—or at least scare—subjects in our clinical trial."

I didn't want to hear Mendel Lopez's promotional talk to potential investors in his start–up company. I wanted to learn why Jim Jackson had insisted on meeting me in person and yesterday refused to discuss the company's problem on the phone. I decided a direct approach was best. "I'd guess officials at FDA and USDA encouraged you to conduct clinical trials before you marketed the foods to consumers. Forget the hype and tell me what went wrong."

Mendel Lopez grimaced. Jim Jackson gulped.

Maybe I'd been too blunt. I decided it was time to act as I would with one of my former students when they were facing a major decision.

"Look, I know your business is in crisis because you flew from Denver to Albuquerque to see me. You don't have to sugarcoat the problem. Let's see if I can be helpful."

Mendel eyed me before he spoke. "After lots of taste panels, we started a long-term clinical trial with our products at a large meal site for indigent homeless people three weeks ago. We substituted our products for beef, turkey, and fish products in recipes for casseroles, patties, and pasta sauce served at eleven to the test group. A control group was served the same meals—but without our products—at noon."

I'm sure I frowned. "Homeless men and women aren't exactly picky eaters or your target audience. I assume..."

Mendel interrupted, "We weren't trying to assess flavor in this trial. We wanted to check for health effects. It was easy to get their cooperation because we paid for all food costs at the meal site for the duration of the study, gave subjects ten dollars each time we drew a small blood sample, and, of course, provided free meals."

I was surprised. Most execs in food companies assumed their products were safe and would have argued they were simply confirming the safety of their products. "Why did you expect to see health effects?"

Jim looked at Mendel as if for permission before he spoke. "As the director of research, I'll answer your question. FDA has noted many meat alternatives produce allergic reactions in sensitive individuals. So, we..."

Mendel tapped his fingers impatiently on the table as his colleague spoke, perhaps because Jim spoke slowly and pronounced most of his vowels with a hard sound when a soft sound seemed more appropriate. Finally, Mendel straightened in his chair and announced, "We were checking for allergic reactions and sure enough we found them."

Jim grimaced. "Two weeks ago, three men and four women developed hives on their faces and hands and five others complained of a tinglin' sensation in their mouths after eatin' the test meal at eleven. No one in the control group complained of those symptoms. The staff at the meal site wanted to end the study. I filed an adverse event report with FDA, but Mendel didn't think.."

"We immediately hired a nurse to monitor the subjects at the meal site. The nurse found the hives on the affected subjects had almost disappeared by the next day. It was nothing."

Jim nodded. "The nurse observed no one developed hives during the rest of the week, although a number of homeless residents in both the test and control groups claimed their hands and faces had become redder and rougher since the trial began. The nurse drew blood samples from all of them but thought the complaints were due to chapping. We had a lot of snow in late January in Colorado."

Mendel growled, "Greedy scoundrels. They thought they could force us to take over their medical care and they knew they'd get ten dollars every time we drew a blood sample." He cleared his throat. "There's more. A woman from a local church who sometimes served meals at the site developed hives on her hands and arms and began to wheeze severely last Friday" He turned to Jim. "You can explain what the nurse did better than I can."

Jim smiled slightly. "The nurse used an EpiPen and rushed the wheezin' woman to the emergency room of a local hospital. The doctor thought the server had an allergic reaction to latex in her gloves or to something in the food. I filed another adverse event report with FDA."

Something seemed strange to me. "I'm surprised they used latex gloves at the meal site."

"Most of the servers didn't." Jim groaned. "We purchased plastic gloves for the site, but when I asked the site director she said that this particular server refused to use the gloves we supplied because they were too large and brought her own."

"Did you find her gloves?"

Mendel stood and didn't give Jim a chance to answer. "Then it happened. One of the men in the test group died Monday. He keeled over fifteen minutes after he ate while smoking outside the shelter. Talk about bad publicity."

Jim nodded. "It was awful. To make matter worse, twenty other subjects that day also developed hives or rashes. The nurse..."

"Took more blood samples from all the diners at the site." Mendel pointed to his research director. "Jim called officials at the FDA and USDA."

"They insisted we file a follow up on our initial adverse event reports within a week after the medical examiner determined the cause of death of the one subject. We were also required to collect food from the meal site for analysis as they had required the previous times. I'm not sure what..."

Mendel interrupted Jim again. "I felt better after Jim talked to the medical examiner. His preliminary analysis was that the man died of anaphylaxis—they tell me that's an extreme allergic reaction—to an insect bite or sting because he had a tiny red lump on one wrist. I wanted to continue the study, but..."

"How many people are in your study?" I noticed Mendel reddened. I guessed he didn't like being interrupted. However, I thought it was likely that something in one of Miracle Foods's products was toxic to sensitive individuals. Also, I doubted anyone would go into anaphylaxis from a bedbug or flea bite. They were the only insect bites or stings I'd expect to see in the middle of winter, but I'm no expert on insects.

"Fifty-one in our test group. Fifty in the control group." Jim shifted in his chair and swallowed hard. "FDA and USDA officials thought it wise to end the study."

That conclusion was obvious. Almost one-half of the subjects in the test group had reacted adversely to the meals and one subject had died, perhaps of unrelated causes. "What do you expect me to do?"

Jim gulped repeatedly and spoke slowly. "The officials at FDA and USDA doubted our product caused *all* these problems. They even agreed with me that it was possible someone was intentionally tryin' to discredit our product. Then the Inspector General at USDA mentioned your name. He said his office had worked with you on a recent case. You were good at tracin' scientific details and gettin' to the root of a problem."

Mendel finally sat down. "And that's why we're here. If news of these incidents leaks out, my company will be ruined. In 1982 when someone laced Tylenol tablets with cyanide, Johnson & Johnson barely survived the bad publicity, and they had a huge public relations staff."

I agreed partially with the two men. If I was tactful and didn't put them in a defensive position, Jim might share information honestly. "These four incidents don't look like random events. However, if this is a case of intentional tampering, the perpetrator is extremely sophisticated." I stood. "I'd better get us beverages before I start asking questions. I should warn you I don't make coffee. So, your choices are tea, water, or soft drinks." I paused trying to think where to begin. "Let's start our discussion with any adverse responses noted among taste panel members during the development of your cultured meat."

CHAPTER 2: Sara on Friday

"Sometimes I don't understand you." Sanders suddenly focused on his steak and began sawing it like it was shoe leather, which certainly wasn't the case. The historic High Noon Restaurant and Saloon in Albuquerque might have a rough history as a brothel and gambling parlor but there was nothing tough about its steaks.

I had brought Sanders to this restaurant after I picked him up at the airport because I hoped this interesting setting, with its more than two-hundred-year history, would set the stage for a relaxed discussion on something besides work. He had a high stress job managing security concerns in the State Department. I had consulted for him mainly through the auspices of USAID, the U.S. Agency for International Development, on scientific and public health issues in Bolivia and Cuba. Soon our friendship blossomed into a romance and finally a committed relationship without marriage.

I knew Sanders was a bit annoyed with me because of my professional decisions during the last week. Then, at the airport when he saw I'd changed my hairdo from a bob to a short pixie style, he sniffed and said, "Your hair is such a beautiful color, like champagne. I can't understand why you don't show it off more." I figured that wasn't a compliment.

I hoped a good meal in this unusual setting would brighten his mood. I suddenly felt a cold chill on my back. "Gee, I think they're overdoing the air conditioning. I just felt a blast of cold air." I tried to be funny. "Or maybe the resident ghost just blew by? You know this building was featured in the Travel Channel's *Dead Files* show on paranormal behavior."

He arched his eyebrows which emphasized his slightly receding hairline. "I think it's warm in here, and neither of us believe in ghosts."

My attempt at humor had failed.

Sanders resumed sawing his meat. "Why did you refuse the USAID assignment in Brazil?"

It was best not to rile him so I chewed slowly and thought before I spoke. "I'm tired of being shot at by drug smugglers and testifying in court for the prosecution in murder and racketeering cases."

He stopped sawing his meat. "That was just bad luck in Bolivia and Cuba. This Brazilian assignment has nothing to do with drugs. You'd be a neutral party brought in to be a liaison between environmentalists trying to protect the Amazon and Brazilian business leaders seeking to improve the economy. Both groups have already recognized your expertise as a practical scientist with no apparent conflicts of interest."

I wanted to scream when he said *apparent*, but I controlled myself. "I've been a consultant enough times to know my limits. Brazil's leader doesn't really want public health reforms. Furthermore, Brazil can be dangerous. A friend recently emailed me about pirates attacking passengers on Amazon cruises. He, his wife, and other passengers were held at gunpoint until they gave the pirates all their cash, jewelry, and watches on a recent Amazon cruise. Most of all, I'm tired of struggling with lost causes. I need a break."

Sanders brushed a wisp of hair from my face. "I understand." He paused. "But how could you agree to consult for Miracle Foods?" He shook his head. "What type of start-up company selects such a sleazy name?"

Usually I'm amused when Sanders acts like an East Coast snob. After all, he can trace his elite family's history in the U.S. to before the Revolutionary War and he did graduate from Princeton. However, today I didn't find his snobbery funny and debated calling him by his first name—Eric—which he hates. I decided to stick to the facts and not display any pettiness. "The project at Miracle Foods is interesting. They're developing new meat substitutes and ran into puzzling findings in a clinical trial. They're based in Colorado so I can drive there with Bug from New Mexico. Bug manages the flights to Washington well, but he can't endure long international flights anymore and prefers drives with me."

"I should have known Bug would be part of this discussion. And..." He stroked my hand. "I enjoy your—and Bug's—company." He said more slowly, "I need and love you."

I could feel the heat rise up my neck and it wasn't due to sexual desire. I was annoyed—no, *nervous* was a better word—that Sanders had forced this discussion in a public place. I guessed it was inevitable and swallowed hard. I fingered the ring on my right hand and then stroked the matching ring he wore on his left hand. "I love you and enjoy the time we've spent together." I paused knowing this could be a bombshell, "But I think it's time for us to see if our relationship works when we aren't working together on the same or interlinked projects. Then I'd be willing to take another assignment part-time in Washington."

His faced reddened. "Does that mean this assignment with Miracle Foods—I think you called it a small, short-term project.—is a test? I don't like tests." He stood. "I think I need to visit the restroom."

I watched the proud man disappear behind a roughly stuccoed wall framed with dark wood and feared I'd been too honest. No, *insensitive* was a better word. We'd shared too much to have a blow up over a silly consulting assignment, but I needed—we both needed—to understand our relationship better. I felt like crying but feared I'd have plenty of time to cry later. Sanders was… special… in so many ways. After what seemed like a long time, probably ten minutes, Sanders returned to the table. I noted he now was standing straight to his full six-foot height and his pale skin was no longer flushed.

"I've made several decisions."

I'd continued to eat while he was gone because I was hungry and thought he might insist we leave the restaurant without finishing our meals. Now I looked at my empty plate, squirmed in my chair, and braced for what I'd hear next.

Sanders sat down and reached across the table so he could hold my hands. "You're right in one sense. We need to explore more of each other's lives outside of shared mutual projects. You certainly have gotten to know my daughter. She thinks I'm less stodgy when I'm around you."

I gulped. This was another touchy topic. "You're not stodgy, but you want a position as a deputy chief of mission in a major embassy or as a deputy assistant secretary in the State Department. I think you should go for it. You've got a lot of seniority in the foreign service and broad experience in technical and security issues not only in the Western Hemisphere but also in Russia and the Middle East. At this point, you can't afford to make mistakes or be misquoted. So, you're cautious. I want to help you reach your goals but let's be honest. I have no political clout and I'm not a social butterfly in Washington society." I felt his hands loosen the grip on my hands. "I'm just an epidemiology professor who took early retirement from Michigan State because I hated working in a politically-charged, tightly structured environment."

He shook his head. "Not true. You're one of the best consultants any of us in the State Department has seen—smart, honest, and practical with a folksy flair that works with peasants in Bolivia, scientists in Cuba, and law enforcement agents in the U.S. Besides I've seen you work the room at a reception—you're good. My boss—an assistant secretary of state—just now said on the phone, 'Sara can make your career.'"

I couldn't believe—no, I was *appalled*—that Sanders had to seek advice or report to his boss even when he was in the middle of a crisis with me. Maybe that was why I'd been unwilling to marry him. He was already married to the State Department. I bridled my comments. "Let me explain the problem from my perspective. Although I want to help you, I really hate schmoozing at receptions. That's what I learned during the five years that I was the head of the Epidemiology Department at Michigan State and one reason why I didn't seek a deanship somewhere. I also learned when I'm forced to conform to rules I don't respect, like in the male-dominated world of statistics and epidemiology, I lash out and step on toes. That's why I like short-term consulting assignments and did so many overseas research projects."

He patted my hands. "You had reason to be unhappy at Michigan State."

"Please let me continue. Unfortunately, what I learned from all those international projects, including the ones I did for you, is I don't want to live overseas. I'd be miserable in a foreign embassy for more than a month. And when I'm unhappy, I lose my tact and say what I think. That's seldom a good idea. I do well in New Mexico because I have Bug. He calms me, but he couldn't take a move to an international site. You'd soon not enjoy my company."

He leaned back in his chair. "We've had this discussion before, but you've never been so frank. I guess I made the right decision just now. I told my boss I would take the vacant deputy chief of mission position in Brazil. I'll be leaving for Brasília in two weeks. I doubt I'll be in that position for even a year, but it will enhance my resume and give me a chance to decide if I want to be based overseas anymore."

I think I flashed him a genuine smile, but I felt tears welling up in my eyes. "Congratulations. You'll never be satisfied until you've had the chance to be in second in command—next to the politically appointed ambassador—at an embassy. You deserve your chance."

Sanders gazed above my head as he spoke. "I'd hoped... However, I told my boss on the phone just now that you wouldn't be accompanying me." He shook his head. "Two of things I love about you are that you know your limits and you understand me." He turned to scan the room but didn't see the waiter. "I'll go to counter and pay our bill."

I grabbed his arm. "Wait. This doesn't have to be the end of our relationship. It could be a growth period when we both figure out what we really want now. Either one of us could decide we were wrong or decide that our goals have changed. Besides, I'm willing to listen to your challenges and consult for free. And we both know I'm a klutz at languages. It's doubtful I'd ever speak passable Portuguese and would be an embarrassment to you in Brasília." I wiped my eyes. "When you want a break from Brazil, you're welcome here in the Albuquerque area or I can meet you in Washington."

"We'll see." He rose and walked rapidly to the counter.

I slowly sipped my water and wiped my eyes before I joined him at the door. I thought putting a happy spin on the next three days while he stayed at my house could be difficult, but I was determined to not have a bitter taste in either of our mouths when he returned to Washington. Our relationship had been—and still could be—a good one.

Then again, this weekend might turn out well. Sanders would enjoy the reception later this afternoon in honor of Ulysses Howe's retirement as the director of the Albuquerque FBI field office. While Sanders had directed many of the U.S. efforts to uncover and track the shipment of coca and cocaine from Bolivia to Cuba and then to New Mexico, Ulysses Howe had directed U.S. law enforcement activities against the involved gangs in New Mexico. They had worked well together for the last two years. Sanders also knew the man who would replace Ulysses on an interim basis. FBI agent Paul Carbonne had worked security for Sanders at the U.S. embassy in Cuba. Then Carbonne had followed drug cartel members from Havana to Albuquerque, where he stayed on tracking gang leader often under the guise of a homeless man. I had also worked easily with both FBI agents but was particularly fond of Carbonne because he, like me, had an antiestablishment streak.

***

I'd never seen the FBI parking lots off Luecking Park Avenue so crowded. "Honey, do you think I should just give up and park down the street? More people have been invited to this reception to honor Ulysses Howe than I expected."

Sanders pointed toward a guard at the entrance to the inner lot. "Ask him."

The guard motioned me forward. "Dr. Almquist, it always makes me nervous to see you park here. You know you're the only one who has had a car blown up while parked in these lots."

I was used to being ribbed about that episode and replied. "That only happens once a year. I'm not due for another bomb yet."

The guard continued, "We saved a spot for you in the inner lot. Where's Bug? He's usually with you."

"I figured a formal reception was too much for Bug." The driver behind me beeped his horn. "I better stop blocking traffic. Thanks."

As I parked my SUV, I said to Sanders, "You know I've spent too much time consulting for the FBI when even the parking guard recognizes me. Too bad I couldn't bring Bug. He likes parading down the halls of this building."

"Please—we're almost late." Sanders rushed me toward the door. After we cleared the security checks, we entered the area around the central staircase of the building. I'd always thought it strange that an FBI field office would have a curved double staircase which looked like the beginning of a double helix of DNA, at the core of its building. Now I realized it made a perfect place for a reception with plenty of room for tables of refreshments and milling guests, while speakers stood at the top of the stairs.

I scanned the crowd. There were lots of men in navy and gray suits—typical FBI agents. I recognized a number of them because I'd reviewed their files for Ulysses Howe. That was hardly the basis of a pleasant conversation. Then I spotted the U.S. attorney who had prosecuted the gang leaders in recent federal trials. He eagerly shook my and Sanders's hands and thanked me again for providing crucial data for the conviction of the drug gang leaders. Then the attorney said, "Did you accept Ulysses's and Carbonne's offer of a position with the FBI in Albuquerque or take another assignment with the State Department?" He winked at Sanders.

I thought, *oh dear, is nothing private in my world?* but said, "You know I always do the unexpected. I'm also tired of the glamour of working with government agencies. I'm doing a small project for a start-up company called Miracle Foods."

Sanders snorted. The U.S. attorney reddened. "Oh, you're tired of being shot at?" He mumbled something to Sanders before he faded into the crowd.

Finally, a man in a black suit appeared at the top of the stairs. He introduced himself as a division leader in the FBI and presented Ulysses Howe with a plaque honoring Ulysses for his twenty-five years of meritorious service. Ulysses, looking more rested than he had in a long time, gave the usual round of thanks to staff. I was surprised when he noted, "I owe special thanks to Sara Almquist for her unique scientific insights, good instincts on human behavior, and daring." The rest of the program was led by Carbonne and consisted of various tributes from agents and other who had worked with Ulysses. I thought the program was like the retirement parties held for faculty members—boring and sad. That's why I'd asked colleagues not to arrange any farewell parties for me at Michigan State when I left.

During the ensuing reception, Sanders was more attentive than usual. He kept a hand on my shoulder much of the time. Usually, we separated at events in Washington and worked the room individually. Perhaps I'd threatened his peace of mind by refusing his proposal to work in Brazil. That had not been my intent.

As soon as we got into the car, Sanders said, "I'd never thought before about what I wanted when I retired. Most of the reminiscences were corny and not interesting or amusing. And it was obvious, Ulysses didn't know what he wanted to do next. Sad and depressing. Do you think others felt that way?"

I pointed to Carbonne and his girlfriend Barbara Lewis who were walking to their car. I'd worked with Barbara bit on two cases with the FBI. "Barbara asked me about half-way through the program, 'Do you think I'm being too harsh, even as a millennial, to say this program is lame?' She also asked if we'd like to hike at Tent Rocks National Monument tomorrow with her and Carbonne."

CHAPTER 3: Sara on Sunday

The rest of the weekend had been fun after the reception. The challenge of keeping up with physically fit FBI agents, like Carbonne and Barbara Lewis, had been invigorating to both Sanders and me. Moreover, the eerie cone-shaped rock formations at Tent Rocks National Monument were amazing. Now, after taking a much happier Sanders to the airport, I was ready to think about the plight of Miracle Foods.

The worldwide market for alternatives to meat was competitive with hundreds of companies producing a variety of products. Many were already on the market. For example, one national hamburger chain was now selling soy-based burgers. At least one major firm was successfully marketing internationally beef-, pork-, and sausage-like products made with mycoproteins. I wondered how many consumers of this product realized they were eating protein from a relative of common molds. Besides the products already on the market, inventors at universities and start-up companies, such as Miracle Foods, were trying to create meats in cell culture. The so called "test tube meat."

Even though the potential for industrial espionage and intentional tampering with rivals' products was great, I doubted all the adverse events in the clinical trial run by Miracle Foods were due to tampering. Maybe it was because I doubted Mendel was being honest with me. He said several times, "You don't need to see the taste panel data, especially the early stuff when we were perfecting our product."

On Thursday, Mendel and Jim only shared with me a summary of their most recent data from test panels. I wanted to see the early raw data because I didn't see how adverse reactions appeared during the clinical trial but not during the taste panels. I'd served on taste panels when I was an undergraduate because it was a way to augment my income by getting free food. As I remembered, the graduate students conducting the taste panels had encouraged us to write in comments. For example, I would have noted if the product I tasted made my tongue tingle. I bet others would, too. Of course, it was amazing how little you needed to taste of some products, like tomatoes stored too long, to complete a taste profile.

Those tomatoes had been gross. Accordingly, I knew exposure to toxic compounds in foods during a taste panel could be small. Even so, I would insist on seeing the raw data from the taste panels.

I also wanted to learn about the taste panelists. Were they employees of the company who couldn't afford to be negative? One of them might have something interesting to say when questioned privately.

Perhaps my suspicions were also aroused because the research director Jim Jackson had focused his attention in the clinical trial mainly on allergic reactions. It didn't make sense. According to the medical literature, allergies to beef, chicken, or other meats were less common than allergies to cow's milk, eggs, peanuts, tree nuts, soy, wheat, and shellfish. Miracle Foods's meat products were produced from the muscle cells of healthy cattle, turkeys, or fish that were cultured in big, closed, sterilized vats in the lab to produce large volumes of meat-like product. Thus, I postulated allergic reactions to cultured meat would occur no more frequently than allergic reactions to the originating meat products.

Then my cynical side took control of my thoughts. I suspected the leadership of Miracle Foods wasn't looking for allergic reactions of subjects in the clinical trial to prove the safety of their products, per se, but to use in advertising to point out the weaknesses of competing products made with allergenic plant proteins. Their plan had backfired. At least one subject and a server had shown severe allergic responses, linked ostensibly to an insect sting and latex sensitivity, respectively.

Then again, I might be over thinking the point. Miracle Foods may had been unlucky and the indigents participating in the clinical trial may have had a larger number of meat allergies than the general population. After all, as many as three percent of adults are estimated to have some type of food allergy. Moreover, I guessed the symptoms developed by the majority of the participants in the study weren't due to allergies, per se. The medical literature is awash with descriptions of adverse responses to foods, including bloating in the gastrointestinal tract, hives, eye irritations, and headaches, which aren't due to allergies.

The problem was there were so many possibilities. I decided to check something less complicated—the background of the two men. Jim Jackson had an unremarkable history. He received a BS in food science from Clemson University, worked in the poultry industry for ten years, and then earned a MS in biomanufacturing and biotechnology from Colorado State before being hired by Miracle Foods four years ago. He was married and had a son in high school.

Mendel Lopez's background was more interesting. He had inherited a large cattle ranch in Colorado from his mother, earned a degree in accounting from the University of Nevada-Reno, and worked in the gaming industry for fifteen years before he became a real estate broker. He'd acquired a brewery in Fort Collins seven years ago, but converted it to a biotechnology start-up company about five years ago. Along the way, he'd been married several times and had one son now in college.

Possibly because I had a science background, Jim's resume inspired more confidence in me. Besides, I'd sensed Jim knew more about the products at Miracle Foods.

As I debated what to do next, I studied Jim's business card and was surprised he'd written his home phone number on the back. I never gave out my home phone number during my years as a professor. Perhaps, he was inviting me to learn a secret. I scolded myself for being theatrical and called Jim even though it was Sunday afternoon.

The phone rang several times before a man answered. "Mr. Jackson? This is Sara Almquist. Do you have time to talk to me? I have a few questions?"

There was blur of sounds as the man seemed to order someone to leave the room. Doors slammed, and then, silence. "This is Jim Jackson. I'm glad you called. We'll have fewer kibitzers here than if I was at the plant. How can I help you?"

"I'm not an expert on allergies and wanted to be sure I have my facts straight. I can see why many of your competitors using plant-based ingredients—like peanuts, peas, or almonds—are concerned about allergic reactions to their products. However, I wouldn't expect your product produced by cultured animal cells to activate common food allergies. As I remember meat allergies are relatively rare."

Jim chuckled. "You're right. I was never much concerned about allergies. That was the boss's hang-up. But I *was* concerned about reports of individuals who developed rashes and swellin' of the face and neck when they consumed fermented products because our meat is produced in cultures that in some ways resemble the fermentation processes used to produce beer and wine. Actually, those responses aren't allergic reactions but are signs of histamine intolerance."

I was struck again by his Southern accent, in which he dropped g's and pronounced vowels with hard inflection. It wouldn't be polite to comment, and I wanted to focus on the topic. "Why didn't you say that when we spoke before?" I decided my tone was too sharp when I heard Jim gasp. "Can you get me up to speed on research regarding histamine levels in food?"

"It's complicated."

                                      J. L. Greger

That wasn't the answer I hoped for. "Start with basic info. Have you measured the levels of histamine in your cultured meat?"

"Yes."

I knew I was being demanding but quickly spat out more questions. "Do the histamine levels vary with batches? On the days when individuals developed rashes and itching, were the histamine levels in other foods on the menu higher than usual? For starters, were there other fermented products on the menu on those days?"

Jim sighed. "Slow down. I'm takin' notes."

I heard banging noises like file drawers being opened and closed and the rustle of papers.

"I had the lab measure histamine levels in our turkey and beef products twice. The four samples contained slightly more histamine than regular beef and turkey. Even so, a three-ounce servin' of our product would contain less than a half-milligram of histamine. That's much less than the amount of histamine in a servin' of spinach, pickles, or many cheeses."

The new information swirled in my mind. "So the basic menu served at the meal site could contain considerable amounts of histamines on some days?"

After a long pause, Jim groaned. "Suppose so."

"Did you ever analyze the meals served for their histamine levels?"

"FDA made us save samples of food from the meals served on the three problem days. They're in a lab freezer because Mendel didn't want me to waste money on unnecessary analyses." He paused. "And I didn't know what to analyze."

I thought of the phrase—penny wise and pound foolish—might apply to this situation. "Was there anything unusual about the menu on the three days when the study participants developed symptoms?"

I could hear the rustle of papers. Then, "Oh," and a long pause. "I hadn't noticed this before. Pickles were on the menu on two of the problem days. They're fermented. But the servers were pretty chintzy with the pickles. I doubt the diners would have gotten much histamine from the pickles."

I interrupted. "You know pickles are the type of food people pick off each other's plates. Your responders could have eaten more pickles than others at the meal site."

"Dang it—there's no way of knowin' that." He paused. "I'm goin' to need a beer after this conversation. I know we should have gotten the help of a dietitian before we began the trial, but the boss didn't want to waste money on unnecessary help."

I suddenly thought of another problem. "Did you ever ask the homeless participants about what they ate and drank when not at the site? For example, do you know anything about their beer and wine intake? I assume some beers and wines, as fermented products, have a fair amount of histamine, but I don't know."

Jim sighed deeply. "How soon can you come to Fort Collins and look at all the data? We're under a tight time line. We want to get FDA and USDA approval of our cultured meat ASAP. We thought we were ahead of our main competitor in California until last week. And FDA has demanded a preliminary analyses of our problems by the end of this comin' week."

He sighed more deeply than before. "Guess I should tell you that someone broke into our plant last night. I couldn't find anythin' missin' in my office, but our competitors would only need copies or photographs of my data sheets or lab protocols."

"Were any other offices entered? Was anything of value taken?"

"Our personnel officer thought several of her files were missing, but she wasn't sure. The burglars, if that what they were, turned over two file cabinets in the main office, but they didn't take a thousand dollars left in a desk drawer."

CHAPTER 4: Sara on the Road to Colorado on Monday

I studied a map on Sunday night. It was a little over an eight-hour straight shot on I-25 from my home in the gated community of La Bendita in New Mexico to Fort Collins, Colorado. I considered briefly taking a scenic route but reality set in. Driving on twisty, narrow mountain roads made me nervous. I decided sticking to I-25 with the Rockies to the west was best. Besides, I'd be lucky to complete the drive in ten hours because I would need to stop three or four times, not because Bug would need bathroom breaks, but because I would.

***

Bug was strapped into his elevated dog seat next to me in front and the cooler filled with water, diet colas, and bags of cut up vegetables and cheese cubes was wedged in the well behind my seat by six on Monday morning when I left the gates of La Bendita. The little dog seemed eager and sat at attention. Some dogs bark in excitement when they hear the words "treats" or "walk." Bug, who never barks, comes running with his tail wagging whenever I say "road trip." Of course, I call the forty- to sixty-minute drives to the hospitals in Albuquerque where Bug does pet therapy "road trips." When I turned north on I-25 instead of south toward the hospitals in Albuquerque, Bug sat up even straighter and, instead of looking at me, peered out the front window. He already knew we weren't going to do pet therapy today. He'd be the perfect navigator with his great sense of direction, if only he could talk.

During the drive northward in New Mexico, my thoughts kept returning to one question—what at Miracle Foods was worth stealing? I knew there was such a thing as industrial espionage but hadn't understood how complicated the manufacture of cultured meat was—and accordingly how much could be stolen—until my discussion with Jim Jackson yesterday on the phone.

First off, cells removed from the muscles of real animals are grown in culture media with nutrients and growth factors in sterile, stainless steel bioreactors, somewhat similar to the fermenters used in breweries. Second, the media and gases are altered so that the primitive stem cells differentiate into muscle cells that merge to form tubules. Third, these myotubes are allowed to grow and clump on a biological scaffold, often made of fibrin, collagen, or alginate. Several researchers, including Jim Jackson, had found the application of an electrical current caused the cells to develop a more meat-like texture. Fourth, the cells are interspersed with fat and flavor components because the strands of muscle cells produced in culture are dry and lacking in flavor when cooked. The composition of the broths, media, gels, and scaffolds used to produce strands of muscle cells vary among start-up companies. In other words, a start-up company, such as Miracle Foods, might hold a couple of patents but have many other "secrets" because their processes had not been perfected enough to be patented yet. It was an area ripe for industrial espionage.

Then my mind drifted to other questions. Why hadn't thieves stolen files from Jim Jackson's office? As the director of research, he would have any secret information which hadn't been patented yet. His explanation that industrial spies didn't have to take the data, but could copy the materials, didn't ring true because presumably the same burglars had stolen personnel files. Couldn't they have photographed them, too?

It also bugged me that Jim said, "the burglars, if that is what they were." This added phrase suggested he knew of a motive for the break-in besides industrial espionage. I figured I was being silly to attach importance to his off-hand comment, but Jim left me with the impression that Miracle Foods was not a happy place to work. I didn't think the source of unhappiness at Miracle Foods was a shortage of funds. Several major business experts on the web claimed Miracle Food was one of the fifty most promising start-up companies in the U.S. The retention check that Mendel Lopez gave me on Friday had been large, but not unreasonable considering the potential size of his problem. No money per se wasn't the root of the problem at Miracle Foods.

I also wondered why had the personnel officer left a thousand dollars cash in a desk drawer over a weekend. At Michigan State, I'd seen business officers and departmental administrators severely punished for that type of mistake. Maybe universities were different than small businesses, but I doubted it.

Sanders was right. It may have been a mistake to accept this consulting assignment.

My bladder overrode my interest in the Miracle Foods's problems as I approached Las Vegas, New Mexico. The city merited only a quick bathroom stop and I was on my way to the Ratón Pass. It's on the border between New Mexico and Colorado. At an elevation of 7,000-feet through the majestic Sangre de Cristo Mountains, the Ratón Pass is subject to high winds and heavy snowfall in winter, but I was lucky on this sunny February morning. There was heavy snow on the surrounding mountains, but the road was clear. Even so, I didn't allow myself to think about anything but driving until I reached Trinidad, Colorado.

Last night I thought Trinidad might have several interesting historical sites. It had a colorful history with the legendary Bat Masterson as its sheriff in the 1880s. A century later it was called the "sex change capital of the world" because of a skillful and extremely busy local surgeon. All I noticed as Bug and I wandered about the town was its many marijuana dispensaries. Their booming business reflected the fact that Colorado had legalized the sale of recreational marijuana before New Mexico and Texas.

As I left Trinidad, I decided to take a break from thinking about Miracle Foods and turned on the radio looking for classical music with no interruptions for political commentary or sporting events. That's another thing Sanders and I have in common. We're both into visual arts— painting, sculpture, architecture—but not much into sporting events or concerts, other than an occasional classical event.

During the final segment of my trip to Fort Collins, I thought about what Jim Jackson had said about the history of Miracle Foods. Mendel Lopez had acquired The Fatted Calf Brewery and Cafe seven years ago when he married the owner who was an adjunct professor at Colorado State in the field of fermentation science. Five years ago, the husband-wife team of Mendel and Leslie Lopez had closed the brewery and converted it into a start-up company. This was more logical than it sounds because the space and some of the equipment from brewery formed the basis of a pilot plant for culturing cells, and the restaurant's kitchen and service areas were converted into lab and office space, respectively.

I achieved my goal and reached the biotech firm before five. I wanted to case out the facility, at least its exterior, before sunset. The building was easy to identify because a large sign said "Miracle Foods." It looked like the owners had painted over the sign which once had listed the brewery's name. The paint was peeling. Otherwise the building with red aluminum siding, a steep roof, and a large empty brick patio looked in good repair.

I parked my car in an adjoining lot for a laundromat and watched two men and a woman saunter out of the building. A pickup truck, a SUV, and an old Corvette were left in the lot. Soon, a tall woman with long, dark hair arrived. About ten minutes later, she trundled a cart with three boxes to her car. Jim Jackson was with her and helped her hoist the boxes into her trunk before he gave her a hug. Then they both drove away in the same direction. I wondered who she was and expected Jim might not be willing to talk about her because they appeared to be *good* friends. Finally a short women with dyed red hair strutted to the SUV.

Bug convinced me he needed a bathroom break and we walked to the back of the building. I saw two large stainless steel vats behind a floor-to-ceiling window at the back of the building. A man rolled a garbage can out on the loading dock and emptied its contents into a dumpster. The pickup truck in the front lot must be his because there were no vehicles in the back lot. As Bug and I finished circling the building, I noted the lower five feet of other windows on the sides and front of the building were covered with black vinyl siding. Evidently Miracle Foods didn't want their work watched by others.

The air was nippy and I was glad when Bug had finished his business. We headed for a nearby motel, our home for the next two or three days.

CHAPTER 5: Sara in Fort Collins on Tuesday

My first question was answered when Bug and I entered Miracle Foods at eight on Tuesday morning. A tall woman with long dark hair—the woman I saw last night wheeling boxes out of the building—greeted me. "Hello, I'm Leslie Lopez. My husband won't be here this morning." She appeared to be twenty years younger than her husband—at most she was in her early-thirties. The main thing I noticed about her was how she teetered in purple suede boots with three-inch stiletto heels.

When Leslie saw Bug, she turned abruptly and led me to a small conference room. "This will be your headquarters while you're with us. You really won't be able to see much of our building because your dog can't enter the lab area or pilot plant."

I smiled. "I agree Bug doesn't belong in the lab or pilot plant but that doesn't mean I can't leave this room. Mendel assured me it was okay for me to bring Bug along."

She eyed me doubtfully.

"Bug's a pet therapy dog in two hospitals in Albuquerque and has spent days in the FBI building in Albuquerque with me. You'll see he won't be a problem." Bug must have realized I was talking about him and waved his tail like a flag.

Leslie didn't appear to notice how cute Bug looked. "Just like Mendel to..."

I thought it was best to change the subject. "Can you or the personnel officer supply me with a list of all employees and their functions?"

She snapped, "Why do you need that for a scientific evaluation?"

I was surprised by defensive tone. "Your husband seemed sure the problems in the clinical trial reflected tampering or industrial espionage. That suggests someone working here may have been involved. Besides, an organizational chart will get me oriented."

"You just saw Mendel's suspicious side. We hired you for scientific advice." She stared at me.

"I'd still like a list of all Miracle Foods's employees and past employees—even maintenance workers and student helpers. If it's too much bother for you, I can talk to the personnel officer myself." She winced. That must be another sore point. I decided it would be incendiary to ask what was in the three boxes she took out of the building last night. Instead, I said, "I know your offices were broken into over the weekend. So I'll understand if it takes a while to find the information I requested. Thanks."

She shook her head in apparent disgust and strode out in her purple boots. I knew I was being catty, but I imagined the scene when she took the boots off. I bet the purple dye in the boots left streaks of purple on her legs and socks, especially if the boots became wet with snow or sweat. I banished that amusing image and organized a back corner of the conference room for Bug with a water bowl, food dish, and bed. Instead of a cage, I had a rolling cart for him. Over the years, I found that was the easiest way to move him and his supplies quickly. As Bug lapped the purified water I'd brought for him, I heard raised voices in the background. Communications among staff at Miracle Foods didn't appear to be optimal. I also noted an occasional waft of a chemical odor—like I've noticed in some breweries and wineries. I wondered whether that indicated problems in their fermenter.

Jim Jackson stuck his head inside and then glanced backward before he entered the conference room. "Seems Mendel and Leslie aren't on the same page." He added more softly, "As usual."

"Oh dear. I hate to start off on the wrong foot."

Jim sighed. "Can't be helped. Your request is certainly in line with Mendel's orders to you. However, Leslie likes to consider herself as the chief operatin' officer Miracle Foods, not merely the personnel officer, although that is her official title."

I swallowed hard and pulled a can of diet cola from Bug's carrier. "Do you have time now to answer a few questions and warn me of other hot spots here?" More to myself than to him, I said, "I can't believe I've stuck my foot in my mouth twice in my first five minutes here."

Jim smiled. "I'll get my coffee mug and an employee chart—It won't be as complete as Leslie's—from my office. We'll have plenty of time because Leslie's on the phone with Mendel now. Their conversations are seldom short. But wait and see, she'll be her bouncy self when she comes back in here."

I petted Bug and sipped my diet cola. There were two ways to view Leslie. One, she wasn't happy about much at Miracle Foods or two, my request for a list of current and past employees confirmed her own suspicions. It was easy to imagine that the list of unhappy, perhaps even vengeful, past employees could be long in this seemingly hostile workplace.

Jim slid an organization chart with several penciled cross-outs in front of me before he plunked down and began to slurp his coffee. "I have four full time employees in the lab and pilot plant." He coughed. "I'm not much into the pretty talk of personnel officers. My staff all have fancy job descriptions, but in essence two handle the initial cell culture process. Bioreactors take constant monitoring. The other two focus on ways to cause the differentiated cultured muscle cells to clump together and form meat-like fibers on an organic scaffold."

That description and the omnipresent odor didn't whet my appetite. I studied the organizational chart. "I see lots of cross-outs among the employees listed as laboratory assistants."

"The cross-outs are student interns. Usually we have two whom Leslie recruits from the food science majors at Colorado State. Most stay only a semester although a few have worked here for over a year."

"Who runs the taste panels and takes care of the day-to-day management of the clinical trial?"

"Leslie does that with the help of Viola Sanchez. About four years ago, Leslie convinced Viola to leave her position as office manager for the Department of Food Science and Nutrition at Colorado State to become the business officer of Miracle Foods. Viola also does all our orderin' and sees we comply with federal regulation and safety rules."

"So, she oversees nearly the same things she did for the academic department, except she doesn't handle personnel?"

"Leslie's more hands on than most department heads."

I wanted to explore how Leslie's apparent micromanagement affected Jim. "Why does Leslie run the taste panels, instead of you? You're a food scientist with training on taste panels."

He laughed. "Leslie as an adjunct professor teaches a course on taste panels and runs all the taste panels for the Food Science and Nutrition Department which includes the Fermentation Science and Technology Program. She can do the panels in her sleep."

"So, who was in charge of the clinical trial?"

"Leslie figured runnin' a clinical trial wouldn't be much different than runnin' taste panels. It's one of the rare times when Viola argued with Leslie. Viola thought we should hire a dietitian to plan and manage the clinical trial. I was surprised when Mendel supported Leslie." He shrugged. "But then no one would call me a personnel expert." Jim laughed but he was amazingly tactful when it came to Leslie.

"Did Miracle Foods hire anyone else to work on the clinical trial?"

"We hired a nurse once we encountered problems, and her salary is comin' out of my lab budget. Mendel bribed—I guess I shouldn't try to be funny—*outsourced* the day-to-day management of the clinical trial to the church which runs the meal site." He shook his head. "They got way more money than the cost of the food and supplies. I don't think they earned it."

"I saw…" I had to stop in mid-sentence because I'd almost admitted I'd cased out Miracle Foods last night and knew a maintenance man appeared to be there after everyone else left. "I noticed the building is in good repair. Do you outsource maintenance too?"

He frowned. "That's an odd question? I guess it just proves I'm not into personnel."

I was bothered by Jim's self-deprecating comments because I doubted they were sincere. He knew more than he admitted, but I wasn't sure how to draw him out. "Sometimes the invisible employees, such as maintenance crews, are involved in break ins. They usually have keys."

"Our handyman is not invisible. He's a jack of all trades and does basic repairs in the lab plus general upkeep of the place."

I didn't look up from my laptop because I was busy taking notes. "Any other employees not on the chart?"

"Not that I know of."

"I think I've got the general lay of the land. Let's go back to the taste panels. Who served on them?"

"Depends. Early ones were done here with everyone in the buildin' participatin'. Later ones were done at the university. Sometimes Leslie used her class as panelists. She called it givin' them 'real-world' experience." He chuckled. "Sometimes she ran our taste panels through the tastin' facility on campus. The Food Science and Nutrition Department basically runs a small testin' business for breweries, restaurants, and researchers at the Lory Student Center. I don't know who served on those panels." He grimaced. "Make it easy on all of us and don't ask Leslie. Just go to Viola. She keeps all the signed informed consent records." He paused. "I always figured consent forms for human subjects was another example of stupid government red tape because I reckoned not much could happen to a taste panelist." He closed his eyes.

"And now?"

"I'm glad Viola insisted we go by the book and keep all those records. Food allergies and reactions to histamine—or God-knows what else—in foods can be scary, especially now. However, I didn't believe that when we started. I cut corners in regard to informed consent on the early taste panels here."

I typed a note to myself to ask Viola for the informed consent records. Without looking up from my laptop, I said, "I suspect that would be true for all early product development. Years ago, I served on taste panels as a student. We were allowed to write in comments, even though we used a standardized check sheet. How about here? In the early panels, did anyone complain about hives or tingling sensations after a taste panel."

He nodded. "I'm prepared for that question because you kept askin' about the panels last Thursday. I looked through the sheets from our early taste panels. No one complained of hives, but no one admitted to a history of food allergies, either. However, the comments included: 'I wanted to vomit after tastin' the product,' 'It feels funny in my mouth,' 'Rubbery,' 'Tasteless,' and 'Yuck.' Actually the last one was the most common written in comment. I'd forgotten how brutal they were." He shook his head and stared at the ceiling.

I thought those sheets might make amusing reading in front of the TV tonight. However, good lab policy dictated raw data sheets shouldn't leave the lab. Jim wiped his eyes. I decided he needed sympathy. "Must have been discouraging."

"No kiddin'. There were a couple of times I thought I'd be fired." He shook his head. "You wouldn't believe how much fat and salt we had to add to develop a meaty flavor in cultured muscle cells or how difficult it was to create a decent ground meat texture. We're still workin' on creatin' a steak texture. The good news was once the product was pretty good, Leslie took over the taste panels. That was about a year ago."

Leslie swept into the room with a heavy, short woman in tow. I guessed it was the redhead who was the last to leave the building, except the janitor, the night before. "Viola can answer your questions. I have to get to my class. As a former professor, you know students expect us to be prepared and interesting, even when topic is not." She flashed a big smile and rushed out without giving me a personnel list.

Viola waited until the door clicked shut before she sighed. "Jim, do you know why she's so touchy this morning?"

Jim walked to the door, opened it, looked down the hallway, closed it, and returned to his seat. "She figured out last night what was missin' from her office—the personnel files of several student interns." He turned to me. "When that was the first thin' you asked for, she panicked."

I considered the comment a compliment. I must be on the right tract. My thoughts were distracted when Viola's eyes narrowed as she stared at Jim. "Did she mention anything else was missing?"

Jim waved his hand in dismissal. "I'm not dumb enough to ask questions that might set her off."

What type of quagmire had I stepped into? As usual, Sanders was right. I shouldn't have accepted this consultation, but this wasn't a time to pout. I needed to gain Viola's trust fast. I tried to sound relaxed as I said, "Viola, looks like you're the glue that holds Miracle Foods together. Mendel thought industrial espionage was a possibility. So I need to review everyone with access to the building."

Viola pulled a couple of pages from a folder and slid them across the table to me. "No problem. Jim and I agree with Mendel even though Leslie doesn't. That's why I printed out a corporate organizational chart and a list of all our employees, even our current and past student interns while Leslie was on the phone with Mendel." She tapped one page. "I've given you email addresses and phone number for everyone, but those for students are apt to be outdated."

"Thanks." I appreciated the woman's organizational skills and calmness.

"Do you need anything else?"

"I'd like to see the consent forms and data sheets from the taste panels. I want to see whether any panelists had a history of food allergies or health complaints and see if any claimed they developed hives or other symptoms after participating in a taste panel."

Viola flashed a broad grin. "Now you're thinking like Leslie. Last night she took home all the records from the taste panels. I don't think you'll find much because the forms didn't encourage comments and had only one health question." She shuffled through the pages in her folder. "Shoot, I thought I put sample questionnaires in this file. I'll be right back."

I didn't think this was a good time to tackle the next point on my checklist—why was Jim fixated on histamine. Instead, I asked Jim to describe the taste panels facilities that Leslie used on the Colorado State campus.

He had just begun to explain the brewing industry's investment in the university's Ramskeller Pub and tasting facilities at the Lory Student Center when a young woman slammed the door open and screamed, "Leslie's had an accident! Her car spun out of control on a patch of black ice. Viola is trying to reach Mendel." She began to sob. "Leslie's in bad shape."

                                              J. L. Greger

CHAPTER 6: Sara's Field Trip

I retreated to the back corner of the conference room with Bug during the next furious five minutes of activity. After Jim had left for the hospital, I fretted because I'd planned to focus on Jim and the analysis of histamine in collected food samples for the next two hours. Then I felt ashamed of myself. How could I have so little empathy?

I walked slowly to Viola's office. She motioned me to a chair and placed her hand over the phone. "How badly do you want to see those consent forms and taste panel sheets?"

"I'd like to review them and talk to you while Jim is at the hospital. Or I could introduce myself to the lab technicians and interview them if you're busy."

She removed her hand from the receiver. "We want the boxes right away. I will pick them up at the police garage in the next hour. Thanks." She hung up and looked at me. "As a middle-aged woman, you've probably guessed the situation here. I can save you the time and effort of discreetly asking questions so you can focus your thoughts on the technical problems." She looked at her empty coffee cup. "Maybe we should talk as we drive over to the police garage to get the boxes."

"Can I bring Bug?"

"Sure. Most days I bring my dog with me to work. She helps me relax."

"Dogs have that effect on their owners."

She nodded her head and looked down the hallway. "I'll be waiting in my car at the front door."

***

Bug and I felt right at home in Viola's car. It looked as "lived in" as my SUV.

Viola slowly turned out of the parking lot. "I didn't want to admit inside that I bring my dog to work because Leslie hates dogs. When my collie is in my office, Leslie spends less time grousing about Mendel."

That answered another question. Bug had been a bad surprise for Leslie. Now for the next question. I tried to be discreet. "It's hard to work daily with a spouse."

She cackled, "Yeah, Leslie and Mendel are a real pair. She wanted to marry a rich man who would back her dream of heading a start-up company. He wanted a young princess for a wife and a good investment. They both got what they wanted."

"What about you and Jim?"

She delayed her reply until she'd made a turn onto a major street. "Me? I needed a job that paid better than my university job did to support my two kids and me. My daughter Elena is a senior in the biotechnology program here; my son is a freshman with no idea of a major. I have no choice but work my buns off to make Miracle Foods succeed, but it won't if the clinical trial identified a real problem with our product."

I reminded her of my previous question. "And Jim?"

"On bad days, he always says, 'Anything is better than overseeing the slaughter of thousands of chickens daily as I did while I was an undergrad.' He was Leslie's choice to head up research. Not sure he's ever got Mendel's full support."

She suddenly made a sharp turn and we faced a gate in a chain link fence. "Leslie's car was totaled but the police were able to open the trunk and retrieve the three boxes. As you know, these boxes should have never left our facility, but Leslie wouldn't listen to me yesterday."

A man tapped on Viola's window. "Got your boxes."

Viola exited her car and chatted with him as he loaded the three boxes in her trunk.

As we drove away, I said, "Gee, he was cooperative."

"Should be—he's my brother-in-law. As he said, 'Those boxes will just sit in the warehouse for months waiting for someone to come get them.'" She was silent for few seconds as she tapped fingers on the steering wheel. "Seems the police don't believe Leslie's story about black ice. There could be an investigation of the accident."

"Why?"

"She hit a pedestrian."

***

Twenty minutes later, Viola threw the lids of the three file boxes on the conference room table and spoke rapidly in Spanish as she rummaged through the boxes. She had guessed correctly I didn't understand Spanish, but I recognized a few words, mainly the curses and the phrase *perra loca*.

"What did Leslie do?"

Viola looked surprised. "I'd hoped our queen left a summary of her discoveries from last night. As expected, she didn't." She uttered one more expletive before she said, "Here's the plan—I'll sort through the boxes for the personnel records while you pull the files on taste panels." She shoved nine yellow pages at me. "These sample copies of the nine taste panel forms Leslie used should help you determine whether we still have a file for each panel." She walked to the door. "I'd better call the hospital."

***

I was deep in my search when Viola yanked one box off the table and threw it on a cart. "How's Leslie? How about the pedestrian she hit?"

Viola rolled the cart toward the door without looking at me. "Leslie is in surgery having her leg set. Her injuries are more severe than the police first thought. Jim will stay at the hospital until Mendel arrives. Seems she didn't have her seat belt on." The cart banged the door.

"How about the pedestrian?"

I thought she murmured, "Don't know," as she slammed the cart forward. I guessed she was closer to Leslie than she had admitted. Maybe she was scared about the future of Miracle Foods and accordingly her future. I decided I should say something upbeat and blurted out the first thing that entered my mind. "Leslie did a good job of organizing the files on the nine taste panels. A tally page on green paper was at the front of each file."

Viola stopped slamming the cart against the door and snorted. "I had student interns prepare those summaries after Jim and Mendel repeatedly asked for results from Leslie." She muttered under her breath. "Then she wonders why she is stuck in an adjunct position at the university. The students in her classes think she's glamorous. The faculty in food science and nutrition call her 'the bimbo.'"

I couldn't think of an appropriate response, other than, "I see you had the interns record how many participated in each panel. So far, I don't think any of the forms are missing. The number of completed forms in each file corresponds with the tallies." I stood. "Here—let me hold the door open for you."

Viola didn't respond as she rammed the cart forward down the hall.

I don't like surprises. I don't think most people do, and I quickly developed a plan to reduce the chances of more surprises. I figured Viola knew most of the secrets at Miracle Foods and might be annoyed enough with Leslie—and everyone else—to share some of those secrets now.

Accordingly, I hurried to catch up with Viola. "I'm impressed by the number of panelists recruited. The four panels marked 'Class' have only about twenty responses each, but the ones identified as 'Lory Center' have fifty to eighty responses each."

Viola snorted. "Don't be impressed. We bribed panelists with vouchers for two dollar off orders at the Lory Student Center's Ramskeller Pub."

When we came to the main office, I opened the door. Viola threw the box onto her desk and said, "I'm sorry but I don't have time for more questions."

My plan had failed. The only thing I'd learned was Viola knew a lot about all aspects of Miracle Foods but only shared secrets when she was in the mood.

***

An hour later, I concluded the questionnaires were of limited value to me. Leslie's primary purpose had been to determine which cultured meat products were marketable. My quick review of the forms indicated casseroles and meat loaves made with the Miracle Foods's products got "good" to "very good" ratings, but slices of cultured meat in sandwiches were unacceptable to the majority of tasters. No wonder Jim had focused the work of two of his assistants on developing meat-like texture in Miracle Foods's products.

I also recognized Leslie's secondary purpose had been to determine which segments of the population would accept cultured meat products within the confines of a one-page questionnaire. Accordingly, she asked panelists four key questions: their age, their gender, the amount of time spent in food preparation weekly, and their major or field of work. The first three questions made sense to me, the fourth didn't.

Although I searched the two boxes in the conference room thoroughly, I didn't find any folder with analyses of the taste panel data in terms of age, gender, and background of the subjects. I was surprised because I always find it exciting to see my hypotheses tested and assumed Leslie would, too. Of course, Leslie might have done the analyses but elected to not share her results with others. I made a note to ask her when she recuperated a bit and focused on the one question on the form that related to the occurrence of allergies among tasters.

Only thirteen panelists of the five hundred or so who completed forms admitted to having food allergies. Those panelists claimed to have allergic reactions to peanuts, seafood, and/or milk. It was likely those reporting an allergy to milk were really lactose intolerant and not allergic to milk, per se. Thus, the incidence of food allergies among the panelists

J. L. Greger

seemed to be lower than the estimated incidence of food allergies in American adults nationwide. I reasoned that wasn't surprising because those with food allergies might have been afraid to participate in the study.

The questionnaires had been designed so they could have been answered on computer answer sheets, but those sheets weren't used. Perhaps because Leslie had allowed space for comments on the back of the form. However, I found only six forms with scribbled comments. My favorite comment was: "The meat does not look as good as the chick with the forms." None mentioned hives or any other health reactions to the food tasted. However, those reaction aren't instantaneous, and usually occur fifteen minutes to two hours after ingestion of contaminated food.

As I pawed through the boxes, I saw about thirty purchasing files. I quickly recognized each file was labeled with the year and one of six codes: *LAB, TP*—I assumed that stood for taste panel not toilet paper, *CT*—I assumed that stood for clinical trial, *OFFICE, EQUIPMENT, MAINTENANCE*, and *OTHER*. There was a color associated with each code; these were obviously Viola's handiwork because she seemed to be big on color coding.

The *LAB* files—all with blue labels—had been subdivided by vendors. A forensic accountant would love the organization of these files, but I doubted such a specialist would be needed to solve this case. No one had mentioned missing funds.

Out of curiosity, I examined the contents of the six *CT* files. All had green labels. The three thin ones contained the contracts and correspondence with the meal site, the nurse, and a medical laboratory. One *CT* file was thick and had the paperwork associated with paying participants in the clinical trial. That reminded me that I needed to see the consent forms for the clinical trial and get a list of the participants.

The fifth green labeled file contained check sheets for each of the sixteen days of the clinical trial. Each check sheet listed the amount of each food served in the lunch. Most of the pages had grease stains and were signed and dated, most likely at the meal site. There were also signed sheets recording the preparation of the main dish on each of the sixteen days. I set this file aside because I realized it contained data essential for my analyses.

The sixth file was odd. It obviously had been fat. The middle ribs had been folded to allow for at least an inch of inserts. Now there were only a couple purchase orders and receipts for paper goods in the file, although it was labeled *CT-food*. I speculated someone, probably Leslie or Viola, had removed all the purchase orders and receipts for food from the file. That was interesting because Viola had hinted more than personnel files might be missing.

I slipped *CT-food* file into Bug's cart under his treat bags. This would be my chance to test Viola's and Leslie's honesty. I wondered whether either of them would admit this file was missing.

I wandered into Viola's office. "I'm done with the taste panel files. I'd like to xerox a few of the forms and your summary tallies for each panel." I thought further explanation was unwise. "Have you figured out which personnel files are missing?"

Viola smiled. "Yes." She pushed several pages at me. "Here's the printouts of the computer records of the three student interns whose paper files are missing. All three worked here for less than a semester."

"In other words, they might have not been pleased with their experience here?"

"I thought that, too, but there's nothing odd in our computer records. Of course, when one of us has a problem with an intern, we usually put a note in the paper file but not in the computer records."

I wanted to interview those three students but didn't want them forewarned. I forced a smile and changed the topic, "One more thing puzzles me about the break-in. I was told the thousand dollars Leslie had in her desk drawer wasn't taken."

Viola looked surprised. "Jim talks too much."

"Why do you think Leslie had so much cash in her desk drawer?" What I really wanted to know was whether the money was a payment for an illicit activity.

Viola's voice was higher pitched than before. "How would I know Leslie's plans?" Then she gave a harsh laugh. "If the money had been found in Mendel's desk drawer, I would have thought it was for his bookie. He likes to bet on sports teams." She looked at the ceiling and swallowed hard. "Or the hound dog could have been paying off a lady friend."

CHAPTER 7: Sara Meets the Police

Everyone was pretty subdued at Miracle Foods on Tuesday afternoon as I talked to Jim Jackson and his lab crew. The surgery to pin Leslie's right femur because of multiple fractures had been a success but doctors had induced a medical coma to limit damage from swelling in her brain.

Then thing got even worse. I was in Mendel's office when two police officers arrived and announced the fifth-grader Leslie hit had died. Mendel coldly announced that he knew nothing about the accident and would answer their questions only with his lawyer present. The police suggested I leave his office.

An hour later the police arrived in the conference room where I was sorting through the menus served at the meals site during the clinical trial. There is one thing good about a clinical trial forced to end early—there were only sixteen menus.

The short male officer stared at me for several seconds before he said, "We were told you'd solve all our problems."

"Doubt it. I only arrived here this morning. And I don't see how the death of a homeless man last week presumably from an anaphylactic response to an insect bite or sting in winter—which doesn't make sense—after he ate a presumably safe test product in a clinical trial is related to Leslie's accident." I resisted chuckling. What I'd just said was double-talk to anyone not immersed in the clinical trial, and I waited for the officers to ignore me or ask for an explanation.

The male officer rubbed his hand over his graying buzz cut and then turned and looked down the hall before he closed the door. The tall, thin female officer with mousy brown hair pulled into a ponytail said, "Paul Carbonne in the FBI office in Albuquerque said you were a scientist and rambled a bit, but it would be worth our effort to get your help."

I felt a headache coming on. "Why did you talk to Carbonne? How did you get his name?" I squinted at the female and then the male officer. "There's something important that you've not told me. What is it?"

The officers introduced themselves as Officer Esther Scofield and Sergeant Bart Western. Scofield sat down at the table and extracted her phone from a pocket in her jacket while Western said, "Mendel Lopez bragged he hired you on the recommendation of USDA and FBI officials. We talked to an Agent Carbonne. He thought we should save ourselves headaches and be frank with you from the start. That's not our standard procedure with a bystander." He cracked the door open and scanned the hall.

Scofield looked up from her phone "Leslie's accident might not be an accident. You're the only one here who doesn't have a motive and what you're investigating may be helpful in determining one."

"Let's both stop the double-talk. I heard Leslie was driving too fast as usual, hit black ice, spun the car, and hit a pedestrian. That's an accident, isn't it?"

"You've heard our official line." After Western nodded, Scofield continued, "Officers found a slick spot that smelled fishy, like brake fluid, at the accident site but no ice. When a mechanic at the police garage reported that a brake line on Leslie's car had been cut, we were called to investigate."

I took a sip of my diet cola to give me time to think. "Who knows about the grease spot and cut brake line?"

Scofield sighed. "No one in this building. We explained our visit here as a routine follow up on a tragic accident."

I smiled because I was about to rise in their estimation. "Did you know that the brother-in-law of Viola Sanchez works at the police garage? Viola and I picked up three boxes that had been in the trunk of Leslie's car this morning."

Western chuckled, "Glad I didn't take Carbonne's bet." He pointed at me. "He guaranteed you'd be useful if I gave you time to think. Filly, how do you know that?"

Scofield pursed her lips and expelled air slowly before she began to tap out a note on her phone.

I couldn't decide it the man meant to be insulting or had an old-fashioned—and inappropriate—sense of humor concerning women. "Thanks for calling me a filly not an old gray mare. I needed info on the taste panels and clinical trial conducted by Miracle Foods. All the data were in boxes that I saw Leslie and Jim load into Leslie's car last night around five. I..."

Western interrupted. "I thought you got here today."

"You discovered one of my secrets. Before I checked into the motel last night, I cased out Miracle Foods from the next-door parking

                                                J. L. Greger

lot." I paused thinking. "Getting back to my story. This morning—around nine—I walked into Viola's office. She was on the phone. After a quick side conversation with me, she told the person on the phone that we'd be right down for the three boxes in Leslie's trunk. When we got there, she popped out of the car to talk to a man." I tried to recall the man's appearance. "Sorry, all I remember about him was he had a knit navy cap pulled over his ears and wasn't tall—not much taller than Viola."

Western shook his head. "That was outside proper police procedure. Do Albuquerque police always do you favors?"

I didn't like his tone. "I'm no expert on police protocol, but I thought it was odd that Viola didn't have to sign any paperwork. So, I commented on how cooperative the man was. Viola admitted he was her brother-in-law, and he figured the boxes would just be left untouched in the police evidence room for months."

Western gave me a puzzled look. "You must have really pushed Viola to get her to go for the boxes. She's not known around town as a pushover."

"I didn't. She wanted to see them, too."

Both officers stared at me.

"This is one of the boxes." I pointed to the box on the table. "It contains the company's personnel records and files from the ill-fated clinical trial. I spent over two hours combing through the files in the other two boxes this morning and then gave them to Viola around noon when we exchanged boxes. Those two boxes contained data files on taste panels conducted by Miracle Foods and what looked like all the company's purchasing records for the last five years."

Scofield whispered to Western before she scurried from the room. He looked bored as he cracked the door and gazed after her. "Why was Viola eager to see those files?"

"She wanted to determine which files were missing. Leslie had told Jim several were missing before she left for the university. He thought—or maybe assumed—they were personnel files. That's why Viola took the box with the personnel files first."

Western closed the door when Scofield scooted back in. "Did Viola tell you which specific files were missing?"

"Yes, when we traded boxes around noon." I pulled a pink sheet that Viola had given me from one of the files in the box. "Here's a list of all past and present employees of Miracle Foods. The starred names are those of three student interns who worked here for less than one semester. Their files are missing."

Scofield coughed. "How did Viola have contact information for them if their files are missing."

"Computer records, which Viola said were less complete than the paper files."

"That's all you've got?"

I swallowed hard because I thought he was being unnecessarily sarcastic, and I hated to admit what I'd done. "From the start Viola seemed concerned that Leslie had discovered files, besides the personnel ones, were missing. When I paged quickly through the purchasing files. I spotted an interesting one labeled *CT-food*. It looked as if someone had removed pages—like an inch thick wad of purchase orders and receipts— from the file."

"Do you know who removed items from the file?"

"No. Most likely either Viola or Leslie." I stepped to Bug's carrier. "The overall impression I've gotten is they don't like—maybe *trust* is the better word—each other." I pulled out the *CT-food* file from Bug's cart. "Now you'll learn my other secret. I hid the file that I think is missing purchase orders and receipts for foods bought for the clinical trial. I planned to see whether Leslie or Viola noticed." I shrugged. "Maybe not a good idea but I think it might be central to discovering what happened at the meal site."

Western grabbed the *CT-food* file. "Probably the best thing you did today. Do you know what it's missing?"

"Not exactly." I pointed to the materials spread out on the table. "However, I can make educated guesses after I study the menus served at the meal site." I paused and noticed Scofield was frantically typing on her phone. "I also spent an hour talking to Jim and the lab crew to learn what data they had from the clinical trial and what they'd given Leslie. Everything they mentioned—which wasn't much—seems to be in the box, but there's a problem because..."

Western shook his head in apparent disgust. "Viola had these files for several hours while you worked on the other two boxes."

I nodded.

Western snorted and glanced at Scofield. "Pardner, not sure if the junk in these boxes is worth claiming."

Scofield pursed her lips and controlled her breathing again. "They were inappropriately taken from a car impounded at the police garage."

Western pointed to the pages I had spread over the table. "Put that junk in the box."

"Please let me copy the menu file. Then I can assess which purchase orders are missing from the *CT-food* file and suggest which

                                                                J. L. Greger

analyses are needed to determine how the homeless guy died. Besides, I need the info for my preliminary reports to FDA and USDA. They want them by Thursday."

Western's lower jaw dropped an inch. Scofield stopped typing and said, "Oh, my."

I wasn't sure what I'd said that had alarmed them and I began to dither. "FDA required Miracle Foods to save samples of the food served on the three days when people at the meal site developed rashes and hives or allergic reactions. But I don't know where those samples are located yet or what to test them for yet. All that needs to be in my preliminary report."

"Yeah, yeah, but what interested me is your comment about telling us how the homeless guy died. You know the medical examiner here is an M.D. and pretty smart." Scofield coughed after Western finished his comment.

I knew I'd overstepped professional boundaries. "Somehow, I doubt the man died from an anaphylactic reaction to a flea or bed bug bite. They're the only insects around in the middle of winter. I'd really like to talk to the medical examiner tomorrow about a hypothesis I'm formulating."

Western thumbed through the contents of the *CT-menu* file and handed it to Scofield. "I'm sure the medical examiner will be game."

"Good. Please don't mention these files to anyone. I've let everyone here think I'm focusing on the taste panels because I don't want them to know, like Leslie, I'm studying the data in the *CT-food* and *CT-menu* files."

Scofield gasped. "What are you trying to say?"

I debated internally whether my next comment would make me sound irrational. I figured it didn't matter. "I think there might also be relevant information at the meal site, but someone from Miracle Foods might try to destroy or steal it if they knew of my interest. Of course, security at the meal site may be poor enough that the relevant items may already be gone."

Scofield wheezed a bit. "You may have answered another of our questions. Leslie's accident was only a block away from the meal site—not on campus"

Western who had been staring at the ceiling, stopped softly cursing. "We'll confiscate all the boxes. I want you to protest loudly. We'll be a little bit nasty." He handed the files labeled *CT-food* and *CT-menus* to Scofield. "We'll deliver copies of these two files to you with a pizza from Paisano's Pizza. How about sausage and pepperoni?" He winked. "You'll recognize the pizza delivery boy." He pulled out a photo from his wallet. "My son works at Paisano's."

"Make it a pepperoni and mushroom pizza."

CHAPTER 8: Sergeant Bart Western's Views

Sergeant Bart Western of the Criminal Investigation Unit of the Fort Collins Police Department rarely got a call for a suspected homicide in the college community of Fort Collins. After all, this relatively small community of less than two hundred thousand was rated regularly as one of the best places to live in the U.S. Most of the calls he and his assistant Officer Esther Scofield handled were classified as aggravated assaults. Thus, he was surprised when traffic officers reported that the cause of a fatal accident was suspicious. He knew this February day was going to be a bad one when mechanics later informed him the brakes lines of Leslie Lopez's car had been cut.

His uneasiness about the case was not only because a child had been killed and the cause of the accident was suspicious but because the driver was Leslie Lopez. What could he say? Leslie had requested a restraining order against a college student who stalked her last year. Western had felt sorry for the twenty-year-old student because Leslie was a snotty cat and had led the boy on. But that wasn't an appropriate thing to say nowadays.

Mendel Lopez, her husband, also made him nervous. He had annihilated anyone who opposed him as he amassed his fortune over the last thirty years. Mendel had generally won his battles because his hired guns—lawyers and consultants—were always the best available. That was why the medical examiner had taken the coward's way out and stated in his preliminary report that the cause of death of the homeless man at the meal site was "anaphylaxis from an insect sting." *Come on.* Bees and wasps don't swarm humans in February in northern Colorado.

He looked across his desk to Esther Scofield as she practiced her breathing exercises and studied a file. The poor woman had asthma and had moved to Fort Collins for health reasons six months ago from Los Angeles where she was a sergeant in the drugs unit. Generally she was a quiet woman, except she was a bit touchy on what he would call protocol issues.

"Pardner, looks like we'll be investigating an accident, which probably wasn't an accident today. He explained the case. "You're sweeter than I am. See if you can wrangle anything from the EMTs. The police at the scene thought the driver was dazed but couldn't smell alcohol on her breath. I'll try to talk to her husband."

***

Thirty minutes later, he had battle scars from Viola Sanchez's tongue but hadn't been granted access to Mendel Lopez. Viola was the type of special assistant every executive wanted. She was one smart Rottweiler. However, Viola had given him the name of the hired gun whom Mendel had hired to save Miracle Foods from embarrassment because of the death of a homeless man. Her name was Dr. Sara Almquist. Her references included the Inspector General at USDA and the interim head of the FBI field office in Albuquerque—Paul Carbonne.

When Scofield said she'd dealt a bit with Carbonne, he called the man. Western wasn't prepared for what he heard. Mendel had outdone himself this time. Besides being a scientist with extensive forensic experience, Dr. Almquist was known for her integrity. Carbonne had described Sara as smart with a sense of humor, but he noted "she might seem a bit spacey at times."

With that information, he and Scofield set out for Miracle Foods ostensibly to talk to Mendel Lopez and his employees, but really to pick the brain of Mendel's current hired gun.

***

As expected, Mendel refused to talk about Leslie or her accident with Almquist present. He was sure Mendel and Leslie had presented themselves as a loving couple to the consultant. However, many in town had observed at least one of their spirited discussions. The mechanic who found the cut brake line had even said, "Mendel must have wanted to save himself the cost of another divorce."

Western agreed but knew better than make any unsubstantiated claims to Mendel, especially with a witness present. It was wiser to play dumb with Mendel. Accordingly, Western waited for Almquist to leave and then asked. "Any reason why Leslie was driving fifty in a thirty-mile-per-hour zone? That's important when we're investigating a vehicular homicide."

Mendel looked at him calmly. "Talk to my lawyer."

***

As Western and Scofield wandered down the hall to talk to Jim Jackson after having an equally unproductive conversation with Viola

Sanchez, Scofield said, "Leslie's accident didn't faze either of them." She wheezed a bit. "I think someone in the department leaked info."

"Maybe we're just smelling money. Mendel's family—at least the Drakes on his mother's side—have maintained a big cattle spread near here for generations. And Viola's family has been their trusted employees for most of that time." He whistled. "Our next interview is with a good old boy from South Carolina who came here for an MS and stayed on. Rumor has it he and Leslie might have been an item six years ago, but his marriage seems stable now. He and his wife sing in our church choir. His boy Tom attends Front Range Baptist Academy."

Scofield murmured, "Hmm. You like Jim."

Western frowned. "Hard not to feel sorry for him. Miracle Foods isn't a happy place. His wife asks for prayers for 'peace in the workplace' almost every week at church."

The conversation with Jim also yielded little, except Jim expressed disappointment that the hired consultant had focused too much attention on the taste panels and seemed oblivious to the real problems at Miracle Foods.

***

After he and Scofield had interviewed Sara, he yelled hoping everyone heard him, "I don't care what you think. This box and its contents are police property." He repeated his statements again as Scofield opened the door to the main office just in case anyone at Miracle Foods hadn't heard him the first time. Then he closed the door and said quietly to Sara, "Don't forget a Paisano's pizza will be delivered to your motel room a little after six."

He hoisted the lone box from the conference room table and whistled as he sauntered to the main office where Viola was screaming as Scofield handed her a receipt and rolled a cart with two boxes and a few loose pages forward. He plunked his box on the cart as Scofield pushed it out the front door.

When Western hoisted the boxes into the trunk, Scofield said, "We acted just in time. Viola wasn't upset when I announced the boxes shouldn't have been removed from police custody until we catalogued their contents." She smiled. "But she lost it when I emptied her wastebasket onto the cart. Looks like she was discarding a few pages from the taste panel files."

He glanced at the loose pages after he and Scofield were in the car. "Maybe the hired gun will know why?"

"Hmm," said Scofield. "They're just four taste panel forms. But... Viola sure didn't want us to find them."

"Xerox them and the stuff in the two files the hired gun wanted. Let her earn her fees. Now we'd better gallop to the meal site before the director goes home."

"No rush. She's waiting for us because I told her we have a contribution to the meal site."

She smiled for the first time this afternoon. "Did I tell you that you're writing the meal site a check for fifty dollars to match mine?"

"Why?"

"We're building good will." She didn't pause for him to reply. "It's time for you to modernize. I'm not xeroxing the two files Sara wanted and these loose pages. I'll scan them with my phone and send the pages electronically while you drive." She breathed deeply and blew out the air slowly several times. "And what was that silliness about your son? He quit Paisano's Pizza before Christmas. Were you trying to flirt with Sara? Let me give you a tip—don't call her a hired gun or a horse again. She frowned every time you made your cute remarks."

"Yes, ma'am."

Scofield coughed violently.

Western knew he was lucky to have Scofield as a partner. She never—well seldom—corrected him in front of the bosses or during interviews. But she was wrong on one point. If he was going to flirt, it would be with her not Sara. That wasn't possible as long as he was technically her boss.

J. L. Greger

CHAPTER 9: Sara Picks at Details

The city park was probably pretty in summer but it was depressing at twilight on a windy, cold day. The thin coating of water on the shoveled walks was rapidly freezing into a glaze. Bug handled the problem well. He avoided the slippery paths and hopped through the deep snow leaving imprints of his furry seat.

I wasn't as graceful as I alternately slipped on the ice or plodded in the snow. Part of my problem was my leather boots were old. They had sat unused in my closet for years—ever since I came to New Mexico from Michigan—and must have developed cracks. My feet were cold and wet when I got to my car. I decided I was not willing to risk frostbite in my toes to learn what had attracted a small crowd of people and dogs to the picnic benches at the far side of the park.

The sidewalk and the drive to my motel reminded me why I liked living in the desert of New Mexico. I seldom had to deal with shoveling snow, slipping on ice, or worrying about frostbite because of wet socks. Still Colorado was a good change of pace. Although several of the characters I met today hadn't been friendly, they hadn't threatened me as gang members sometimes had during previous cases. Moreover, I felt I was doing something positive. Cultured meat could be ecologically useful if an acceptable product could be manufactured at low cost.

Then I realized that no one had asked me to taste the products of Miracle Foods. I would have thought they'd be proud of their products and would promote them to everyone who entered the building—perhaps even have samples for tasting in the main office.

I called Sanders and told him about my day. After my long dialog, his comments were succinct. "So far, you've only learned what they want you to know. You described a group that has lots of secrets. Tomorrow you have figure out which secrets are relevant to the death of the homeless man at the meal site. Then the rest will fall into place. Have they even told you his name?"

He was right, as usual. I'd collected and analyzed lots of details but perhaps missed the forest for the trees. It reminded me how good a pair Sanders and I were professionally. I hoped we were as good on a personal level. "Thanks honey for the best advice I got today. Now it's your turn. How was your day?"

***

I'd received the files from Scofield on my computer just before I finished my conversation with Sanders. The loose pages Viola had tried to discard were interesting. One was the form with the unusual comment—"The meat does not look as good as the chick with the forms." The profiles for the individuals who completed all four discarded taste panel ratings were the same—a college-age male interested in engineering and with unspecified allergies. I wondered why Viola had tried to discard these pages. My first thought was her son had filled out these forms, but I couldn't imagine why the information on these forms mattered. Unless she was ashamed her son had a crush on Leslie.

Shortly after I emailed my observations to Scofield, my pizza arrived. Only the delivery boy was Western, not his son. He seemed pleased with what he called "my tips," warned me not to open my door again for anyone until morning, and told me to call him if anyone from Miracle Foods contacted me. I couldn't decide whether his last two comments were reassuring or made me more nervous.

Bug snuggled next to me as I watched a rerun of the 2017 version of *Murder on the Orient Express* with Kenneth Branagh and studied the menus from the clinical trial. I was now sure that Leslie and I had honed in on the same discrepancy because I noted her penciled comments on several pages. I emailed Scofield and asked if I could meet her at the police station at nine. I hoped Western wouldn't be present because he didn't have the patience to appreciate my argument.

***

Sanders and I usually talk every morning between five-thirty to six my time. That's seven-thirty to eight his time in Washington, D.C. Although I'm an early bird, five-thirty seems awfully early some days but that was the price of living two time zones away from my partner. This morning was an exception. He'd forgotten to alert me last night that he was catching a seven-a.m. flight from Washington to Miami. Thus, he woke me at four-thirty to say he'd was about to board a flight to Miami on his way to Havana. I thought he'd already completed his work in Cuba, but there was no time to question him.

The purpose of his call was two-fold. He didn't want me to panic when I couldn't reach him at our usual time. He also wanted me to call him sometime between ten to noon his time—that was the time he would be in the Miami airport before his flight to Havana—about our weekend plans. After I heard in the background the hollow sound of an airport announcement, Sanders spoke more rapidly. "Thought about your case last night. Any chance the mischief at the clinical trial was the first round of a nasty divorce? Got to go. Love you."

I decided there was no reason to go back to bed and made a list of what I had to get done before I met with Scofield at the police station. The most important item on my list was to call FDA officials in Washington and determine exactly what they expected in the report from Miracle Foods on the adverse events that had occurred in the clinical trial. Then I had to talk to Mendel, which was apt to be unpleasant.

I was confident that the FDA would expect analyses to be run on the saved foods samples. Although allergenic proteins and histamine were the usual components in food causing rashes and hives, it was possible that the inappropriate application a disinfectant or a pesticide at the site could have caused rashes in a few unlucky diners. However, the fact that the rashes were seen only in diners in the test group made the second supposition unlikely. I hoped FDA would only require analyses of histamine.

If Mendel refused to pay for the analyses or insisted as Jim had that the analyses be done in the labs at Miracle Foods, the FDA would probably want the Fort Collins police to confiscate the frozen samples and move them to a safe location to wait analyses.

FDA would also want to know whether the apparent toxicity of several of the meals in the clinical trial was due to sloppy mistakes by Miracle Foods or to intentional sabotage. I was awash with data but had no answer to that question yet. The wafts of odd chemical odors I'd noticed at the plant could reflect early signs of spoilage and poor quality control at Miracle Foods because of incompetence or unwise short cuts in production. However, I couldn't rule out industrial espionage or malicious sabotage by a disgruntled employee.

The saboteur, if he or she existed, had a lot of scientific knowledge. Histamine toxicity per se is never fatal. That suggested the saboteur didn't want to kill anyone but wanted to disrupt the clinical trial and presumably devalue Miracle Foods and its intellectual property without really hurting anyone permanently. The most likely candidates were Jim Jackson, Leslie Lopez, and the technicians and interns employed by Miracle Foods.

My conversations with the technicians had convinced me that they focused on their individual tasks and didn't even know that Jim had monitored histamine levels in any of the cultured meat products. The reports in the files from student interns in the personnel files suggested they also had been kept uninformed about the "big picture" at Miracle Foods. All the interns referred to tests they performed on coded samples; none referred to their results in terms of beef, turkey, or fish forms of cultured meat. That meant Jim and Leslie were my most likely suspects. Of course, there was Viola Sanchez. She was smart enough to have broken the codes. She certainly had taken charge of the data from the taste panels.

I decided I needed to talk to the three interns whose files were missing, particularly a Troy Pitkin. I'd found a letter of recommendation from Jim Jackson in the computer version of Pitkin's personnel file. Jim had noted that Troy had modified a method for histamine analyses from the literature and applied it to cultured meat samples.

That left the dead homeless guy. Technically, the FDA and I were only interested in his death *if* it was due to what he ate at the meal site. I'd read his preliminary autopsy report several times, but how it related to the rest of the problems at the meal site remained a mystery. One thing was clear—high levels of histamine in the product couldn't have induced the allergic reaction that killed him. I needed to talk to the medical examiner.

Then there was the last mystery. Why had someone tried to eliminate Leslie? Granted she was unpleasant but that wasn't a reason for murder. From my perspective, the main question was: What did Leslie know about the snafus during the clinical trial? Perhaps, she'd have something to say when she came out of her medically induced coma. Then I realized she may have shared her suspicions with Mendel on Monday night.

When I find my mind is running in circles, I try to relax and let my subconscious digest the data. Accordingly, I walked Bug for twenty minutes before I called FDA officials and then the Inspector General's Office of USDA in Washington. They agreed with my suspicions and referred me to their field agents in Denver and Fort Collins. Most of all they reiterated they expected a preliminary report from Miracle Foods by Thursday. They also noted that Viola Sanchez had notified them I was responsible for the report.

***

I walked into Scofield's office at one minute after nine having barely finished all my calls and emails to federal officials. I felt discombobulated, not ready for another serious discussion. "Be patient with me like you are with Western. I'll get to a conclusion eventually, but it only will make sense if you listen to my reasoning first."

Scofield gave me a one-sided smile.

"Jim Jackson has repeatedly stated that he thought the symptoms of individuals at the meal site were caused by high histamine levels in food, not allergies, per se. So last night I calculated the histamine levels in the menus served." I pointed to a spreadsheet on my laptop. "He kept emphasizing fermented foods, such as pickles and sauerkraut, and certain vegetables, such as spinach, tomatoes, and eggplant, were major sources of histamine. However, when I considered the amounts served at the site, none of the meals would have contained more than a three-quarters of a milligram of histamine. From what I see in the literature, that level of histamine wouldn't produce the rampant symptoms of histamine toxicity observed among test subjects at the meal site."

"Okay. He was wrong."

"Not totally. The symptoms, at least the rashes and hives, in the homeless at the meal site are consistent with histamine poisoning. So I thought maybe several of the homeless men or women had induced histamine symptoms by drinking too much booze. Not uncommon among indigents. But I found a six pack of most beers contains less than a tenth of milligram of histamine. Then I noticed you could get maybe three milligrams of histamine by drinking a liter of certain red wines. Red wines also contain other substances that intensify the response to histamine."

Scofield coughed. "Is histamine why my face sometimes flushes when I drink red wine?"

"You could be one of the sensitive individuals."

"Now I've got a reason for not liking most red wines." Scofield spoke more slowly, "It's my experience most sots here favor beer not wine. Besides meal site officials don't admit anyone who shows sign of drunkenness. They're too apt to get rowdy or make a mess."

"That's what I figured. So I decided I'd reached the limits of my food composition tables. A certified food testing lab, needs to analyze the samples saved from the three problematic days at the meal site for histamine."

"Yes, I remember FDA officials ordered Jim to freeze food from the meal last week when the one subject died. Our deputy medical examiner had laughed, 'Poor Jim has no idea what to look for in that garbage.'"

"That's what I figured. Then I checked which methods were considered best for histamine analyses of foods. That's when things got interesting. Most of the methodologies focused on analyses of fish. It seems scombroid poisoning is really histamine poisoning."

Scofield stared at me with her mouth agape. She swallowed hard. "When I worked the docks in L.A. looking for drugs, we sometimes noticed red inflammation on the arms and faces and wheezing among fishermen. Especially if the catch stunk. Those were the ones most apt to be shipping drugs in the fish."

"You've hit the nail on the head. Seems histamine levels can go sky high in tuna and mahi-mahi when the fish start to spoil, even before the fish stinks or tastes bad."

"But meal sites for the homeless don't serve fresh fish."

"Doesn't matter. Several of the most severe documented cases of scombroid poisoning have occurred when individual ate canned tuna."

She didn't look at me but texted rapidly on her phone. "The server at the site had made a tuna casserole on the day she became ill."

I thought Scofield was awfully observant to have noted and remembered that detail. I'd also noticed she hadn't wheezed or done any of her breathing exercises this morning. "How did you remember that detail?"

"The deputy medical examiner mentioned it to Western and me before he released the preliminary autopsy report."

"Wait. So, the deputy medical examiner doubted the homeless guy died of an insect sting even though he mentioned the insect sting in the preliminary report?"

Western entered the room without knocking. "Hired gun, you've caught up to our investigation in about a day. Better than I expected."

Scofield straightened, pursed her lips, and slowly expelled her breath. "We hoped to draw out the truth by making everyone nervous. The medical examiner wanted to let the killer know he'd found a small wound on the corpse, without mentioning a drug injection."

My mouth was agape. This was one slick police unit. "Let me see if I can add to the puzzle with my other observations. Tuna casseroles were served on the two days when individuals developed symptoms that sound like histamine poisoning."

"But only individuals in the test group developed rashes. Damn— that means we can forget the canned fish theory." Western shook his head. "No luck on this case."

I smiled. "No, I think we can conclude the fish product made at Miracle Foods sometimes contained high levels of histamine or some other toxic substance."

"But not always?" said Scofield.

"That's what I'm guessing because fish was served six times during the three weeks of the clinical trial. Individuals in the test group developed symptoms on only two of the days. Leslie must have reached the same conclusion because she penciled in what looks like batch numbers for the cultured tuna on the menu sheets."

J. L. Greger

Western began to pace. "Hate to bust your bubble but the church woman got sick after she made the fish casserole with real tuna." I must have looked surprised because he added, "You know—tuna from a can not the fake stuff."

I gasped. "I didn't know that, and it sure complicates our story. I wonder… could it be? Perhaps we have two sources of toxic contamination—canned tuna and sometimes cultured tuna." I thought for a few seconds. "Maybe Leslie noticed the incongruity and pulled the purchase orders and receipts from the *CT-food* file. She wanted to trace the source of the canned fish."

Scofield quietly took notes as Western blustered. "Do you think Viola is involved?"

It was now my turn to be flustered. "She's the purchasing agent for Miracle Foods. She placed every order I saw in the files."

Western stopped pacing. "And you thought Viola seemed to know more than personnel files were missing."

"And I'll add to our confusion. I can't believe Jim didn't mention spoiled fish was the usual source of massive amounts of histamine. He kept trying to divert my attention to fermented foods." I paused to think "There's another thing that bothers me. Jim told me he'd analyzed samples of the beef and turkey products for histamine. He didn't mention any analysis of the cultured fish."

Scofield looked up almost demurely at Western as he continued to pace. "You mean pious Jim who sings in the church choir might have lied?"

I winked at her because this was the first time I'd heard her mock her pompous partner. "Or worse. The problem is both Jim and Viola would lose their lucrative jobs if Miracle Foods folded because of bad publicity on Miracle Foods's products. Of course, if they received a large bribe, they might not care. Similarly it doesn't make sense for either Leslie or Mendel to undermine their own company."

Scofield looked up from her phone and taking notes. "Unless one of them wanted to decrease the value of Miracle Foods prior to seeking a divorce."

Western stopped pacing. "God knows their marriage appears to be rocky…"

"And boisterous," said Scofield.

Western's phone buzzed. After he said, "We'll be there right away," he winked at Scofield. "The meal site was broken into last night. Several cases of food and all their records are missing."

I surmised they had a secret, and they didn't plan to share it with me, yet.

CHAPTER 10: Sara at the Meal Site on Wednesday

As I looked at the trashed storage area at the meal site, I thought this break-in wasn't really for theft but was designed to destroy evidence. Of course, I didn't know *what* evidence. The perpetrator could have been trying to hide something about the death of the homeless man or attempting to disguise how contaminated food had been fed to the homeless.

My assigned task was to determine what food was missing and it wouldn't be easy. The cook was busy talking to Scofield. His scrawny assistant Mike, probably at least once a homeless man, sat dejectedly in the dining area cursing. I couldn't blame him. Dozens of cans and plastic canisters of food doused with pickle relish and broken glass lay on the floor of the storeroom.

Careful to avoid glass shards, I dropped to my knees and started to read the labels. All the cans were tuna and all the canisters were dried cheese. I studied the metal racks that lined one wall of the storage area across from institutional refrigerators and freezers. Only one rack was empty. On one side of this rack, canned fruits and vegetable were still neatly stacked. On the other side of the empty rack, plastic pails labeled as pinto beans, peas, lentils, and black beans were lined up on the lower shelves of the rack. On the top shelves were bags of rice and boxes of dried pasta. I guessed the empty rack had been the storage area for canned meats, dried cheese, and the unfortunate jars of relish.

I pulled the assistant cook Mike into the storeroom. "What was on these shelves?" I pointed to the top two shelves.

Mike scrunched his face. "Relishes and dried cheese. Things we don't use much."

I looked at the debris on the floor. "Did you have four or five gallon jars of relish and six large canisters of cheese?"

He scrunched his face again. "Sounds right."

"Beside canned fish, what else did you have on the lower two shelves?"

Mike rubbed his unshaven lower face. "Hmm—maybe canned chicken? Maybe not. The cook likes to buy fresh turkey and chicken thighs. Taste better." He shook his head. "We serve fish a lot—too much." He nodded as if he was agreeing with himself. "Yep, bottom shelves were all cans of fish. We got a big shipment in early last week." He scratched his greasy looking hair. "Then we got a second small order."

"Do you know when?"

"Look lady, I just help cook and clean. One of the church ladies keeps the records."

That reminded me that I'd like to talk to the woman who experienced the extreme toxic reaction last week. "You've been helpful. I'll talk to the officers and see if you can clean up this mess."

He shuffled away. "Better or lunch will be late. Makes the guys and gals grouchy."

I interrupted Scofield's conversation with the cook. "They took only cans of fish. The dried cheese and relishes fell when they removed the cases of fish. I need to see the receipts next."

The cook, a slightly younger and cleaner version of his assistant Mike, nodded. "Sound right." He nodded his head again and again. I was beginning to think he had a degenerative nervous disorder. "Problem is the drawer with the inventory and all of last week's receipts was empty when I looked. Damnedest thing. Who takes paper?"

Scofield thanked the cook profusely for his help and sent him off to his kitchen. When he was out of earshot, she said, "Western and I feared—maybe hoped—this would happen. I got the inventory and receipts from the church secretary last night, while Western installed a camera. We purposely waited until the cook, his assistant, and all the clients had left for the day." She looked around the room. "The problem was it was too late to get our lab crew out for a non-emergency. Western is not good at technical details. I hope the camera worked."

Western came from a side door whistling. "We got photos, such as they are. Guess we can leave now."

"Wait." I pulled Western's sleeve. "Can we talk to the server who developed the severe reaction last week?"

Western stopped whistling. "No need."

"Are you sure?"

Western stomped to the door. Scofield laughed. "He should have admitted he set up a meeting with the server and our deputy medical examiner." She looked at watch. "It's in thirty minutes at a local coffee shop."

                                    J. L. Greger

I thought of my promise to call Sanders. "Sorry, but I need ten minutes now to make a call."

Western grimaced. "Hurry—we'll be waiting in my car by the front door."

***

Sanders was in a good mood. He was traveling to Cuba with an expert on LIDAR, a type of laser system using pulsating light waves to create three-dimensional images. Only this expert from the National Oceanic and Atmospheric Administration—which Sanders always called NOAA—was focusing on pulsing waves in the range of green light, not the usual infrared range, because light in part of the green range could detect objects under fairly shallow water. Sanders claimed this technology could be used to increase security of the U.S. embassy in Havana. As I listened to him talk, I suspected the system was more likely to provide data on activities in the coastal waters of Cuba. I knew better than comment on this idea on a non-secure phone line. Instead, I said, "I've been thinking about your suggestion this morning. Scofield told me Mendel hasn't stopped by the hospital or called to check on Leslie. That makes me think a divorce is imminent."

"Agreed, but I doubt he cut her brake lines. Then he'd be worried about what she might say if she came out of the coma and would be regularly checking up on her."

"Hadn't thought of it that way. And there are two individuals who have checked on her three or four times each."

"Do they have any possible involvement in the problems at Miracle Foods?"

"Yes."

"Too bad. I'd hoped you could ignore her accident and focus just on the meal site. I'd really like you to finish up this case and be able to meet me in Miami this weekend."

"Doesn't matter. The cold and snow here have convinced me I need to get out of here."

"Only the cold and snow makes you want to come to Miami?"

"Don't be coy. I'll know my plans tonight when we talk. Love you." I rushed to Western's waiting car.

***

Shortly after Scofield, Western, and I were seated in in the far corner of a rather average looking coffee shop with an impressive display of bakery items in a glass case, a man with a denim jacket and a Stetson hat strode in with a wiry woman with purple streaks in in her almost white hair. When they approached our table, Western said, "Abigail, I see you've recovered from your little bout last week at the meal site."

Before the woman could answer, the man reached out his hand to me. "I'm Sam Drake, the guy who did the autopsy on the homeless man who died at the meal site." He held my hand tightly and stared into my eyes. "I want to start this partnership right. The one thing I'm sure of is the man at the meal site died of anaphylaxis, in other words an allergic reaction. Everything else is debatable."

I knew I'd reddened because my face felt warmer. "I appreciate your honesty. May I quote you to the FDA officials who want answers from me?"

Sam nodded. "Half of the confusion is due to Jim Jackson. Last Sunday after church he kept rattling on about histamine in fermented foods."

I must have looked confused because Sam put his arm around the old woman's shoulders and said, "Mom and my family go to the same church as Western and Jim Jackson. Trouble is Jim's theory doesn't make sense, at least not for the dead man. High histamine levels aren't fatal."

Abigail flashed an annoyed look at her son. "And because the man died from an allergic reactions, he made me get all sorts of useless allergy tests. I kept telling him I may have asthma and be allergic to latex and cats, but I'm not allergic to fish. The tests proved I was right. Besides the tuna didn't taste right. It was hot—no… peppery."

"Bingo!" Everyone stared at me. I must have spoken too loudly. "Certain fish, like tuna, can develop high—like off the charts—levels of histamine when they aren't processed properly. The histamine levels are sometimes elevated before the fish stinks or has an off flavor. However, many say the fish tastes peppery."

She smiled at her son. "See? *She* wouldn't have made me take all those allergy tests."

Sam put his hand over his mother's. "But the fish was canned. That should have destroyed any toxins."

"Canning doesn't destroy histamine. Several of the worst cases of scombroid poisoning, a fancy name for histamine poisoning, have been caused by canned tuna." I turned to Abigail. "But I don't understand why you were the only one who got sick."

"That's easy. The cook was off that day. His assistant Mike was preparing the meal. I got to the meal site two hours early because I planned to check the casseroles before they were served." She bit her lip. "I might as well say it. I don't trust the old sot and tasted the first batch

J. L. Greger

of the casserole before he put it in the oven. I told him it was too peppery."

Sam touched his mother's arm. "You never told me that. You know raw foods aren't safe to eat."

She removed his hand from her arm. "Remember I *was* a dietitian. There were no raw eggs in the casserole. It was safe to eat." She looked back at me. "Mike began to argue with me when I told him the casserole didn't taste right because he said that it had been made with canned tuna not the cultured tuna. We both knew everyone who got sick the week before had eaten a tuna casserole made with the cultured tuna."

I interrupted, "Did that earlier casserole taste funny?"

Abigail shrugged. "I don't know. I wasn't there that day." She frowned. "Now, where was I?"

"I'm sorry I interrupted you," I said. "You were telling us what you did when the casserole tasted funny."

Abigail smiled. "Oh, yes. I made Mike taste the casserole and show me one of the cans the tuna came from. It wasn't our usual brand. We decided to make a new batch of the casserole with tuna from cans with our usual labels. The next batch tasted fine. That's what we served."

Sam said, "I don't understand why Mike didn't react to the histamine, too."

His mother clicked her tongue. "Who would notice? His skin is always red and he coughs all the time." She looked at me. "He also tasted less. He hates fish."

I said, "Did you also supervise the preparation of the casserole made that day with the cultured tuna?"

Abigail smiled. "Of course, it tasted fine. You know the cultured meat products are quite good in casseroles, but less so in salads."

"What did you do with all the unused casserole made with the first batch of canned tuna?" I decided to be optimist. "Were portions of it saved?"

Abigail frowned. "How did Mike answer that question?"

Everyone stared at her.

Abigail frowned again. "Mike takes all the leftovers from the meal site and gives them to the homeless men and women who meet at the city park at sunset. Supposedly it's for their dogs. I don't think the cook knows. I just stumbled onto him doing it about a year ago and thought it was harmless." She looked at her son. "We can't serve the leftovers to anyone. It seems a shame to waste the food."

I wondered whether a number of the city's vagrants and their dogs had scratched for "fleas" that night but I decided that would be impossible to trace.

At this point Scofield was taking notes frantically. Sam was quietly scolding his mother. Western yawned. "And that's why I hate eye witness accounts. We wasted so much time talking to staff and homeless at the meal site and didn't get the real scoop."

I wanted to miss Scofield's response to Western and said, "Why don't I go the display case and pick out five baked items. Then we can cut them up and each sample several." I placed my hand on Abigail's shoulder. "While I'm gone, try to remember the labels on the cans of the bad tuna—their color, pictures, anything."

Western winked at me. "Make that three. None of us need the calories."

As I gazed at the muffins, sweet rolls, and coffee cakes, I realized why most people in Colorado seemed fifteen to twenty pounds lighter than my friends in the Albuquerque area. Five of my friends in Albuquerque would have eaten five items.

When I returned to the table with a pumpkin muffin, a slice of cinnamon crumb cake, and an iced jelly roll, Abigail looked at me triumphantly. "I remembered that most of our tuna comes in cans with blue or green labels with a picture of a fish. The labels on the can of bad tuna were red and didn't have a picture. The brand name began with a C." She flashed a smile. "Don't worry I'll keep thinking about it and will tell my son if I remember anything more."

"Well, now we know what the burglar took." I said, "The cans on the floor of the storeroom this morning were all green or blue. I didn't see any cans with red labels."

No one was paying any attention to me. Scofield had cut the baked goods into pieces and everyone was sampling them. After my first taste, I decided I would come back to this coffee shop. Then I collected my thoughts and looked at Sam. "Does the coroner's office here often give preliminary guesstimates, like calling a small wound an insect sting, on autopsy reports?" I'd avoided being insulting and saying *false statements on autopsies.*

Sam didn't look annoyed. "We have a drug problem here that we don't discuss. The funding for the homeless meal site is shaky now. They didn't want bad publicity." He thought a second. "And the police and my boss thought there was no need to annoy a prominent and—let's be honest—contentious citizen like Mendel Lopez with an inflammatory speculation on the autopsy report."

Scofield nudged me. "You may not have realized the report was marked as a preliminary autopsy report, pending tests. The body is still in the morgue waiting for the right tests."

Western finished savoring his piece of the jelly roll. "Let's cut the crap. A lot of people here are suspicious of the so-called 'cultured' meat. Many would like Miracle Foods to fail because they think it undercuts ranchers. You know it's not real meat. A few have real reasons to dislike Mendel Lopez. That gives us dozens of people with a motive for tampering with the food at the meal site. When Sam here found the tiny wound on the guy's wrist, we thought it might be important." He forked the last piece of crumb cake and pointed to Scofield. "Pardner can explain."

"We thought the small wound could be an injection site and that would suggest someone intended to kill that particular victim. That ruined our theory that he was killed by an activist for natural foods or a competitor to Miracle Foods because they would have picked a homeless victim randomly." Scofield frowned. "The coroner's office ran standard toxicological tests. Nothing was obvious. We hoped mentioning a puncture, albeit as an insect sting, in the preliminary autopsy report might make the killer nervous and..."

Western interrupted, "Cause him or her to act stupidly like raiding the meal site last night. We figured your appearance also would make a killer nervous. We certainly told everyone you were a super sleuth for finding odd ways to use chemicals to kill."

All I could say was, "OMG."

Sam frowned. "These two make my report sound more creative than it was. The slight swelling and redness around the wound made it look—with a little imagination—a bit like an insect sting. I was buying time and hoping someone would suggest the right toxicology test." He peered at me. "What do you suggest?"

CHAPTER 11: Officer Esther Scofield's Perspective

Scofield was pleased she'd convinced Western to invite Sam Drake and his mother Abigail to coffee. She'd learned more about the meal site from Abigail than she had from Mike, the cook, or for that matter the director of the meal site. Now she had a much better idea of what to look for as she scanned the cache of files she removed from the meal site the night before. First, she slowly thumbed her way through the receipts and purchase orders in the *Orders* file. It was a mess. The file was as disorganized as the meal site director seemed to be.

Then she opened the file labeled *Miracle Foods*. In it was a memo from Viola Sanchez. Scofield said a silent prayer of thanks for Viola. She really hoped this woman had not dirtied her hands at Miracle Foods because the Fort Collins Police Department could use an employee with her organizational skills and her ability to cut bullies down to size. Even Western was afraid of her. She'd be a perfect boss for the evidence room, and Scofield suspected Viola might need a new job soon.

The memo listed all the foods and paper goods purchased by Miracle Foods for the meal site as of last Monday. The list included purchase order numbers, brands, and quantities of food ordered. However, Scofield was troubled because she couldn't find any entry on the list to correspond to the shipment of canned tuna with a brand name that began with C.

The last file she examined was labeled *Odds & Ends*. She thought that was a good name for its contents. There were letters of complaints about the food, a list of items in the lost and found, and odd memos. One from the meal site director to the cook last week was interesting:

I found three cases of canned fish today with no receipt or purchase order. I assume it was gift. From whom? Better taste it before you serve it. I never heard of Cook's brand tuna.

Scofield realized either the cook and/or the meal site director were forgetful or were hiding information. No one had mentioned that the source of the small order of canned tuna was unknown. Perhaps that wasn't surprising. Abigail said the church had replaced the meal site director a year ago when Abigail and another church lady learned the former director augmented his wages by selling food from the site at reduced prices to a local bar. The church officials had decided to not press charges. Scofield thought the former director had not garnered much extra income because most food at the meals site wouldn't appeal to bar clients.

She called the hospital to check on Leslie. A nurse reported Leslie was still in a medically induced coma but the swelling in her brain hadn't decreased much. Scofield checked with the police officer guarding Leslie. No one had stopped by the hospital to see her, not even her husband. However, the officer had intercepted thirteen phone calls. Jim Jackson and Viola Sanchez had both called four times each. Men, who blocked their phone number, had called twice. The officer believed the unidentified male callers were really one person because the background noise was similar both times. A young woman with a shrill voice, who also blocked her number, had called three times. The officer had determined these three calls were long distance ones.

Scofield thought Western was wasting the city's money by having a guard posted at the ICU. But Western was obsessed with the idea that whoever cut Leslie's brake lines would try to again to kill her.

Scofield meandered down the hall to the photo lab thinking about Mendel's apparent lack of concern about his wife. She dreaded the scene she expected to see and hear in the photo lab. Western had been proud of his tape initially. It showed only one masked person had entered the storeroom. The timer on the tape indicated the entry occurred at fifteen minutes past midnight. However, after Western reviewed the tape several times, he realized it proved little except the break-in was not a random event. The robber had stood in front of the shelves, apparently reading labels, for several minutes before he removed three cases of tuna. Western had sought the help of a photo technician to improve the resolution of the tape in hopes of gaining more information.

She knew the technician had been unsuccessful when she opened the door and heard Western say, "Play the useful section one more time. Maybe Scofield will spot something we missed."

The tape jerked forward to show an individual with a dark hoodie, dark stocking cap, and jeans remove three cases from a shelf in the storeroom and then knock everything else off that rack with a broom. The individual was thin and probably a male because his shoulders were broad. He was young or at least his movements were agile. Unfortunately, he also wore gloves and a mask.

Scofield was ready to say the tape had little value, when Western shouted, "Look at his hands now. He must have removed his gloves. How did I miss that?"

"Maybe they got sticky when the relish jars broke," said the photo technician as he slowed the tape.

Scofield thought the mystery man in slow motion moved like Frankenstein's monster in old movies. That made her think. She calculated the three cases of tuna cans must have weighed seventy pounds. The robber appeared to lift all three together easily. "Our mystery man is pretty strong to handle those boxes so easily."

Western only grunted as the film moved on in slow motion. When the mystery man reached high on the rack and shook it so the last jar of relish tumbled to the floor, Western shouted, "Got you." Western shouted again when the mystery man touched the wall outlet as he turned off the lights.

Scofield was already dialing the meal site when Western yelled, "Tell them to leave the storeroom immediately without touching anything. I'll get someone from the lab to dust the rack and light switch. If I'd noticed the guy took off his gloves two hours ago, we'd have solved the case by now."

Scofield doubted Western's optimism but she couldn't blame him for the probable loss of evidence. Western had watched the tape several times at the site before he gave the cook permission to clean up the storeroom.

***

Scofield thought Western lived a charmed life. The cook and his assistant Mike had been too busy preparing and serving the meal to clean up the storeroom.

The forensic technician identified several fingerprints on the frame of the top shelf of the empty rack. He tried to not only get images of the fingerprints but also lift the DNA from those prints, but the technician decided the prints around the light switch were hopelessly smudged.

While the forensic technician worked, Western glad-handed indigents eating their meals. Scofield sometimes wondered whether Western planned to run for office when he retired. She avoided the crowd of homeless men and women in clothes that hadn't been cleaned in months—probably since the first major snow fall in late October. The

J. L. Greger

odors emanating from the crowd were enough to trigger an asthma attack. Instead, she showed the site director a copy of her memo to the cook about the Cook's brand tuna.

The director sighed. "It's not unusual for church members and other good citizens to lug in cases of foods or serving items. The problem is they expect a thank you note." She paused. "I worry more about things that disappear. You wouldn't believe the things that go missing."

"Try me."

"Leftovers."

"Anything else?"

"Miracle Foods gave us twenty new salt and pepper shakers sets at the start of the clinical trial. They were red clear plastic with Miracle Food seals on them. I thought they shouldn't be used after the man died until the seals were scraped off the shakers and told Mike to clean them." She shook her head. "This morning I couldn't find them. Mike claimed he didn't know where they were." She shook her head again. "Why would anyone take them?"

Scofield decided not to alert the director to watch Mike, even though she surmised Mike had a penchant for stealing. She guessed a bar might pay him several dollars for those red salt and pepper shakers.

***

As soon as Scofield was seated in the car, Western announced, "Guess what? Two of our outstanding citizens wandered by the meal site last night after the bar down the street closed at midnight. They observed a car parked in the lot by the back door."

"Did they see the driver or anyone entering the building?" Scofield wondered how lucky Western would be this time.

"Yeah, a man in black. Not enough to be useful" He smiled. "But their description of the car was much better. I suspect they were casing the car out. I'll have to check their histories."

Scofield held up three fingers. "I can think of three—no four—young men who might be our man in black. Viola has a son in college here. And doesn't Mendel have a son in high school or college? How old is Jim Jackson's son? And didn't Leslie file a restraining order against one college student last year. We've not even checked his file."

"Good girl." Western turned into an empty parking lot. "Let's talk. I immediately thought of Viola's boy but not the others. The technician said the angle of the fingerprints on the rack suggested the man was about six-feet. I bet Viola's son isn't much taller than her. At most, five-eight."

"Too bad. I was imagining we had an explanation for why Viola tried to pitch several taste panel forms."

"Come on girl, you knew we couldn't be that lucky. Besides, I've been thinking. Viola's smart. Smart enough to have put the four forms in the waste paper basket because she wanted you to notice them."

Scofield pursed her lips and exhaled and inhaled slowly trying to ignore him while she tinkered with her phone.

Western continued, "I noticed last Sunday that Jim's son, a sophomore in high school, is almost as tall as Jim when they stood side by side in the church choir. But he's skinny as a rail. I doubt he could carry seventy pounds, but then it's easy to underestimate the strength of teens." He paused. "Been awhile since I've seen Mendel's son Wendell, but Mendel is about six foot. The boy's a junior in engineering here."

Scofield felt like screaming, but managed to say calmly, "Why didn't you think of that earlier? Wendell fits the profile of the person who completed the four forms Viola pitched. An engineering student who was in school already a year ago at the time of the first taste panel."

"Nah, boys don't think of their mothers—or even their step-mothers—as sexy like the one questionnaire comment indicated."

"Are you sure?"

"Shoot. I don't like where this could go."

Scofield wanted to laugh because Western liked to act as if he was worldly-wise but he was actually rather prim and proper. She looked up from her phone. "I found Leslie's restraining order. It's against a young man of twenty named Seth Evers. Police records indicate he's five-eleven with brown hair and a student here at Colorado State. No indication of his major."

"I'd hope I could avoid interviewing Seth. I talked to him a year ago when Leslie made her complaint. He's such a smart-ass. I had trouble worming anything from him."

Scofield stared with him with her mouth agape. "He must be bad. I've watched you interview college students. You get them to say more than anyone else on the force."

"I don't let them scare me with their BS because I know the BS is just hiding chicken..." Western winked at her. "To protect your tender ears, I'll say excrement but you know what I mean."

Scofield coughed. She often sensed Western cursed less when he spoke to her than when he talked to his buddies on the force or to street people, but he'd never admitted it before. She didn't know whether to be glad or worried that he wanted to impress her. Although he was a widower, he seldom spent much time with women. Actually, she didn't know the latter point but that was the rumor in the police department. However, she wasn't interested in Bart Western. He was too much like her former husband. She'd vowed to never get involved with another extrovert. But she also didn't want to insult Western. He wasn't a bad partner *if* you ignored his bluster. Actually, he was a good partner and certainly knew the long-term residents in Fort Collins like the back of his hand. And her asthma was much easier to control in the relatively clean air of northern Colorado than in the smog of L.A.

She suddenly realized he'd stopped blustering and was looking at her expectantly. He seldom seemed to notice when she tuned him out or answered with a non sequitur. She hoped that was true now. "We don't have time to interview the college kids now because we're due at Miracle Foods a little after one."

"I'll bet that's a fiery session."

CHAPTER 12: Will Sara Be Fired?

I was rather proud of myself when I knocked on the door to Mendel Lopez' office at one. I had had made two important discoveries since I had left the coffee shop mid-morning.

Mendel continued to peck at his computer as I began to speak, even though I had warned him, or at least Viola, that I was almost ready to send a preliminary report to FDA after I spoke to him.

He seemed to ignore me as I explained how I arrived at my hypothesis that three separate sets of crimes had been committed at the meal site. "The first involved the intentional serving of bad batches of cultured fish and resulted in the two outbreaks of rashes and hives among diners at the meal site."

He didn't look away from his computer screen. "It was an accident not intentional."

His phrasing suggested he knew some of the cultured fish product wasn't safe to eat. Perhaps the man knew more about the production problems in his company than he'd admitted. I spoke more forcefully as I made my second point. "The second crime was the murder of a homeless man at the site."

Mendel stopped typing. He stood and pounded his desk. "Stop exaggerating. It was lousy bee sting."

I lowered my voice because I'd gotten his attention. "It appears he was intentionally exposed to an allergen that induced anaphylaxis. I've spoken to the deputy medical examiner. It sure sounds like murder to us."

Mendel's jaw dropped. His face turned bright red.

"The third set of crime involves multiple small offenses. The delivery of a small shipment of 'bad' canned tuna to the meal site was an act of at least criminal mischief. It appears that the 'bad' tuna was an attempt to thwart any investigation of the symptoms developed by subjects who were previously fed your cultured tuna. This plan was foiled by Abigail Drake, and she was the only one who became ill." I noticed Mendel was slowly crushing a wad of paper in his clenched fist. "But the criminal mischief caused her bodily harm. Finally, there's the theft of the cans of 'bad' tuna and vandalism at the meal site."

"Who cares about those petty crimes?"

I realized he must be extremely annoyed because I could see saliva spray from his mouth as he yelled. "I think you'll find the police agree with my summary of events. Here's what you need to do to decrease the liability of Miracle Foods and yourself in these apparent crimes, because I believe FDA and USDA will find all the mayhem relevant to any decision about the safety of your cultured meats."

Mendel suddenly returned to his chair and sat down.

"Histamine analyses need to be performed on at least several batches of your cultured meat. I also think..."

Mendel interrupted, "Just order Jim to run the analyses."

"It's more complicated than that. First, Jim has analyzed batches of both the beef and turkey forms of your cultured meat. Although he claims the fish form of your cultured meat has similar levels of histamine, he's been unwilling to show me the raw data."

"Oh really."

"On the basis of his limited analyses, I think the histamine levels in your cultured beef and turkey might be slightly higher than literature values for beef and turkey." I noticed Mendel's face has become red again. "There's no need to panic. A three-ounce serving would still contain less than a half-milligram of histamine. My concern is with your product cultured from tuna cells. I'd guess on the basis of the subjects' responses that some of your cultured tuna contains far more than the FDA limit of five milligrams per hundred grams of fish."

I now had Mendel's rapt attention. "What would you suggest?"

"First off, you should have histamine levels tested in your products by an outside laboratory with experience in doing histamine analyses. Jim and your lab should do histamine determinations on duplicate samples but without knowledge of the results from the other lab."

"I see. You don't trust Jim's work."

I saw no reason to be brutally honest. "Every lab needs to validate their results by comparisons with other labs. That's especially true because FDA and USDA will want to review these data before they approve your products."

"That means we'll have to make new batches just for your little project!" His sarcasm was heightened by the loudness of his voice.

I thought *this man has a short fuse*. Few employees or spouses could endure this for long. I decided to stay calm and ignore his bad humor.

The worst that could happen to me was Bug and I would drive home tomorrow. "No. I know Miracle Foods made over ten batches in preparation for the clinical trial. You have plenty of samples for analyses."

"And these histamine analyses will solve all my problems?" His voice was again loud and his mannerisms aggressive as he leaned across his desk toward me.

I tried to not act nervous as I delivered more bad news. "The histamine analyses will help FDA and police officials decide what other tests are needed. Moreover, the histamine levels in the cultured tuna probably have no relevance to the man who died. I've talked to the deputy medical examiner and FDA officials. You may have to allow other tests on the food Jim collected from the meal site."

"Fine, if they pay."

I wasn't going to get in a discussion of finances. "They want to remove the samples from your freezers here."

I was surprised when he merely sighed. "What do I care about the garbage?"

I felt braver. "I will report to FDA that you are cooperating with the necessary steps. I know this is very trying for you. I'm sorry but if we do this right, your company should emerge from these unfortunate occurrences with limited damage to its image." I looked at my watch. Western should be here by now. "Do you know anyone named Herman Preuter?"

I expected him to say *that's the man who died at the meal site*. Instead he answered I thought too quickly. "No."

"Look you don't have to answer me, but I'm pretty sure you'll get this question from the police soon."

Mendel stood as if to dismiss me. "I'm busy."

I didn't think I could stall much longer. "I have another question. No one has offered me a chance to taste your cultured meat. Why don't you offer samples to everyone who stops by your office? The taste panels results were quite good."

He sighed. "You sound like my wife. Jim and I were afraid of industrial espionage."

I frowned. "Surely a competitor couldn't learn that much from a taste." I thought a second. "But I'm no expert on marketing. You'd know better."

He just stared at me, and shook slightly. I was relieved when Western, without knocking, entered with Viola and Scofield behind him.

Western slowly looked around the room. "I hope you two are about through with your discussion. Mr. Lopez, I have FDA and USDA

                                                                    J. L. Greger

officials with me and a search warrant. They're going to remove materials from your freezers for analysis." He glanced at me. "I think Dr. Almquist has told you what we'll be looking for. If not, the search warrant gives details. As I told Viola we've also brought along a police computer technician. He will download Miracle Foods's financial and personnel records. We need to compare them to the files, which were in Leslie's car at the time of her accident and accordingly are in the evidence room of the Fort Collins police."

I couldn't believe my eyes or ears when Mendel with his head down meekly said, "Fine."

Viola began to cry which seemed like an unusual response.

***

Scofield found me shortly after I emerged from Mendel's office. "The FDA official in Denver you talked to earlier today and local USDA official are already collecting the samples from the freezers here. Your emails were clear about the location of the samples and the importance of keeping them frozen. The Agricultural Research Service labs of USDA here in town have also confirmed to me that they're prepared to receive these frozen samples as you arranged. The computer technician has downloaded larger files from companies and should have no trouble today. I think Western did a good job, as he would say, of introducing the fear of God into Mendel and Viola."

I tittered. "He certainly frightened them into silence."

Scofield looked toward the ceiling. "Probably his favorite part of the job." She looked back at me. "That means we have only two problems. Jim left the building through a side door as soon as Western walked in the front door."

"He must have a guilty conscious."

"I decided he was small fish at this point. I didn't want him to distract us."

"What's the other problem?"

"We have an unhappy puppy in the back seat of the squad car. Western and I were glad you dropped off Bug at our offices before you went in to see Mendel. We understood you were afraid someone might try to retaliate against you by harming Bug. However, he's not been the confident, tail-wagging dog we've seen with you. He's sat in the corner of our offices and the back seat of the squad car and whimpered."

"Poor baby. This has been a bad day for him. He was alone in the motel room most of the morning. I shouldn't have brought him, but I hadn't thought this consultation would be quite so complicated and ugly."

She pointed to a uniformed officer. "He'll help you collect your coat and papers from your make-shift office and retrieve Bug. Will you leave For Collins tonight?"

I was surprised because I hadn't thought about my precarious situation. I was used to working on investigation for the FBI or the State Department not working for a specific company. "Oh." I thought a couple of seconds. "No, Mendel hasn't fired me yet, and he paid me for a week's work. I'll continue to try to help sort out the mess at Miracle Foods as I finish my report to the FDA. Who knows you may be getting more emails from me."

Scofield looked like she was about to hug me, but instead she shook my hand. "Good luck."

When the officer opened a back door of the black and white sedan, Bug bounced into my arms. He kept licking my face as if I've been gone for days. It made me feel guilty and we started on a long walk. We hadn't gone far when I remembered a major point I wanted to tell Scofield.

Scofield and Western both looked surprised when Bug and I walked back into the main office. I laughed. "Bad pennies always return. I just realized that I should remind you to talk to Troy Pitkin, the intern who did the histamine analyses."

"What did you say?"

Western vehemence surprised me. "I... I didn't mean to be insulting or bossy, but Pitkin is the only one besides Jim—and maybe Leslie—who knows anything about the histamine analyses. His personnel file was one of the missing files."

"Say the name again."

"Pitkin."

"How could I have missed that?" Western stepped closer to me pulling Scofield with him. He whispered, "The first officers on the scene at the scene of Leslie's accident said she kept screaming, 'Pit' among other things." He glanced at Scofield. "She told me you're worried about your job here. Don't be. The FDA official just told Mendel you saved his ass."

Scofield coughed. "I doubt he used that phrase."

CHAPTER 13: Sara on the Colorado State Campus

I was surprised when I heard Scofield's grainy voice on the phone an hour later. I hadn't thought about it before, but her voice did sound as if she was getting over a bad cold. Maybe many of her coughs weren't a reflectance of her annoyance with Western, after all. "We decided it was time to interview all the college kids in this case. Western thought you might be helpful when we interview Pitkin."

"I don't want to leave Bug again."

I heard Western voice in the background. "Tell her we have a small K9 vest here. Bug can wear it. Then he can enter any building. We'll pick her up at the motel in ten minutes."

Scofield coughed. "That's an irregular solution, but you heard him."

***

As soon as Bug and I were situated in the back seat, Scofield said, "We have two purposes—to gain information and to make Mendel and Viola nervous enough to talk." She bit her lip. "There are a couple of details in this case which we've not revealed to anyone. Details you may need to know as you formulate questions. The first officers to arrive at the scene of Leslie's accident claimed she was hysterical. She kept screaming 'Pit,' 'Endel lied,' 'V wrong' over and..."

"Yeah. Mainly she screamed, 'stairs.' They had trouble restraining her enough to take her to the hospital." Western shook his head. "One reason the docs induced a coma—to stop her screams."

Scofield pursed her lips and took a couple of long slow breaths. "The medical staff noticed her heart rate and blood pressure rose dangerously when she screamed. They hoped by inducing a coma they would relax her and more importantly could reduce the accumulation of fluid around her brain. Unfortunately, the swelling isn't abating."

Western glanced away from the traffic to look at me. "What she's trying to say is: Leslie is a goner if the docs can't lessen her brain swelling soon. Are you sure Leslie didn't say anything useful to you on Tuesday morning?"

I thought a second. "We talked less than ten minutes total. She said little, except to convey her annoyance at Mendel for allowing me to bring Bug. Of course, if I had to live with Mendel, I'd be touchy too. That man expects to always get his way."

Western snorted. "Yeah, enough to make employees act criminally." He turned into the parking lot by Green Hall, the home of the CSU Police. "Now you're seeing one of the big perks to our job—a reserved parking spot near the center of the Colorado State campus."

Without looking up from her phone, Scofield said, "I've arranged to meet the Sanchez siblings at the nearby Lory Student Center. They aren't suspects, but they could give us insight into Wendell Lopez because they went to high school with him."

Western chuckled. "And to make their mother nervous. I'm going to talk Seth Evers. I talked to him when he was stalking Leslie last year. Felt sorry for him." He paused. "Come to think of it that's how I met Leslie. She screamed that I was incompetent when I didn't arrest Seth Evers and just warned him to stay away from her."

Scofield turned to me. "What do you know about Troy Pitkin?"

"As you know, Troy Pitkin's file was one of three missing files at Miracle Foods, but Viola let me peruse the computer versions of the three files. Pitkin's file was the only one with a letter of recommendation from Jim." I squirmed. "Only the letter wasn't really a recommendation. Jim just stated that Pitkin modified a method for histamine analyses in the literature for use in the lab and applied it to cultured meat samples. That got me thinking. Jim knew for several months about the levels of histamine in the cultured meat because Pitkin started the project last August and quit in early November. If any batches were contaminated with high levels of histamine, Jim should have acted before the clinical trial

"Do you think Pitkin will talk to you?"

"I don't know. He's more apt to agree to meet with you initially, but he's apt to say more in response to questions from an old professor alone."

I was lucky Troy Pitkin answered his cell phone immediately. However, he was reluctant to answer questions about his experiences at Miracle Foods until I mentioned that if he preferred, he could talk to Sergeant Bart Western of the Fort Collins police.

Pitkin's voice became sharper. "You're politely saying I don't have a choice. It's not convenient to meet you in my dorm."

"I'll meet you in front of Lory Student Center."

"No. Someone might see me. Let's meet in front of the microbiology building in twenty minutes."

I figured he had a class in the microbiology building, but I was wrong. He loped up to me from the north of the campus. I wasn't surprised that he spotted me easily. I was the only middle-aged woman with a small dog in sight. He was about six feet and wore a black knit cap, black parka, and jeans.

Pitkin looked over his shoulder several times as I began to question him. Finally, he said, "We'll be less obvious if we walk as we talk."

I decided I'd better address the problem in a straightforward manner. "Is there a reason you don't want to be seen with me?"

"Look, I know about the hives and rashes at the meal site.... and even the death. I don't want anyone associated with Miracle Foods to see me with you."

I decided to not ask who he was avoiding—at least not yet. "How did you learn about the problems in the clinical trial run by Miracle Foods?"

He blinked. "Word gets around. As you know, I did histamine analyses for Miracle Foods. I wasn't surprised when people in the clinical trial got sick because a couple batches of cultured fish had high—like a hundred times normal—levels of histamine."

I wanted to shout *hurray* but decided I shouldn't let him know that Jim hadn't shared that data with me. I also wanted to put a positive spin on his comment. "Sounds like you were really into your work at Miracle Foods. Why did you quit in November?"

He looked over his shoulder again. "I was working late in the lab one night and heard Mendel Lopez yelling at Jim Jackson. I didn't hear the conversation clearly but afterwards Jim had my lab notes up on his computer screen. He usually wasn't that eager to see them. The next day, he told me we were going to change the focus of my research." His Adam's apple bounced as he gulped repeatedly. "I thought about it, talked to my advisor and resigned from my internship. Didn't you see my letter of resignation? You said they gave you full access to their records." He stared at me.

I figured I had to say something. I didn't want to lie. "I saw Jim's letter of recommendation for you."

"Some rec. He said what he assigned me to do, partially. Nothing on the quality of my work. Useless. Glad I didn't finish the semester. He gave me an A anyway." I must have looked surprised. "I'd signed up for three credits for my internship last semester."

I wanted to move on to key questions before he realized I hadn't answered his question. "How many batches of cultured meat did you analyze?"

"Five batches of each of the three forms—beef, turkey, fish—of cultured meat." He looked off in the distance.

"You were telling me about the samples you analyzed."

"Yes." He lowered his head. "I guess I should have said *I think* I analyzed five batches of the three products. Everything was coded. I wasn't supposed to know which was which, but it was easy to tell the fish form. It smelled like fish and the texture was different—finer, less stringy. You could tell the beef because it was a darker color. I didn't say anything to Jim because he was so worried about Miracle Foods's secrets. Knew he'd freak out. That was dumb because his codes were obvious. They included the date the batch was made and a B, T, or F."

"What did you find?"

Pitkin frowned. "You know they made me sign a nondisclosure statement when I started to work at Miracle Foods."

I exaggerated a bit. "Don't worry—Miracle Foods wants me to give them a thorough report."

Pitkin nodded. "Not much histamine in most of the samples. Less than a half-milligram in a hundred-gram serving of the beef and turkey samples" He leaned down to pet Bug. "I broke lab rules and kept a few notes on paper towels that I shoved in my jean pockets. We had to do all our calculations and keep all our records on the lab computers. I wasn't allowed to make copies of the lab files." He looked back at me. "You were a prof. You know I had to be able to say something about my results."

I smiled hoping to encourage him. "How about the samples which you thought were fish?"

He shook his head. "Funny thing. Two samples were low like the beef and turkey samples. One sample had probably about a ten-fold higher level of histamine, but two samples had more than hundred-fold more histamine than the beef and turkey."

"What did Jim say?"

"Which time? He told me I contaminated a couple of my samples the first time and told me to start over and analyze the fifteen samples again. The second time, he said the same thing. The third time was the night I heard Mendel Lopez yelling at Jim."

"Were the results similar all three times?"

"Pretty much. Can I go now?"

                                        J. L. Greger

"First look at these photos. Do you know any of these people?" I showed Pitkin photos of the Sanchez siblings.

Pitkin shook his head.

"How about these?"

Pitkin pointed to the photo of Seth Evers. "That's the guy who bothered Mrs. Lopez. Her class on taste evaluation was one of the reason I wanted to work at Miracle Foods." He pointed to the last photo. "Wendell Lopez is a real jerk."

I thought Pitkin was becoming more interesting as I spoke to him. "What do you mean?"

"Mrs. Lopez didn't deserve the jokes Wendell and Seth pulled on her. When they got caught, only Seth was punished." He gulped. "I really got to go." He bounded away before I could ask another question.

The kid was scared. Suddenly I was, too. Mendel and Jim had both lied to me. What type of game were they playing? Maybe Leslie had been grouchy with me initially because she thought I was part of their game. They had hired me, and Leslie was as Western said, a "goner."

***

Bug has a thick coat and likes to play in the snow, which he rarely gets to do in the Albuquerque area. But even Bug was glad to hop into the warm police car with Scofield and Western after he and I returned from our meeting with Pitkin.

Evidently Scofield had arrived only a few minutes previously because she was quizzing Western on how he got his interview done so quickly. He replied, "At least, you didn't say I was lucky again."

Scofield sniffed and in a monotone voice summarized what she learned from Viola Sanchez's children. "You were right," she said as she glanced at Western. "Neither of them is tall enough to have left fingerprints on the upper frame of the rack at the meal site. I talked to them separately but their answers were consistent." She looked at her notes. "Neither admitted to allergies. Both claimed their mother had advised them not to participate in Leslie's taste panels. I thought that strange. The younger one is nineteen and still a sweet kid who seemed to make no attempt to be discreet but knew little. He summed up his knowledge of Miracle Foods by saying, 'I don't ask Mom about things that upset her. It's easier that way.' The daughter who seems to be a younger, thinner clone of her mother said, 'I avoid the Lopezes.' She's really quite pretty but seems as calculating as her mother."

Western sneered. "You got nothing."

"No." Scofield snappy response suggested she was annoyed by his condescending attitude. "I got the son to admit he'd seen Seth Evers with

Wendell Lopez several times on campus." She paused. "By the way, the girl said your son is a 'good guy.'"

"Of course, because he is." Western cleared his throat. "I found Seth Evers in his dorm room. He liked talking about Leslie Lopez. Claimed she strutted around the taste panel room with high heel boots like a corner hooker." He checked his notes. "I want to quote him correctly. He read aloud, 'I didn't even know they made boots in purple leather until I saw hers.'" Western started to chuckle as he looked up from his notes. "Gave me quite a critique of her looks. He's got a vivid imagination. He..."

I didn't think Scofield wanted to hear any lurid descriptions because she interrupted Western, "Okay, but does he have allergies? Did he participate in the taste panels? How many?"

"No food allergies. Participated in at least four of the taste panels Leslie conducted." Western checked his notes. "Claimed he just checked the boxes. Never wrote anything else on the forms at the taste panels." Western paused. "But he's a BSer. Wouldn't trust anything he said."

I looked back and forth between the two officers. "My turn now? Jim lied to me. He knew their cultured fish—at least several batches— wasn't safe to eat because of high histamine levels three or four months ago. Second, Wendell helped Seth harass Leslie."

Scofield nodded. "Basically confirms the comments of the Sanchez brother and sister."

"My third point is based not on what Pitkin said but how he acted. He's scared and seemed to think someone is following him. One of you officially need to talk to him and perhaps faculty in the Fermentation Science and Technology Program. The director of the internship program is apt to have a copy of Pitkin's final report on his internship. It will identify two batches of cultured fish with high levels of histamine." I gulped. "Pitkin probably has a copy of his report, but I didn't want to admit to him that his personnel file at Miracle Foods was missing. The instructor should also have the final reports of the other two interns whose files are missing." I shrugged. "They might be useful."

Scofield as usual had recorded my comments. She turned off the recorder before she spoke. "Again we're getting questions not answers."

Western started to whistle before Scofield had finished her sentence. "Don't worry, pardner. I may have found as answer. Remember I said two of the indigents at the meal site this morning spotted a car at the meal site last night?"

Scofield gave a tired smile.

J. L. Greger

"A blue 2000 Corvette. Guess what? One is licensed to Mendel Lopez, but Wendell has gotten a speeding ticket while driving it."

Scofield coughed. "I was surprised the old sots at the meal site remembered the car. Now I understand."

"That's the end of the good news. Jim Jackson has a blue 2000 Corvette, too." He shook his head. "I'd hoped Jim wasn't involved."

"Hard to think one of your church friends could be guilty?" Scofield chuckled. "All three—Wendell, Mendel, and Jim—fit our description of the vandal at the meal site—around six feet and physically fit."

Western whistled. "Don't be negative. I remember when I was kid an old man called Ramone Lopez ran a repair garage at the edge of town. Closed years ago. It's now the site of a Chevrolet dealership. Guess who owns it?

Scofield rolled her eyes. "Mendel Lopez."

"Yeah, that piece of land was the only thing Mendel inherited from his dad. Everything else came from his mother. His parents divorced when Mendel was a kid, as I remember."

Scofield began her breathing exercises.

Western glanced at her. "You think I don't know, but I do. You breathe harder when you want to yell at me... or at least correct me."

I wished I could disappear. This conversation was deteriorating into a spat—the type between an unhappily married couple. The smart thing to do would be to remain silent. I decided to live dangerously. "What made you suddenly remember Ramone Lopez?"

Scofield mouthed her thanks at me.

"I had an investigative assistant check out Mendel's history."

"Logical—but why now?" I asked.

Western's voice became lower. "I saw how Mendel looked at you and heard much of your conversation before I entered his office. Nothing should have provoked such anger. Either the man doesn't like advice from smart women, you were getting close to the truth, or you reminded him of Leslie."

Scofield sighed. "Finally, you've gotten to the point. You think Mendel tried to kill Leslie by cutting the brake lines in her car or had someone else do it. Right? Have you hypothesized a motive—besides a bad marriage?"

"Something to do with Miracle Foods. As I doubt that Mendel cares about cultured meat, per se, I assume it relates to the value of the company. Of course, the value is most likely important because it will affect their divorce settlement."

Scofield groaned. "We're really no better off than we were yesterday at this time. By the way, what did you promise the investigative assistant to get her to dig up all the dirt on Mendel?"

Western stiffened. "I thought I did a good job of presenting the data in a colorful way."

"Problem is your memory of the good old days isn't that good." Scofield resumed her breathing exercises.

I squirmed a bit. I didn't want to be drawn further into their long-term disagreements. "Could you take me back to my car? It's parked at Miracle Foods. Sam Drake and I have both been studying the literature on food allergies. We want to brainstorm a bit."

Western whistled. "Sam's a real lady's man, but he's married."

I knew why Scofield started her breathing exercises whenever Western whistled. His whistling and comments were annoying.

CHAPTER 14: Who Is Herman Preuter?

The brown brick building occupied by the Larimar County Coroner was surrounded by trees. Sam Drake was waiting for me by a side entrance and guided me down a back hallway to his office with Bug nestled in his cart. It was a cloak and dagger operation because dogs weren't allowed in the building.

We both laughed when I unzipped the cart. Bug snorted repeatedly, jumped down, and stalked around Sam's office.

"How are you enjoying our Croak Squad: Cough and Crow?"

"What?"

"That's what those of us in the coroner's office call Western and Scofield. They're our main police contacts because they are the primary homicide detectives in Fort Collins. They're almost a comedy routine at times, but they do solve cases."

"I think they basically admire each other. If I said something against one, I'm sure the other would turn on me like a pit bull. So, I won't say anything about them." As I spoke, I poured water into a bowl for Bug and then took a swig from the bottle. Water flew in all directions as Bug eagerly lapped the water, and I'm afraid water drizzled down my chin as I gulped the water. I hoped Sam hadn't noticed.

He must have because he smirked and asked, "May I offer you coffee?"

"Thanks, but I'm not into coffee."

He sipped his coffee. "Couldn't live without regular doses of caffeine." He looked at his computer screen. "I've got my autopsy report on our indigent—Herman Preuter—up on the screen." He turned the screen so I could see it as I moved my chair closer to him. "The edema I noted in his lungs and upper airways is consistent with anaphylaxis. As I noted this morning, I sent blood samples to our lab for analyses of antigen specific immunoglobulins." He grinned as if to ask if I understood.

I smiled. "I'm aware that labs can determine whether someone is allergic to a specific allergens by testing for proteins, called immunoglobulins that are specific to various allergenic proteins. I didn't know those immunoglobulins could be tested in autopsy tissues."

He nodded. "Yes immunoglobulins are stable in blood." He tinkered with his computer. "Anyway, I got the lab report this afternoon. My observation of the small wound at the wrist seems to be extraneous. There were no specific immunoglobulins to any of the proteins in bee venom or other insect's saliva. There were also no elevations in the immunoglobulins specific for meat, milk, or seafood, but..."

I scooched my chair close so that I could see the report better. "Wow. The levels of immunoglobulins specific for peanuts are high."

"Yes—high enough to have induced anaphylaxis. That's why I called you. You're the one who has studied the menus served at the meal site. Fatal anaphylactic responses to foods usually occur within minutes of the consumption of the food. These data indicate Herman Preuter must have ingested peanuts at the meal site."

I pulled out my laptop. As I searched for the menus, I said, "The director puts up warning signs at the meal site when they serve cookies with nuts or peanut butter. She also told me she never prepares peanut butter sandwiches on site. If they are served, like the cookies, they are kept separate from all other foods. Thus I think accidental ingestion of peanuts is unlikely."

Sam stood and looked over my shoulder.

"I don't see anything on the menu for that day with peanuts." I thought a second. "But it would be easy for someone to add finely ground peanuts to the applesauce or for that matter the tuna casserole which was served. I don't think most people would notice the taste or texture of a small amount of finely ground peanuts."

Sam sat down. "If the person who added the peanuts to the food knew Herman was allergic to peanuts, he or she committed murder."

"The FDA required Jim to freeze samples of the food served on the three days when someone developed symptoms, but peanuts might have been added to only Herman's food and then wouldn't be in the saved samples. If you need them, those samples are all now in a secure location."

"Western told me that, but he failed to tell you I extracted the contents from Herman's stomach. They're frozen here."

I had new admiration for Sam. "You've thought all along that the food at the meal site was poisoned—well maybe that isn't the right word, but you know what I mean. Why didn't you indicate that in the preliminary autopsy report?"

"If I asked for the food samples, I was afraid someone might destroy them. Besides, Western and I figured the fancy consultant who the FDA and USDA forced Miracle Foods to hire would find the samples."

I felt heat rising up my neck. "What?"

"You didn't think Mendel Lopez would have hired you if FDA hadn't forced him clean up his operation with an outside consultant?" He smiled. "Now with this new lab report and the frozen samples secure, I can amend the autopsy report and issue a final version."

I wanted to complain about being duped by everyone but decided that was counterproductive. "Mendel and Leslie weren't the only ones who might have tried to destroy evidence. I've caught Jim Jackson in several lies."

Sam frowned. "I think Jim is too timid to do more than lie. I think Leslie plotted this scheme to devalue Miracle Foods before she divorced Mendel. He found out and attempted to have her killed. Of course, I'm not paid to assess live individuals only the dead."

"You really don't like Mendel."

"No one does, and it's no secret that he and Leslie argued a lot."

"That's what Western said. In any case, we'd better talk to Western and Scofield."

Sam looked at his watch. "They should be here any minute. I wanted to check you out before they arrived."

"Check me out?"

"We all were suspicious when Mendel hired you. We figured he thought you were too dumb to get at the truth or he'd bought you off."

I felt my confidence draining. I must have looked pathetic because Bug licked my hands. He often did when he sensed I was nervous. I don't know why but he was usually right in his assessment.

Sam put his hand on my shoulder. "I stated that wrong. You've convinced me you're a capable, honest scientist."

I suddenly had a brain flash. "Wait—we've missed the obvious. Are we sure of Herman Preuter's identity? Did you check his fingerprints? Lots of guys on the street use several aliases. Maybe Jim and Mendel had a reason for being afraid of industrial spies."

Sam sighed. "Fingerprinting is a standard part of an autopsy. I compared his prints with those in the Integrated Automated Fingerprint Identification System. All I can say is no one with those fingerprints has a criminal or military history. He signed in at the meal site as Herman Preuter. There is no criminal or military history for a man with that name and about his age."

"Did he have a driver's license or any identification? Did you try photographing his face or doing DNA analyses and checking national records?"

Sam chuckled. "Now you're checking *my* competency."

"No, I'm brain storming. You know Herman Preuter could have been targeted because someone recognized him from his past life—before he was on the streets."

"I've been thinking along the same lines, but I don't have much. His DNA didn't match those of anyone in the FBI CODIS system. His teeth indicated until recently he had good dental care and was probably only in his early forties."

***

"Whoever gave Herman Preuter the ground peanuts knew a bit, actually probably a lot, about him. You don't tell someone about your food allergies when you first meet them." I remembered a couple of weird dates. "Well, not unless you're a hypochondriac or a health food nut."

Western looked around the conference room in the coroner's office. "I suspect those who are willing to eat that artificial meat would include a *lot* of nuts."

Scofield coughed for the first time since she entered the conference room five minutes before. I thought that was the longest time I'd watched the two detectives together that she hadn't coughed or done a breathing exercise. "His allergies might have been obvious to others because he wore a medical alert bracelet."

"That's an interesting idea." Sam began to scan a file on his computer. "It suggests Herman Preuter was a middle class—or even upper class—man until recently, which is consistent with his teeth." Sam turned his computer screen so we could all see a photo of a dead man's arm. "I can see a slight tan lines suggesting a bracelet or watch band in this photo of Preuter's wrist. Too faint to be sure. But everyone's tan lines fade in winter. What's more a broken prong or catch on such a bracelet could have caused the small wound on his wrist, if it was ripped off his arm while he was alive."

Western stood and began to pace. "Sam, maybe I was wrong this time and Herman wasn't a random victim."

Scofield began to cough so violently I was afraid she was choking. Western ignored her and continued to talk.

CHAPTER 15: Sara's Exciting Night

"I think I'm coming down with a cold. My nose has itched all afternoon."

"Honey, you've just reminded me of my mother. She always said we were going to kiss a fool when my sister or I complained that our nose itched. Then we'd giggle and run and kiss her."

Sanders didn't laugh. "And your point?"

"If you were here, I'd say kiss me. I'm your fool. Mendel and Jim have had me chasing my tail for the last two days. Most of what I've learned they already knew."

"Hmm. I suspect FDA or USDA officials forced them to hire you."

He was right again, and I changed the topic. "Here's my problem. I was so busy I didn't have a chance to book a flight to Miami. Then I got your text to not book any flights. What's up?" I was worried he'd found a more pleasant way to spend the weekend than with me in Miami, but I was determined to keep my attitude positive.

"I finished my business in Havana today and flew home to Washington. The scientist I brought along showed his modifications of the LIDAR technology will meet our needs in Cuba. As we talked, he suggested his modifications might also make it possible to use LIDAR technology to examine what's under a snow cover."

I held my breath. With my luck, he'd want me to meet him for a demo of the modified LIDAR system in Alaska. Well, at least I had winter clothing with me.

"My counterparts in NORAD are interested."

That was good news. The NORAD headquarters was near Colorado Springs. But the local weather report said a cold front was expected to dump a foot of snow on much of Colorado on Friday and Saturday. "Have you heard the weather predictions for Colorado?"

"Yes. We're going to catch a flight from Joint Base Andrews in Maryland and get to Peterson Air Force Base near Colorado Springs tomorrow before the storm hits. The demonstration for NORAD staff will take most of Friday."

"Great. I can finish up my work in Fort Collins by noon tomorrow and be in Colorado Springs by late afternoon. I'll have plenty of paperwork to do if you're busy all day Friday. Or Bug and I may just rest up."

After he hung up I thought about our relationship. His work collecting information for government agencies was exciting. I liked learning about new technologies, and I enjoyed seeing his agile mind embrace new ideas. After a moment, I realized my comment sounded like a teacher enjoying her work with a bright student. There was no doubt about it. We needed to expand our mutual interests.

I scanned sites for tourist attractions near Colorado Springs. The most obvious thing to do this weekend was to ski or snowboard. However, I was terrified by the thought of sliding uncontrollably down a hill of snow, let alone a mountain. I'd fallen too many times just walking on snow and ice. Thus, I hoped Sanders would be worn out by his demo on Friday and would be willing to do indoor activities or wander around the Air Force Academy on Saturday.

Sanders had often said I should learn to play poker because it would improve my ability to bluff. Maybe this was the weekend I'd learn. Just in case I wasn't a challenging enough partner for him, I decided I'd better pick up a jigsaw puzzle or game and a couple of bottles of his favorite wines.

***

I'd just returned from my errand when the phone rang. I figured Sanders had forgotten to tell me something, but it was Western.

"How would you like to go to the hospital with me and Scofield? Leslie is going in and out of consciousness now and screaming again." Western stopped talking, and I heard someone speaking in the background. "We tried to reach you earlier but you were out."

I didn't feel like explaining my errand. I remained silent and heard a voice in the background. Western mumbled something that sounded like, "Don't start that again." Then he said clearly, "We're pulling up at your motel now."

I gave Bug a treat, turned on the television, and sneaked out the door while Bug was busy chewing. Western had the car idling with a large snow pile on one side and a puddle which was rapidly becoming a glaze of ice on the other side. As I avoided the deepest part of the puddle and opened the door on his side, I heard Scofield. "You know she's used to being treated like a lady."

                                                    J. L. Greger

"No, Carbonne said she was treated like one of the boys by the FBI agents in Albuquerque."

I couldn't resist adding, "Actually, they've always been protective of Bug and me when possible." Then I noticed that Scofield had begun her breathing exercises and knew it was best to change the topic fast. "Has Mendel come to visit Leslie yet? I was thinking—Mendel never mentioned her today when I spoke to him. Doesn't that seem kind of callous?"

Western shrugged. "He sent her a big bouquet of yellow roses."

Scofield corrected him. "He paid for the flowers that Viola brought to the hospital but couldn't leave in Leslie's cubicle in the ICU. The guard at Leslie's room talked to Viola when she tried to deliver them. Seems her calls to the hospital were at Mendel's request."

Maybe I was wrong about Mendel. I doubted it, and I was feeling bitchy. "Must be nice to have an assistant who is that loyal."

Western turned onto the street from the parking lot. "You sound as cynical as Scofield. Me, I feel sorry for Mendel after meeting his son Wendell. We just finished a long interview with him."

Scofield turned to me. "In essence, Wendell claimed Leslie ruled the Lopez household. He certainly dislikes her enough to have cut her brake line and hinted so did his father."

"Wendell is a screwup," said Western. "He keeps switching his major and claims his poor grades are caused by boring professors, his father's many demands on him, friends being useless, and illness. In general, nothing is his fault."

I noticed Scofield coughed slightly in response to Western's last comment, but Western ignored her and continued, "I figure Wendell is innocent of any real crimes because he's lazy and not bright enough to understand what's going on at Miracle Foods."

I surmised Scofield and Western hadn't pulled much concrete information from Wendell. "As a-professor at Michigan State, I counseled several guys who resembled your description of Wendell. Generally they were brighter than they seemed. Their immaturity often reflected fear... fear of becoming like their father. Or as one twenty-year-old put it, 'My dad is trapped in a boring job and marriage, and I don't want to make the same mistakes.' Once he admitted his fears, he was able to complete a major. The funny thing was his major was physical therapy—his mother's career path. Is there any chance that Wendell secretly admires Leslie?"

Neither police officer replied to my comments. Western whistled as he parked the car and walked rapidly toward the hospital without looking back at Scofield or me.

Scofield muttered as she and I followed hm. "Our interview with Wendell was a nightmare. Wendell started by asking Western, 'Are you a suck-up like your nerdy son?'" She sighed. "I've seen bullies attack Western verbally. He always ignores them, but his son is his pride and joy. And I must say that Wendell is a champion at finding someone's weak spot and goading them. When I asked him about Mendel's relationship with Viola Sanchez. He quickly said, 'Dad says she was once pretty. Now she's just a good peon.'"

I gasped. "So, he's a bigot and a sexist."

Scofield slowed our pace. "I don't want Western to hear my next comment. I think Wendell was raised to have no respect for women, but he secretly admires Leslie or dislikes his father enough to enjoy seeing him unhappy." We caught up with Western as we passed through the revolving door at the side of the hospital. Scofield spoke more loudly. "We did learn a few relevant points about Wendell. He's allergic to peanuts, which means he knew enough about peanut allergies to poison Herman Preuter."

Western shrugged. "He got one thing right. He thinks cultured meat is a rip-off."

Scofield pursed her lips but didn't cough. I also decided to ignore Western's last comment. "Did he say anything else?"

"He tried to make Leslie's life miserable," said Western. "Claimed that's why he participated in the taste panels and pushed Seth to tail her."

"Oh dear, so all my detective work on the questionnaires yielded us nothing but proof that Wendell was hassling his stepmother Leslie.?"

Scofield touched my shoulder. "No, your groundwork helped us establish the animosity between Viola and Wendell. We're sure now she put Wendell's questionnaires in the trash not to protect him but to call attention to his behavior. He's a troubled young man."

***

A physician met us in the hall outside of Leslie's cubicle in the Intensive Care Unit. "Leslie is starting to come out of her coma. I doubt she can answer questions, but you may find her rantings useful." He paused. "The swelling in her brain hasn't abated as much as we hoped."

Western grimaced. "You're saying she may have experienced permanent brain damage? This is as good as it gets?" The physician nodded.

A hoarse voice emanated from the cubicle. It didn't really sound like Leslie's voice. "He... tried... to kill... me." I decided any scientific investigation was secondary and moved back to and let Western and Scofield enter the room first.

"He... tried... to kill me."

The lines on Western's face softened. He took Leslie's hand and tried to soothe her while he occasionally glanced at her monitors. It was obvious he'd spent time with victims in hospitals before. "Now, now, Leslie. This is the police. We need your help. Who tried to kill you?"

Her eyes widened and she stopped thrashing violently in her bed. "Pushed me... stairs."

"Who tried to push you down the stairs? When?"

The physician whispered to Scofield and me. "It's not uncommon for patients to hallucinate when they come out of coma or to remember something in the distant past."

Leslie squawked again. "He... pushed me... stairs."

Scofield reviewed photos on her phone. She pulled up ones of Wendell and Mendel Lopez and handed her phone to Western.

He tinkered with the phone and asked Leslie to focus on the phone. "Did he try to hurt you?"

"No."

I wasn't sure whether Leslie's answer meant anything because I doubted she was capable of focusing her eyes on the phone, but I respected Western for his efforts.

He tinkered with the phone again and asked, "Leslie, did he try to hurt you?"

Leslie seemed to squint at the phone this time. It may have been my imagination.

"No." She convulsed in tears.

The physician suggested we leave the room. Outside the cubicle, Western said, "She stared longer at the photo of Wendell. Maybe because her attacker was young. As I remember her stalking allegation against Seth Evers included an act of violence. Funny thing is she yelled at me for not arresting Evers but in the end didn't press charges against him."

Scofield and Western were considering their options when I saw a man carrying flowers approaching the nurse's station. He must have seen me because he turned and hurried away. I sprinted after him. The hallway was empty. The door to the stairwell was ajar. On instinct, probably not a good instinct, I raced down the stairs. I heard glass break below me. A few steps before I reached the door to the lobby, I stumbled over a broken vase and flowers. I slammed open the door. Visiting hours were over. I saw no one except a white-haired woman at the front desk.

I panted. "Did... did you see a man... leave... in the last minute?"

She smiled sweetly. "A young man overcome with grief rushed by."

"Can you describe him?"

"Tall, black knit cap, black jacket. Did I say he was young?"

Western ran past me. Scofield checked the men's restroom and then began to question the volunteer in more detail.

I sat down and panted. Someone didn't want me to see him. Why? Was he another threat to Leslie?

I went to the stairwell. The yellow daisies, white mums, and broken glass were still there. So was a card. I thought for a moment, reached in my purse, and pulled out an unused plastic bag. Using the technique I perfected when collecting Bug's wastes, I scooped up the card without my fingers ever touching it and sealed it in the bag.

The door opened. "I've called for backup." Scofield kept the door open with her foot as she watched the front entrance of the hospital. "Did the guy have on gloves?"

"I didn't notice his hands, and I doubt I can add much to the volunteer's description. Six foot. Not overweight, but it was hard to tell with his bulky black jacket and knit black cap." I paused. "Odd, that's the same description I would have given for Troy Pitkin this afternoon, but there's probably more than fifty men on campus who would fit that description today." I waved the bag with the card in front of her. "This was with the flowers. My fingers never touched it."

As she talked to someone in the police lab, she kept watching the front entrance. She muttered almost to herself every few seconds, "What's keeping Western?" She smiled slightly when Western finally sauntered toward us.

Although Scofield would never admit it, she cared about Western. Maybe *depended* on him was a better description. Anyway, they were a team.

"He got away, but I saw a car with its light off leaving the parking lot. I think it had the outline of an old Corvette. Maybe in blue. I called squad cars in the area to look for it."

Scofield frowned. "We'd better go to Leslie's room and give the guard backup until the officers you distracted get here."

Western whistled in his usual out of tune manner. "I already called for more backup. I told the original officers to look for the car for five minutes and then go to the Jackson and Lopez residences and see if anyone is at home."

CHAPTER 16: Sara on Thursday

Bug and I were late getting to the police station the next morning because check out from the motel had been slow. Western began to speak as soon we entered his office. "Both Jim Jackson and Wendell Lopez arrived home after ten last night. Both had on dark jackets, and dark knit caps were found in their Corvettes. Both said they were working—at the lab in Jim's case and at the library in Wendell's case. Neither could name anyone who could back up their story. Hard to believe but I'd say Jim and Wendell were in cahoots and providing alibis for each other."

Scofield pursed her lips and started her breathing exercises. "I must be out of it today. I was thinking the same thing." She looked at her phone. "Now let's discuss our two newest leads. The note that you saved last night was handwritten and said:

I'll do better next time.

The lab is checking it for fingerprints and DNA, but I wouldn't hold my breath."

I murmured, "Odd sentiment for a get well note. Could it be a threat?" I searched my memory. "I'm sorry I didn't focus on the man's face last night."

Western patted my shoulder. "Being a good witness is harder than we admit."

"Yes," Scofield continued without coughing, "Our second lead has potential. A middle-aged woman reported to Denver police late yesterday that her husband was missing. He'd left Denver four weeks ago on a business trip."

Western snickered. "Weird she waited so long to report him missing."

Scofield coughed. "Denver police thought that, too, and checked out her home for evidence of foul play. The report is long but the bottom line is he was going to explore opportunities in a 'food business' in Fort

Collins. The wife said—this is a quote—'He likes to case out business opportunities incognito.'"

My jaw dropped. "Miracle Foods would qualify as a food business. You're wondering if this missing man could be the homeless man in your morgue."

Western chortled. "Stranger things have happened. Now if we keep the pressure up, someone will make a mistake."

Scofield shook her head. "I wouldn't bet on it, except you are lucky."

Western winked at me. "No, just talented."

"Whatever." Scofield tinkered with her phone. "I've asked Sam Drake to send the DNA profile of our homeless man to Denver for comparison to DNA from samples that the Denver police collected. It's a long shot but..."

Western stood. "This morning we're going to split up. Scofield thinks you'd be a better partner than me when questioning the faculty in the university's Fermentation Science and Technology Program. She also wants to know how the lab should analyze the frozen food from the meal site and our dead guy's stomach contents."

Scofield smirked. "He feels more comfortable interviewing his friends at the meal site."

Western ignored the barb. "I felt yesterday that a couple of the indigents might become talkative if I set the stage right. I also want to chat with a couple of divorce lawyers in the area to see whether Leslie or Mendel Lopez had contacted them recently. I need to remind them that they owe us favors. Well—no need to explain." Western opened the door to the office "Scofield won the coin toss and you two get the police car. Our assistant has volunteered to look after Bug this morning."

I must have looked surprised.

"She loves dogs. He'll be safe here with her. Then we'll do a wrap-up at the station around noon so you and Bug can be on your way to Colorado Springs before the storm hits. Besides, whoever cut the brake lines on Leslie's car will become more desperate as we apply more pressure. I don't want you around as a tempting target."

Scofield nodded. "If anyone asks, we'll let them think you're returning home. We'll keep the information on your location in Colorado Springs this weekend secret."

I gulped because I didn't think I was in that much danger.

***

                                          J. L. Greger

Scofield turned on her recorder and then questioned me about the lab tests as she drove to the CSU campus. I concluded my comments by saying: "Ask the FDA for help."

Scofield nodded. "Is there anything else Western and I need to think about?"

"Last night I checked the notes of the nurse who monitored the clinical trial. The twelve indigents who developed symptoms after eating the first batch of the bad cultured fish developed more severe symptoms the second time. And eight more at the meal site developed symptoms in response to the second meal with the bad cultured fish. I hypothesize the histamine levels were higher in the second batch of cultured fish because otherwise the meals were similar." I typed rapidly on my laptop. "I've sent you a list of the names of those affected. You'll note Herman Preuter is not on the list." I paused. "Wait—we've missed the obvious. Has anyone shown the indigents at the meal site pictures of Jim, Mendel, Wendell, Troy, and even Leslie? One of them must have put the peanuts in the meal served to Herman Preuter or paid Mike to do it. That means someone at the meal site must have seen Herman Preuter's murderer."

"Why Mike?"

"Remember how Abigail said he took all the leftovers from the meal site to a city park to feed the dogs of the homeless. I figure he's more apt than the cook or the meal site director to bend the rules."

Scofield called Western and gave him instructions. I was glad I couldn't hear his salty comments because she was extremely thorough— to the point of micromanagement.

***

Scofield had made an appointment to talk to the internship director in the Fermentation Science and Technology Program, so before we arrived the woman had pulled the files of all the students who had done internships at Miracle Foods. While Scofield sorted through the files and scanned all the interns' final reports on Miracle Foods, I chatted with the instructor about problems encountered when managing students in field situations.

After we discussed the problem of not allowing internships to degenerate into cheap grunt labor for companies, I explored another hot topic. "I found sexual harassment was a frequent issue when students were on site during epidemiological studies overseas. Do your interns complain of harassment?"

The woman looked surprised. "We have strict policies. If a student complains of sexual harassment, I must investigate, and in most cases end the internship immediately."

I decided to see if she was naive or just quoting the party-line. "So, students don't report harassment because they'll lose any chance for a recommendation from the internship?"

The instructor nodded. "It's odd you asked about that problem. That was one of Leslie Lopez's big concerns about internships. She asked to see the file of every student who interned at Miracle Foods. I don't know why. No young woman ever hinted that Jim Jackson made her feel uncomfortable." She looked to see if Scofield was busy and spoke more rapidly when she realized Scofield wasn't listening. "Actually, I do know why Leslie was so concerned about sexual harassment. One instructor in the biotechnology program gave her a hard time years ago." She again glanced at Scofield. "At least that's the rumor. I started work here six years ago. By then she and Mendel were married."

Scofield and I interviewed the three other faculty members in the program. All noted Leslie got great teaching evaluations from students.

One male associate professor claimed Leslie liked to brag about managing a company based on research. Then he said, "No wonder Miracle Foods is struggling. She knows little about research and the food scientist she hired to head up research at Miracle Foods is a yes-man."

In contrast, an older male professor claimed Leslie was beginning a promising research career when she met Mendel at a university fundraising event. "She quickly decided she was more interested in becoming an entrepreneur than a tenured faculty member."

Although both men had been in the department for more than ten years, each claimed he knew nothing of Leslie's interactions with anyone in the biotechnology program.

Scofield and I thought our most interesting interview was with the woman who had run the pilot plant for the Fermentation Science and Technology Program for the last ten years. She claimed Leslie had a boyfriend in the biotechnology program at the time she became a part-time instructor in the program eight years ago. "But it was very secretive because he was a married man with a son. Once she met Mendel, she dumped the old boyfriend and held on tightly to Mendel." She winked. "Leslie considered Mendel to be the goose that laid the golden eggs and has put up with all his dalliances because she wants Miracle Foods to be a success."

I wondered whether Jim Jackson had been the lover whom Leslie dumped. He'd earned his MS in biotechnology about seven years ago. He was married and had a son. Scofield doubted Jim had been an instructor in the biotechnology program but planned to check with that program. We both agreed that none of Leslie's colleagues liked her much.

J. L. Greger

***

Bug was happy when Scofield and I walked into the conference room at the police station. Western was not.

"I called five divorce attorneys in Fort Collins and Denver. None would admit they'd been contacted by Mendel or Leslie recently. One was ecstatic at the prospect of having Leslie as a client. She said, 'I saw Mendel on the slopes with three different women last season.'" Western shook his head. "The woman lawyer who represented Mendel in two of his divorces said, 'Mendel never initiates the legal action of a divorce. He just does what he wants and lets his wife decide when she has had enough.'"

I was confused. "Wait—how many wives had Mendel Lopez had?"

"Let's see. His first wife and twin ten-year-old daughters died in a car crash when Wendell was an infant. Within a year, he married his long-term mistress. She lasted less than a year. Then he married the woman who basically raised Wendell. She almost drank herself to death before she got up the gumption to divorce Mendel." Western scratched his ear. "That makes Leslie wife number four."

Scofield cleared her throat. "Your renditions of Fort Collin's history are always fascinating, but let's get back to our current situation. What did you learn at the meal site?"

"I circulated pictures of Mendel, his pathetic son Wendell, Jim, Pitkin, Viola, and even Leslie around the meal site and talked to probably thirty diners. None admitted ever seeing Mendel, Wendell, Jim, or Pitkin."

Scofield winked at me. "He was lucky. He's saving the best for last."

"Sorry to disappoint, pardner."

I wondered whether Western assumed a Texan drawl and emphasized a "d" sound when he said *pardner* to annoy Scofield. It didn't work this time as it usually did. She just smiled.

After a long pause, "The cook and Mike recognized Jim and Viola and noted they always came in together. Mike claimed Jim seldom spoke to anyone, but Viola always had a long talk with the director of the meal site and sometimes the cook."

"What about Leslie?"

"Everyone at the site knew Leslie. The men adore her. Evidently, she flirts with all of them. The women like her because she always asks whether they like the food and often hands out fruit to anyone who wanted more to eat." Western uncharacteristically slouched in his chair. "I was so sure I had the right leads this time."

Scofield put her hand on Western's shoulder. "You're disappointed because you don't like the obvious conclusion. Mendel and Wendell aren't prime suspects for the murder of Herman Preuter, but Leslie, Jim, and Viola are." When he didn't reply, Scofield turned to me. "I've emailed you the reports of the student interns at Miracle Foods. All are shorter than two pages. All are encoded, but you said Pitkin had told you how to break Jim's codes on samples. Once you get to Colorado Springs, please see whether these reports are useful."

Western looked at his watch. "I checked the weather report before you two arrived. The snowstorm is moving fast and will hit Fort Collins early this afternoon. That means it's time for you and Bug to be on your way." He smiled. "And it's time for Scofield to stop mollycoddling suspects and let me start grilling them." He hugged me. "The jokers at Miracle Foods didn't appreciate you. They're all as fake as their meat."

CHAPTER 17: Scofield's Analyses

Ever since the previous day when the police had confiscated the frozen sample meals from Miracle Foods, Scofield had been thinking about how many resources were available in Fort Collins that the police never used. She wondered how many of these limitations reflected a lack of knowledge and how many were due to imagined slights. She doubted she'd get a straightforward answer from Western, but it was worth a try. "I learned something yesterday. I knew the Agriculture Research Service lab and office complex at the southern edge of the CSU campus was a research facility of the U.S. Department of Agriculture, but I'd never been in those buildings."

Scofield waited for Western's response. He was silent. She suspected that meant he'd not been in the ARS facilities either. "I also would never have thought about asking them for freezer space to store the samples we confiscated from Miracle Foods."

Western finally answered after he parked the car by the campus police station. "I'm not sure how Sara so quickly convinced them to be cooperative. All she told me was USDA is responsible along with FDA in previewing and eventually approving cell-cultured food products. I asked her what she meant." He whistled. "Guess that's the fancy term for the fake meat that Miracle Foods is developing."

Scofield smiled to herself because while Western had talked to the director of ARS lab yesterday, she'd talked to the director's secretary. She learned the director had received calls from the Inspector General of USDA, the director of the Denver office of the Food Safety Inspection Service in USDA, and an FDA official in Denver on Wednesday morning. They had all requested the director's cooperation with the investigation that Sara was leading at Miracle Foods. Thus, the director of the ARS lab had agreed to find space for frozen samples from Miracle Foods.

Scofield saw no reason to mention those details to Western. Instead, she said, "Sara agreed to conduct a workshop on cultured meat for USDA scientists and all USDA meat inspectors in this region. And the amount of material we moved to their freezers wasn't large."

"I'd been feeling sorry for Sara because I figured Mendel Lopez would fire her in a day or two. I shouldn't have worried—she'll instead enlarge her consulting business." He shook his head. "I must say I enjoyed our snatch and grab routine at Miracle Foods yesterday. Of course, it wasn't really a snatch and grab because it was legal, but it sure ruffled Mendel's feathers."

Scofield had her answer. Western didn't seek new contacts in Fort Collins because his long-term knowledge of the people of northern Colorado was so deep that it was seldom necessary. However, she'd noticed a downside to his long term memory. Sometimes his memory of past grudges or mistakes blinded him. She feared that was the case with Mendel Lopez. Then again, Mendel had yet to display his good side in this case even though he appeared to be innocent of any wrongdoing other than arrogance and rudeness.

"Let's forget about Mendel and focus of Troy Pitkin. The director of the internship program in the Fermentation Science and Technology Program thought Pitkin was one of their best students, but noted he was always 'rather tense' and since his disagreement with Jim Jackson 'almost paranoid.' That's why she encouraged Pitkin to resign from his internship before the end of last semester and to talk to Leslie."

"You're saying the boy might cry if I push too hard?" He jumped out of the car and started to walk rapidly to Lory Student Center."

Scofield rushed to catch up. "No, I'm saying this young man may have been pulled unwillingly into the..."

"Horseplay at Miracle Foods? And that's your way of telling me you want to take the lead in questioning the boy?"

***

Scofield looked around the food court in Lory Student Center. She counted eight men with dark oversized jackets and dark knit caps. She wondered whether the men were making a fashion statement. They certainly didn't need their coats and caps inside. The space was hot and loud. Even though the noon hour was long past, students swarmed among the various fast-food vendors lining the court.

As she and Western approached the Panda Grill, one of the similarly dressed young men stood up. He was about six foot and could be the man Sara had seen last night at the hospital. "Troy Pitkin?"

"Yes, ma'am," said the young man. He looked around the food court. "Can we talk somewhere else? Where no one will see me."

Scofield tried to give a motherly smile. "Follow me. We'll go upstairs."

When Western suggested they sit near the Aspen Grille, Pitkin said, "I'd rather not. Students in the Fermentation Science and Technology Program work there. They might see me."

"No problem. I noticed an empty room down the hall." As soon as they were seated at a table in an empty banquet room she said, "We're not accusing you of anything. Why are you so nervous?"

"Because a man died at the meal site testing the cultured meat and several others became ill."

Western laughed. "We aren't going to force you to eat the fake meat."

Pitkin literally slid down in his seat.

Scofield practiced her breath control exercise and resisted the urge to slap Western as she focused on Pitkin. "My partner thinks he's being funny. I think cultured meat is an interesting concept, but no one has offered me a taste. Have you tasted it?"

Pitkin smiled. "Yes, the flavors of the beef and turkey are good, but they don't feel quite right when you chew them. They're too rubbery. The fish sometimes has a bit of an off-taste, but the texture is good."

She figured Pitkin had relaxed as much as possible. It was time to ask a big question. "Were you the one who tried to deliver flowers to Leslie Lopez last night? The guy wore a black jacket and black knit cap like yours and was about your height."

She kicked Western's leg under the table when he said, "I thought you were..."

Pitkin took off his cap and traced his finger along scratches on the tabletop. "Lots of guys have caps like this."

"Hmm." Scofield decided a bluff was in order. "If you didn't, I think you know who did. Leslie liked the flowers, but we didn't give her the note. Let's see—what did it say. I think, *I'll do better next time.*"

Pitkin gasped.

She couldn't decide whether he was surprised by the note or the fact she had read it. "What do you think that means?" She waited ten seconds. "I'm pretty sure you know who wrote the note."

Pitkin said, "Not sure," so softly she could barely hear him.

Western put his hand on Pitkin's shoulder. "Look, son. We don't think you've done anything wrong but withholding information from the police is a crime. The sooner we round up the guilty person, or maybe I should say *persons*, the better for you."

Scofield was surprised that Pitkin didn't flinch when Western tried his "son" trick. "My partner is right. We know several guys—like Wendell

Lopez and Seth Evers—gave Leslie a hard time. Sometimes men do that when they want a woman's attention."

"Yeah, but they didn't want her attention, at least not like that."

"What did they want?"

"Wendell—actually several of us—saw her having coffee here with a gray-haired man several times. He had a neat beard and looked like a professor."

"What was unusual about that?"

"Wendell didn't like it."

"Why would he care?"

"He was worried about his dad. Said 'my stupid Dad really loves that...'" Pitkin blushed and murmured something.

Western did his hand on the shoulder routine again. Scofield was worried if Western kept doing it, Pitkin could charge him with inappropriate behavior. "Now, son, we're all adults. What did Wendell call Leslie?"

"A Ho."

Scofield was afraid what Western would say after he stopped snickering and rapidly said, "So Wendell didn't like Leslie because he was worried about his dad. Is that a fair statement?"

Pitkin nodded.

"How did Seth Evers feel about Leslie?"

"He did whatever Wendell asked. And he thought it was funny to make Leslie nervous."

"Why?"

"Don't know... except Wendell makes promises. You know his dad owns several businesses. It can be hard to get a summer job or a first job when you graduate."

Western stood and winked at Scofield. "Mr. Pitkin, I have one last question. Who tried to deliver the flowers to Leslie last night?"

Pitkin shrugged. "Ask Wendell and Seth."

Scofield tried not to show the annoyance she felt. "Here's my card. We know you've not told us everything you know or suspect. The next time we speak it will be at the station and you will be charged with withholding evidence if you continue to be uncooperative."

As they left, Pitkin slumped at the table.

Western said, "I didn't think you'd ever stop mollycoddling that kid."

"There was no hurry. It took time to get the officers in place. The woman officer at the table we just passed will follow..."

Western started to look backward.

                                              J. L. Greger

"Don't you dare." She pulled Western forward. "Like I was saying, she'll follow Pitkin for several hours. Campus police have located Wendell. He should be leaving a business class in about ten minutes. They also know Seth Evers is due at a class in an hour. That's why I took my time with Troy."

***

Wendell Lopez would have been easy to pick out of the crowd of students spilling out from the large lecture hall and down the concrete stairs of Rockwell Hall even if the campus police hadn't identified him. Although it was cold, Wendell didn't pull on a cap over his spiky black hair with fades on the sides. Most students emerged with their heads covered.

Scofield walked directly toward Wendell while Western and the campus police circled behind him. When Scofield was four feet in front of Wendell, she displayed her badge. "Wendell Lopez, I want to talk to you."

Wendell turned, saw the uniformed campus police behind him, veered toward Western on his right, and almost fell on his face. Scofield figured Western had scored again. Western had perfected a routine where he lifted his foot to trip suspects while he grabbed for their arms. To anyone watching, it appeared as if Western was keeping them from falling. Scofield hated to admit it, but it was a masterful dance step.

"Wendell, this is your lucky day. You're going to help me and Officer Scofield figure out who caused your stepmother's accident."

Wendell's face flushed. He pulled Western's hand from his shoulder. "You don't have any proof I was involved in her accident" He flipped out his phone when it buzzed.

"Son, why don't you wait to take that message until we're in our car or at the station? It's awfully cold here."

Wendell ignored Western, turned his back to him, and texted a seemingly long response.

***

Scofield was pleased. Neither Seth Evers or Wendell Lopez had asked for a lawyer. But then why would they? She had plied them with soda and cookies. However, she had tried to create tension for the two young men by keeping them in separate rooms, asking two or three questions, leaving to talk to the other one, and then repeating the process. A uniformed officer followed her as she moved between the two rooms, while Western remained in the observation room between the two interrogation rooms.

Both young men named their usual poker partners on Wednesday night as proof of their location the previous evening. Western and an aide quickly called the named poker players. The supposed witnesses reported both Seth and Wendell had arrived late to the game.

Scofield decided Seth was the weaker link and focused on him. "I think you shouldn't trust Wendell Lopez. He just told me you were late to the poker game. Why would he make it look like you were the one trying to harass Leslie last night?" When Seth gave her a blank stare, she explained someone had attempted deliver flowers to Leslie at the hospital the previous evening. She hinted the attached note was weird, without giving details. Then she pursed her lips and did her breathing exercises as she stared at Seth. The routine usually made Western feel guilty, she hoped it would have the same effect on Seth.

Seth groaned, "I'm tired of taking the blame. Sure, I hit on Leslie but so did other guys. She can strut her stuff better than the babes in our classes. Wendell says his dad's money buys her all the right clothes, especially those boots. But I didn't bother her last night."

"Why were you late to the poker game?"

"I had to finish a report that was due today. Ask my economics prof."

"Okay, I believe your alibi. Do you think Wendell could have threatened Leslie last night?"

Seth supported his head in his hands as he slumped over the table. "No idea. After the restraining order last year, he promised me no more pranks on Leslie. It stopped being fun."

Scofield left quickly and found Western standing with his chest stuck out like a rooster in the viewing room. "He's just a dumb kid. Cut the boy loose. I'll do Wendell." He'd stepped out of the room and then stepped back in. "This may be of interest. The call to Wendell was from somewhere near campus—maybe Miracle Foods."

Scofield shook her head. "Then it wasn't Pitkin."

"Right, timing's wrong. Pitkin made a call almost as soon as we left him. Wendell's call was several minutes later."

Scofield watched with concern as Western started whistling and swaggered into the interrogation room. She hoped he wouldn't do anything stupid.

"According to the lab, the flowers you tried to deliver to Leslie last night were purchased at Walmart. That's kind of cheap for a rich boy like you."

Wendell blinked. "You've got your wires crossed. The flowers old lady Sanchez delivered for Dad to Leslie were from the best shop in town. One thing I learned from Dad is money matters."

"How much did you give Seth to do your dirty work?"

Wendell shook his head. "Look, Seth and I flirted with Leslie. We thought it was fun to annoy her, but Dad sat me down a couple of weeks ago. First time he ever talked to me like a man. He told me the cute bimbos at school would never become interesting women. He said, 'Do you know how boring it is living with a woman who keeps only fruits, vegetables, and booze in the fridge? Think of your last stepmother.' Then he explained that all I needed to do was graduate and get a good job. Then I'd have my pick of women. Dad finished by saying, 'Believe me—Leslie's good in bed, but it's her business sense that I value.'"

Scofield raced into the interrogation room before Western made a true, but inappropriate, comment. She also figured her agitated appearance might scare Wendell. "My partner is being too easy on you. Forget last night. We want to know what you were doing on Monday night and Tuesday morning." She leaned toward Wendell. "You'll remember Leslie had her near fatal accident on Tuesday morning."

Wendell turned pale.

She hoped her aggressive approach wouldn't backfire and cause Wendell to request a lawyer. She reverted to a tried-but-true interrogation technique. She pushed Western out of the room and lowered her voice to sound sexy. "Look Mr. Lopez, I think you're innocent, but my partner is not *kind* to young men. He calls them 'boys' and is jealous of them. Just tell me about your classes Monday afternoon and what you did next. Then we can both go home."

CHAPTER 18: Western's Angle

Western only half-heartedly listened to Wendell as he replied to Scofield's questions. He doubted Wendell had cut Leslie's brake lines because he doubted the boy could have found them. This kid had no future in engineering. Someone should advise him to transfer to the business school. Western smiled as he thought of his son's frequent comment, "If you aren't smart or don't want to work hard in college, you should major in business." He knew his son was a bit of a smart-ass too, but a nice one.

He could see Scofield was determined to wring every useful detail out of Wendell. He suspected she already had, but who knows. Accordingly, Western decided to do what Scofield would do while sitting in the viewing room—read emails.

The one from the guard at the ICU was depressing. Leslie was moaning, and the doctor was debating whether to induce another coma because standard medications hadn't lowered the pressure in her brain. Western ordered the guard to record her moans because it might be the last chance to learn anything from her.

The next email was the best news of the day. The medical examiner had scored a hit. Rapid DNA analyses indicated the corpse of Herman Preuter in the morgue was the missing CEO of a small food company. The man had disappeared from Denver a month ago and his real name was Herb Parson. Western was surprised that Parson's DNA analyses were on file because he'd not been in the military and had no police record. Western guessed the wife must have provided a hair sample for analyses.

Western decided he'd show Scofield he could pay attention to details. He checked the roster of former students in the graduate program in biological and chemical engineering at Colorado State. Jim Jackson was on the list; Herb Parson was not. Western decided to call the program and ask whether Herb Parson had ever been associated with the program. The secretary, who seemed pleasant when he began the call, turned frosty when he mentioned Herb Parson. She transferred his call to the department head.

After a five-minute delay, the department head began the call by asking for Western's badge number. Then he said, "Before I answer your questions, please tell me if you're calling because a woman has initiated legal action against Herb Parson because of his behavior when he was employed by the department as an instructor for two years."

Western knew he'd hit pay dirt. "No, we're not talking about a lawsuit. Would you prefer if I came to your office?" That brought the expected response. The department head preferred to answer questions on the phone. He quickly explained that Herb Parson had been an instructor in the Master's level biotechnology program. He'd been fired after three women complained of his inappropriate behavior.

Western continued to ask questions until the department head said, "All three women dropped charges against the university after we fired him and conceded to their requests. I'm sorry but I can't say more. I think Herb Parson came to legal agreements with each of the women individually. You should talk to the university's lawyers."

Western figured he should notify Scofield immediately. Her interrogation of Wendell was a waste of time. On second thought, he'd let her sweat the interview. She'd argue with him less in the future when he said college boys were pains to interview. Wendell was a jerk but Western doubted he was smart enough to have been involved in the horseplay at the meal site.

After Scofield ended her protracted interview with Wendell, Western summed up his conversation with the university lawyer to her simply. "We now have three suspects, maybe more, with real reasons to kill Herb Parson. Seems he riled every woman he met and physically attacked at least three of them. A regular Don Juan."

"Was Leslie one of them?

"The university lawyer said she'd threatened to file a lawsuit but didn't. No wonder the wife didn't report him missing for a month. She was glad he was gone."

For once, Scofield didn't use her body language to disagree with him. She simply said, "Now we talk to Mendel."

***

Scofield and Western debated possible approaches to questioning Mendel Lopez but in the end agreed no matter how they approached Mendel, he would be annoyed. Accordingly, Scofield said as she barged into Mendel's office at Miracle Foods, "Mr. Lopez, we have questions. Is there a reason you haven't visited your wife in the hospital?"

Mendel stared at her.

"Were either of you considering a divorce or a separation?"

Mendel continued to stare at her.

Western gave his broadest grin "I'll make the question simpler. Were you and your wife having problems? Your son certainly thought you had marital problems."

Mendel frowned as he waved for them to be seated. "Twenty-year-old males aren't good judges of marital problems, but now I understand your questions. Leslie and I have for the last couple of weeks or so disagreed on a business decision." He smiled.

Western couldn't believe his ears. The guy really thought he could charm his way out of any situation. "This isn't twenty questions. This is an investigation of two murders and an attempted murder."

Mendel turned pale. "The hospital didn't call. "His voice shook. "Did Leslie's condition deteriorate? I.... I can't stand to be in hospitals."

Western wanted to say *Grow up,* but before he could speak, Scofield said, "No, Mr. Lopez, your wife is alive, but she claims someone pushed her down the stairs. We have reason to believe this was the man." She shoved the old photo of Herb Parson without a beard at Mendel Lopez.

"Well, who died?"

Western could not resist being sarcastic. "Remember the homeless man at the meal site who ate your Miracle Foods's product and the boy your wife hit when her car went out of control?"

"Oh yes." Mendel sat down and studied the picture carefully. "I don't think I've seen this man. Yet... he looks familiar."

Scofield shoved the morgue photo at Lopez.

Mendel gulped as he stared at the photo. Then he stood and looked out into the main office of Miracle Foods before he closed the door to his private office. "I don't want anyone to hear this conversation. It... it could be..."

Western thought Mendel looked paler and older as he walked to his desk and appeared to be searching his computer files. "I'm searching for my notes on a meeting. It was strange."

Western wanted to yell *Spit it out* but figured Scofield was right when she brought her finger to her lips.

"It's here somewhere." After about a minute, Mendel said, "I had an offer... to buy Miracle Foods about two months ago. I knew Viola and Jim would be hysterical. Viola keeps reminding me, at least once every month, that she left the security of a state job at the university to run our finances here. Besides, she thinks I owe her for something twenty years ago. Jim is making progress, but the damn fake meats aren't ready for market yet. I wonder if they'll ever be." He continued to mumble as his computer screen was filled with opened files.

Mendel was quite pale as he turned to Scofield. "I didn't file my notes on the meeting under 'offers' because that would make it too easy for others to locate. Trouble with owning Miracle Foods is everyone here is smart and nosy, including my wife."

Scofield leaned toward Mendel. "We all have trouble finding files sometimes. Can you search for a key word?"

Western thought she was doing a masterful job of acting concerned while she tried to sneak peeks at the screen. If necessary, the technician who had copied Mendel's computer files yesterday could find it.

"I did and it's not here."

"What was the word, Mr. Lopez?"

"'Hooray.' I thought."

Western couldn't contain himself. "You were that eager to sell Miracle Foods?"

Mendel turned to Western without any of his usual swagger. "I made my fortune by taking chances on land and commodity deals, but nothing prepared me for running a start-up company based on so-called scientific discoveries. It takes iron balls." He blinked. "Leslie says I don't have enough patience." He blinked again. "About three months ago, she admitted we had hired the wrong head scientist. Then out-of-the-blue I got a call from Herb Parson. I knew from the start he was an oddball."

Mendel suddenly straightened. "That's it." He typed rapidly. A new file opened on the screen.

As he perused it, Scofield murmured, "What was the file named?"

"Oddball." Mendel seemed much more relaxed as he turned toward Scofield and Western. "Everything was odd about Parson. He called and wanted to meet with me without Leslie. He didn't want me to tell her about the meeting, either."

Western shrugged. "How was that odd?"

Mendel took a quick glance at his screen. "Leslie and I are partners. We bounce all—well, most—of our business deals off each other. My son and others think we're arguing. We're not. We're thinking out loud." Mendel stared at the ceiling.

Scofield broke his trance. "Tell us about your business deal with Parson."

"We talked on the phone. Parson owned a company that made artificial meats out of plant products and wanted to expand into cultured meat products. It was obvious he knew a lot about biotechnology and the alternate meat market—at least more than I did. I figured he didn't want Leslie to participate in the discussion because he thought it was easier to snow me alone." Mendel paused. "That much was logical. The rest wasn't. He didn't want a tour of our facilities. Told me he had other ways of learning about our facilities. Didn't want to see our financial records. Said he already knew most of the details. Parson just wanted to know how much I wanted for Miracle Foods, our patents, and trade secrets." Mendel frowned.

"Did he slip and mention his source of information on Miracle Foods?"

"No, but I had the distinct impression he wasn't bluffing. That made think he'd already talked to Leslie and had played the same game with her as he was with me. I decided I could play his game and agreed to meet with him sometime in the following week. I figured that would give Leslie and me time to strategize." He shook his head again. "When he suggested I meet him in a hotel room in Loveland, and not in one of my offices in Fort Collins or in his office in Denver, I became impatient. I thought he wasn't making a legitimate deal. He was just—as Leslie would say—on a 'phishing expedition' and wasting my time. I told him so."

"What did he do?"

Mendel studied his computer notes. "We agreed to meet the next day at my real estate office. I..."

Western was tired of the long narrative and was glad when Scofield asked, "Did you tell Leslie?"

"That night at supper I told her we might have an offer to sell Miracle Foods but I didn't mention Parson's name. She thought it was a mistake to enter negotiations until the clinical trial was concluded. She noted that she thought Jim had finally figured out how to prevent histamine build up in the fish product. If that was true and the clinical trial went well, the value of Miracle Foods and our patents should be more than triple our investments. We could get several competing offers."

"What did you say?"

Mendel chuckled. "What was there to say? She was right. The time wasn't right for sales negotiations, but I met Parson the next day. Our whole meeting lasted less than ten minutes. He never took his coat off." He touched the morgue photo. "That's why I'm not sure. The man I met had a neat gray beard and trimmed gray hair. The man in the photo looks more unkempt and his hair is longer, but the head shape and brow are similar."

                                              J. L. Greger

Western didn't feel like waiting for Scofield to carefully unravel details. "When did you tell Parson's name to Leslie?"

Mendel bit his lip. "Leslie was pretty distracted in December and early January finishing one semester, preparing for the next, and planning the clinical trial. Then I got an email from Parson." Mendel retrieved the email and turned the screen so Scofield could read it easily:

You'd better reconsider my offer. It might be unwise to wait until the clinical trial begins.
Herb Parson

"I took that as a threat and showed it to Leslie. She hit the fan. Never saw her so upset."

Scofield was rapidly pecking at her phone and didn't look up. "What did she say?"

"Herb Parson had been an instructor on campus and had been fired for bad behavior. She didn't elaborate, *but* she was adamant. *We couldn't sell Miracle Foods to him.*"

Western was surprised by Scofield's next questions. "Did you tell ever tell Sara Almquist about Herb Parson or his threat?"

"I told her I feared competitors had caused our problems."

"Why didn't you mention Parson's threat or your problem with high histamine levels in your fish product to Sara Almquist?"

"Leslie said I should. Jim advised me that it was unwise to tell our problems with histamine accumulation in our fish products to a consultant with such strong ties to federal inspectors. It would line us for more required tests and red tape." Mendel frowned. "When Sara made it clear she knew we had problems with histamine levels in our products, I was annoyed with Jim and myself. I knew I should have listened to Leslie."

***

Scofield and Western arrived at the police station several minutes later with Mendel Lopez in tow. Western lost the coin flip. Scofield began to question Mendel while he was stuck with the college student Troy Pitkin.

Western quickly decided Scofield was right. Pitkin's skittishness was way beyond nervousness. Pitkin was guilty of something. However, she was wrong on the next point; actually, they both were wrong. They'd figured Jim Jackson would eventually show up at the library in response to Pitkin's call.

Thus they'd been surprised when the woman officer tailing Pitkin notified them a middle-aged, overweight woman had casually sat down by

Pitkin in the library. The officer hadn't acted because the woman had made no effort to speak to Pitkin. After several minutes she'd left, leaving a library book on the table. The officer's suspicions were finally raised when Pitkin pulled a slip of paper from atop the cover of the book, pulled an envelope from the book, and shoved the envelope in his book bag without reading it. The officer stopped him as he left the library and asked to see the envelope. When he refused, she asked him to accompany her to the police station.

After Western's first question, Pitkin requested a lawyer. Western felt sorry for the young man and explained options to him. Pitkin listened politely before he said, "I'm broke. Please get me a public defender." Western contacted the public defender's office.

***

As Western stood in the observation room, an aide updated him on Scofield's progress with Mendel. Scofield had begun the session by reciting Leslie's moans and telling Mendel about Herb Parson.

Mendel asked to see the old photo of Herb Parson and studied it intently. "I met Leslie at a university reception designed to get local business people interested in partnering with the university on start-up companies to develop science and technology projects in the Fort Collins area. She was eager to learn whether I would be interested in a new biotech—she never said 'biotechnology' always 'biotech'—business opportunity, but she was distant. She wouldn't meet me for dinner to discuss her ideas. She insisted we meet in my real estate office."

"How did that make you feel?"

Western thought the question was an unnecessary waste of time. Then he decided that there was no hurry because Pitkin was a dead end until a judge granted them a search warrant and the public defender's office responded with the obvious answer.

"Made me more interested in her idea. She wanted to convert the microbrewery she owned into a company that used biotechnology to produce artificial meat. My family had been cattlemen for generations. The idea of being a co-owner of a company that made fake meat was *embarrassing*. Leslie was persistent. When I tried to charm her, she informed me a man whom she thought was a potential business colleague had become... aggressive. She didn't use the word rape, but she said he'd tried to push her down a flight of stairs." He studied the photo again. "Said she didn't want to confuse business and romance like she'd done before." He returned to staring at the photo.

"And what did you do?"

"I fell in love with her." He wiped his eyes. "I never asked her to talk about the man who abused her." He handed the photo back to Scofield. "No wonder she didn't want to sell Miracle Foods to him. But yet... I'm surprised she didn't admit the whole story to me."

Scofield patted his hand. "Women often don't want to talk about rapes or attempted rapes. They think their husband or boyfriend will think less of them. That's why predators like Herb Parson usually have multiple victims."

He wiped his eyes. "What can I do?"

"Go to the hospital. Talk to her. We need her help to solve this case. She pointed to Western who had just entered the interrogation room, "We think she figured out who sabotaged the clinical trial before her accident, probably last Monday night—the night she brought three boxes from Miracle Foods home."

Mendel suddenly straightened. "I think she'd figured it out earlier because she'd been acting strange for several days—ever since Jim and I returned from Colorado. That night, she was looking for something specific in the files."

Scofield patted Mendel's hand. "How about if we go to talk to your wife now? The doctor said her return to consciousness could be a good sign, but she needs encouragement."

Western thought Scofield had been wise not to add the rest of what the doctor had said. "Or it might signal Leslie's last attempt to cling to life."

CHAPTER 19: Sara in Colorado Springs

There wasn't much good to say about my drive from Fort Collins to Colorado Springs. No snow was falling when I began driving a little before noon. By the time I reached the motel in Colorado Springs at three, the windshield wipers could barely keep up with the snow. The drive should have taken a little over little two hours. It took more than three even though I never stopped.

The last thing I wanted to do when I arrived at the motel was sit, but Bug changed my mind. He quickly tired of plowing through snow that was over his shoulders. Then I decided that plodding through a foot of snow while carrying a squirming dog wasn't fun either.

I scanned my emails. I read the email Scofield had sent before I left the Fort Collins Police Department:

> *Can you decipher anything from these student reports? We expect Pitkin won't cooperate unless you give us something to scare him.*

I expected the attachments to the email to be the internship reports by the two students who had worked at Miracle Foods last summer and Pitkin's report of his work during the fall semester. I was surprised that Scofield had also attached the reports by four other student interns who worked at Miracle Foods during the previous year.

The answer to her question was *no—well, not easily.* I'd decided during my drive to extricate myself from my basically unsuccessful consultation with Miracle Foods. That meant ignoring Scofield's email, finishing my report for Mendel Lopez, notifying FDA I had quit as a consultant, and calculating the total bill for my consultation. To be honest, I thought it better to quit the project than to have Mendel fire me, which I guessed was imminent.

I was surprised when my computer pinged and an email from Mendel Lopez appeared. I braced myself and opened it:

I want to know who in my employ worked with my competitors to devalue Miracle Foods by ruining the clinical trial. The local police aren't up to the task. I will pay your hourly rate for your work with the police.

He didn't add a thank you or further explanation.

I doubted "his competitors" were involved in the sabotage of the clinical trial. I suspected his wife, son, and two key employees—Viola Sanchez and Jim Jackson—all had adequate reasons for wanting to hurt him. I certainly felt little sympathy for him, but I had nothing better to do.

I studied the attachments to Scofield's email. It took a while but I finally saw patterns. Jim had assigned all of the interns the boring task of monitoring the pH, temperature, and levels of several electrolytes in the vats of cultured meat four times a day. Jim had apparently asked the students during the spring semester and previous fall semester to taste the final products. Their comments on the turkey, beef and fish products confirmed Pitkin's analyses of the codes. Samples were coded by the date that batch was started in the vats. The initials T, F, and B stood for turkey, fish, and beef, respectively.

The first question that popped into my mind was why had Jim spent so much time monitoring pH and temperature in the vats of cultured cells? I didn't know much about food science or biotechnology but I'd seen a number of autopsy reports and talked to several pathologists while working with the FBI. They had told me the acidity of a murder victim's muscles increased during rigor mortis because of the accumulation of lactic acid in the muscle. pH is a confusing scientific term to laymen because it basically is the inverse of acidity. Thus, high acidity meant a low pH. I also had been told the pH rises in muscles of murder victims when their muscles begin to degrade after a couple days. I'd been around at least one smelly corpse that must have a very high pH in his muscles. I guessed the same was true in fish and meat. I decided Jim and the students in the spring and previous fall had determined the pH, temperature, and electrolyte ranges that yielded acceptable cultured meat without off-flavors.

My next question was what had changed between the spring semester and summer? Jim had not allowed the students during the summer to taste the final products. He hadn't spoken to them much, while previous students had thought he was talkative. Not surprisingly, those summer interns had complained their projects were boring and quit their internships early.

My third question was why had Jim purposely produced several vats during the summer of the cultured fish at pHs and temperatures that he knew would produce off-flavors? Was that why he didn't allow the students to taste the cultured meats during the summer?

Pitkin's analyses of histamine in samples produced the previous summer confirmed my earlier suspicions. The fish products with high histamine levels were from batches produced at higher temperature and pHs.

Before I began my search of the food science literature on pH of meat and fish products, I checked Leslie's notes in the *CT-menu* file and emailed Scofield:

> *Pitkin's report indicates two batches of cultured fish (Jn9F and Au16F) contained high levels of histamine. I think these batches were served on the two days when subjects at the meal site developed rashes and other symptoms. Leslie seems to have reached the same conclusion according to her notes in the CT-menu file. I'm surprised diners didn't complain of off-flavors in the fish on those days.*
>
> *You might try to discover if anything odd happened at Miracle Foods last May or June. Jim went from being a productive employee to trying to sabotage product development.*

I quickly tired of studying the literature on meat science—which was huge—on the importance of pH on meat tenderness and as an indicator of meat and fish spoilage. I decided I deserved a break and scanned the book I bought last night. *Games for Couples* had at least ten word quizzes besides all sorts of suggestions for risqué modifications of board games and several types of lovers' scavenger hunts. Many of the games were silly and might irritate Sanders, if he wasn't in a playful mood.

However, the "Questions for Private People" section looked promising. The questions, at least the first ones, could spark interesting discussions without prying too deeply into sensitive areas:

> *a) Name the place you would most like to visit. Why?*
> *b) Name the person (alive or dead) you'd most like to invite to dinner. Why?*
> *c) What's your favorite holiday? Why*
> *d) If you were on a quiz show, would you give up $10,000 for a chance to win $100,000?*

That question was followed two other questions of the same ilk but with different prizes. The last questions in the quiz were more intriguing and I hoped we'd get to them:

***

Sanders emailed me at five and suggested I order dinner to be delivered to our motel room at six-thirty because he didn't feel like "cleaning up" for dinner. He also noted he'd be really hungry because he'd spent a lot of time today hiking in snowy mountainous areas trying to test the modified LIDAR system. I didn't need the Lover's Food Quiz to know that he'd want a meaty main dish, and not pasta or seafood.

CHAPTER 20: Western's Outlook

Western thought the scene in the hospital room was romantic, but he would never admit that thought to Scofield. She'd laugh at him.

Mendel took off his heavy winter coat, handed it to Scofield, and slicked his hair back before he entered Leslie's cubicle in the ICU. He gulped several times before he gently touched her hands.

Her eyelids fluttered and the ends of her lips moved upward. "You... came."

Mendel stroked the side of her face. "You thought I didn't have the guts to enter a hospital."

She moved her head from side to side slightly.

Mendel finished her thought. "You knew I was afraid. Both my girls lingered in comas here for days after their accident. I swore I'd never enter a hospital again." He kissed her forehead. "They tell me you're getting better. These officers need your help." He stepped back so Leslie could see both Scofield and Western.

Leslie moaned.

Western wasn't sure, but he thought she said, "Bad... dreams." He wondered whether she had bad dreams or that was what she thought of him and Scofield. He decided to forget the latter idea.

Mendel leaned closer to Leslie. "Why didn't you tell me about that bastard Herb Parson? I would have understood. We couldn't have sold our Miracle Foods to him."

Leslie closed her eyes. "He's... laughing."

When she didn't open her eyes or say more for thirty seconds, Mendel turned to Scofield. "I can't. You ask her your questions."

Western thought Scofield was like a cat ready to pounce on a mouse. No, that was unkind—she acted like an experienced interrogator.

She turned on the recorder before she moved close enough to Leslie to stroke her hand. "Leslie, don't be afraid. Herb Parson can't hurt you."

Leslie opened her eyes. "Not want... to remember."

Scofield pulled Mendel closer and told him to stroke Leslie's forehead. "I understand. Let's talk about what happened Sunday. Why did you go to Miracle Foods?"

"Can't..." A tear rolled down Leslie's cheek.

Mendel waited a few seconds before he said, "We got a call from a technician about a break-in."

Scofield asked Mendel, "Why was the technician there on a Sunday morning?"

Mendel didn't look away from Leslie's face. "At least one technician always gets to the plant every day by six a.m. to monitor the vats of cells and make corrections. I don't know why but the cells seem to be sensitive. The call woke us a few minutes after six. Leslie..." He pulled her matted hair away from her face. "...said she'd take care of everything. She rushed to Miracle Foods."

Western didn't want to wait for Scofield. "What did she find?"

Leslie moaned, "Herb... don't."

Mendel wiped his eyes with one hand and continued to stroke her hair with the other hand "Two file cabinet overturned. Drawers open. She called the police."

Western turned away and pulled up the police report on his phone:

No evidence of forced entry into building or office. Two file cabinets ransacked. Found ten hundred-dollar bills in desk drawer. Not a typical robbery. Leslie Lopez, co-owner of business, could not identify what was stolen but will call when she does.

He walked over and whispered in Scofield's ear, "Mendel's not telling us anything not in the police report."

Scofield nodded in agreement and leaned closer to Leslie. "I think you took the three personnel files—the ones you claimed were missing." Scofield stopped as if to give Leslie time to think.

Leslie didn't respond.

"Okay, let's try something easier. Where did you put the files you took?" Scofield waited a moment before she said, "Your bad dreams about Herb Parson won't go away unless you admit the truth."

Up to now Leslie's monitor had shown her blood pressure increased when each question was asked, but there had been no wild fluctuations or piercing screeches of warning. Now the monitor began to screech and a nurse rushed in.

Scofield voice was steely. "Don't dodge the question. Where did you put the files you took?"

"*Class notes... file.*"

"Why?"

"Ask Pit..."

Western could no longer prevent the nurse from reaching Leslie. The nurse took one look at Leslie and announced, "Everyone out—now." She pointed to the two officers. "This patient can't take more of your questions."

Mendel leaned closer to Leslie. "I love you, darling."

Another nurse pulled Western out of the room. Scofield led Mendel out.

As they stood in the hallway watching the nurses huddled over Leslie, Mendel wiped his eyes. "I knew it was bad luck to come."

Scofield shook her head. "You men always imagine the worst. Stop it. You made Leslie happy."

Western noted Scofield didn't purse her lips and do her breathing routine. He surmised she'd learn more from that session than he had. It was annoying to have such a smart partner, but kind of nice. He didn't have to wait long for a clue.

"We've already searched all of Leslie's files at Miracle Foods and in her small office on campus. Mr. Lopez, we'd like to search Leslie's home office."

***

On the way to the Lopez's home, Scofield tried to softly question Mendel. Western knew she was failing to elicit anything of use because all he heard was the same response from Mendel over and over. "I don't know what files Leslie kept in her home office. I never enter her office, but lately she keeps claiming I've violated her space."

Western took one look at Leslie's office and decided Mendel had told the truth. The walls were a dark purple. He thought a woman would call it royal purple. The upholstery on the desk chair and a side chair were the same shade of purple. It made

J. L. Greger

Western cringe and figured it had the same effect on Mendel. He understood why women liked pink. It was pretty. Purple gave him the willies.

After a five-minute search, Western found a large envelope, not in the file drawer of Leslie's teak desk but in the drawer above the kneehole of the desk.

Files labeled with the names of the three student interns were inside the envelope. Scofield quickly decided these were the files missing from Miracle Foods, but she wasn't satisfied. "There has to be something more," she whined.

Western preferred her to whine rather than do her breathing exercises because the whines made him feel less guilty. As he relooked through the desk drawers, Scofield studied every page in the three files.

Scofield grumbled that she couldn't be sure if the files were complete. Eventually, she mumbled about small red tick marks by several entries. Evidently there weren't any tick marks on the copies of the interns' reports that she'd obtained from the internship director.

All the while Western kept pulling files from the file drawer and scanning them for anything interesting. He wasn't sure he knew what *interesting* meant but figured he'd recognize it if he saw it. Mainly he waited for Scofield to make an announcement. He figured it was imminent because she was now rapidly typing on her phone.

"I checked the last email from Sara. She reached the same conclusion as Leslie. Two batches of the cultured fish are of interest."

"What do you mean?"

"Both Sara and Leslie flagged batches called Jn9F and Au16F." She turned to Mendel. "Did she mention them to you?"

Mendel stopped pacing the hallway outside his wife's office. "Surely you've figured out by now that I know little about the technical aspects of this business. I just keep track of the money. That's why Leslie, not me, should have gone to Albuquerque to talk to Sara Almquist last Thursday. But she had to teach that day and the FDA insisted we engage a consultant immediately."

For the first time, he entered Leslie's office and opened the door to an under-the-counter refrigerator. "Leslie keeps bottles of soda and water here. Wendell likes to annoy her by raiding it. He seems to be doing it more frequently lately, or Leslie has been complaining more lately." He shook his head. "Want one?"

"No." Scofield returned to scanning information on her phone. "I'm going to have our lab scan the download from Jim's computer for these codes."

Western slammed the desk drawers shut. "There's nothing labeled 'class notes' in the desk drawers." He looked around the room and opened every drawer again. A small one in the table supporting the printer contained a dozen thumb drives. "The lab could check these." He looked at a large basket underneath the table. A purple afghan, the type that was all hairy, was neatly folded in the basket. He thought the afghan must be huge to fill the basket. He smiled as he lifted the afghan to reveal a purple leather attaché case. "This could be interesting."

Mendel, who was now sitting in Leslie's desk chair and sipping a soda, stared at the case. "It's odd that Leslie didn't have that with her when she went to class on Tuesday morning. She usually carries her class notes in it." He paused. "That's it."

Western had already unzipped one outer pocket of the purple case. Nothing was there but a tube of lipstick. He unzipped the main compartment and pulled out a file labeled *class notes*. He glanced at the top page. "Seems we were wrong." Then he noticed something else at the bottom of the case—a wad of paper. "I think we've found the receipts that Sara thought were missing."

***

"Look son, there's no reason for you to remain silent. You asked for a public defender but you can't get one unless you're charged with a crime in Colorado. We've not charged you with anything yet. All you did was try to deliver flowers to Leslie Lopez on Wednesday night." Western smiled at Troy Pitkin. "Don't try to deny it. Your fingerprints on the note were clear. I also think you did something else."

Western knew he was on shaky ground because Pitkin had requested a lawyer, but he decided that technicality didn't matter considering the pages Scofield held in her hand. "I think you're the one who turned over the file cabinet on Saturday night or Sunday morning at Miracle Foods. What did you take?"

Pitkin stared at the table.

Western knew he could have told Pitkin that they had found a note from Leslie exonerating Pitkin of the break-in and robbery,

                              J. L. Greger

but he wanted to see the boy sweat. Besides he could tell by Scofield's cough that she was ready to play the "good" cop.

Scofield gave a sad smile and cooed, "I think you were only doing what Leslie Lopez paid you to do. That means it wasn't stealing or even vandalism."

Western hated when she did her motherly routine. Her, slightly high pitched, sugary tone was so fake, but it was effective.

Pitkin began to shake. "I messed up the offices at Miracle Foods but I didn't take anything. Mrs. Lopez told me to turn over a file cabinet in her office and one in Viola's office. She said to throw several files on the floor, leave the key she'd given me in her top desk drawer, and take the money in the drawer, but I couldn't. It didn't seem right."

Western knew Pitkin was telling the truth. Leslie's letter addressed to the police in the *class notes* file had made the same points. He also realized Pitkin was a good kid. He called Leslie "Mrs. Lopez" and hadn't taken the money. "Do you know why she wanted it to look like a break-in?"

"I want a lawyer."

Scofield handed three pages to Pitkin. "We explained your situation to the Larimer County District Attorney. That's the first page. He says we can't charge you with the break-in because you were paid by a co-owner of Miracle Foods to do it and the other co-owner Mendel Lopez has agreed not to press charges. That's the second and third pages." She didn't add the DA opined that Leslie Lopez could be charged with making a false statement to the police.

Pitkin studied the documents. "You're right. I did try to deliver flowers to Mrs. Lopez at the hospital, but that's no crime. I ran because I was scared. I'd seen Wendell's blue Corvette idling in the back corner of the hospital parking lot. He seems to be everywhere I've turned during the last two weeks." He shook his head. "I didn't think my note was threatening. It was an apology. Our plan didn't work. Mrs. Lopez thought if everyone at Miracle Foods thought files were stolen from the personnel and financial offices that someone would talk or make a mistake. They didn't. Instead they tried to kill her."

"Who did she expect to talk?"

"I'm not sure."

Western was tired. It had been a long day. "Spit out a guess."

"Jim Jackson was hiding lab data from Mrs. Lopez. She knew he'd kept the two batches of fish with high histamine levels."

"How did she know?"

"I don't know where to start."

Scofield leaned toward Pitkin. "Just start at the beginning. We've got plenty of time."

Western wanted to curse. It was time to go home.

Pitkin looked at her like a grateful puppy with his big brown eyes. "On the first day of classes this semester, Mrs. Lopez stopped me in the hall of the Gifford Building and asked me why I quit my internship at Miracle Foods last semester. I didn't want to tell her, but she insisted. I told her I didn't like all the secrecy in the lab." He looked at Scofield with a "beaten dog" look.

"What did you tell her?"

"Jim wouldn't tell me anything about the two batches of the cultured fish with the high histamine levels. When I asked if he'd pitched the bad batches, he said, 'They might be useful.' Then he laughed. It made me uncomfortable."

Western said, "Hurry up."

Scofield began her breathing exercises. Western recognized the warning signal and cursed internally.

"What did Leslie say?" Scofield put her hand on the back of Pitkin's chair. "Was she concerned?"

"She marched me down to the internship director's office and asked to see my internship report and those of two other students. She made copies and together we studied them. We agreed Jim might have made the first batch of fish with high histamine levels by accident last spring, but there was no logical reason why Jim would have made two more bad batches last summer." Pitkin looked around the room as if to check if anyone else had entered.

"And what did Leslie do?"

"She told me to tell no one. Said she'd do some checking and get back to me."

Scofield waited and waited. "When did she get back to you? What did she say?"

"It was the third week of classes. People at the site had developed rashes the previous week. She told me she suspected one of the bad batches of the cultured fish had been fed to the homeless at the meal site because she found an almost empty container of one of the bad batches in the freezer at the meal site. Then she

J. L. Greger

found containers of the other bad batch in a lab freezer. She wanted to stage a break-in at Miracle Foods to make Jim and his accomplices nervous." Pitkin gulped. "I didn't want to do it. She wrote a note explaining the situation and put it in her *class notes* file. Said it would be there if anything happened to her." He gulped again. "I was really scared, but she promised me a thousand dollars. I needed the cash." He smiled hopefully at Scofield. "You know the rest."

Western was surprised Pitkin hadn't mentioned the note he received in the library. This boy really was into secrets. "We'd like to see the note you got in the library this afternoon."

Pitkin sat up straight and pointed at Western. "You were watching me?" His voice showed signs of anger. "For how long? You had no right." He turned to Scofield. "The email you showed me. The DA said you couldn't charge me with anything."

Western chortled. "Son, we're charged with maintaining the safety of the public and your safety is in jeopardy. Look at what happened to Leslie."

Pitkin turned white and gulped repeatedly. "I hadn't thought of it that way." He pulled a sheet of paper out of his pocket and handed it to Scofield:

> *Don't be foolish like Leslie. Remember you don't have to talk to the police.*

Western winked at his partner. He figured the rest should be easy. "We know a middle-aged woman gave you the note. Was it Viola Sanchez?"

"No, but I think I've seen her before. Don't know where."

Scofield texted a message before she said, "Instead of questioning you about her, I've asked an artist to work with you to create a composite sketch."

As soon as Pitkin nodded, Western stopped pacing. "Son, we know you made a call after we questioned you earlier this afternoon at the Lory Student Union. Who did you call? What did they say?"

Pitkin's ears turned bright red.

"Remember we're trying to protect you, and you're not making it easy."

"I called Viola, like Leslie told me to do if she wasn't available and the police tried to question me."

Scofield continued to pump Pitkin with questions about Viola, but it was obvious to Western that it was a waste of time.

CHAPTER 21: Sara's Longest Minute

Sanders's coat, cap, and gloves were wet when he stomped into our motel room. "Damn macho men didn't want to see a computer simulation of the modified LIDAR technology's ability to discern what was under snow. We basically did a live scavenger hunt in deep snow today as more snow and sleet pelted us."

As he took off his hat, I saw his hair was wet. I assumed it was from sweat. However, when he took off his coat, I noticed his slacks were wet, too. I guessed he'd fallen in the snow, but I thought a direct question would only remind him of his bad day. So I said, "Poor baby. Did they appreciate you'd brought them a valuable new technology?"

"That's the worst part. The modified technology system worked wonderfully when we viewed submerged vessels along the Cuban coast from the air earlier this week in Cuba, but it was obvious the modifications were insufficient to make the system viable in snow covered areas."

"Well, that means we have all day tomorrow to play."

"No." He sat on the bed and pulled off his hiking boots. "The NORAD scientists and the scientist I brought along are working tonight on making more modifications and devising further tests for tomorrow." He pulled off his wet socks. "As you can see my old boots leaked. I'm beginning to think my days doing field work should be over soon."

I wasn't going to touch that comment with a ten-foot pole. I opened his suitcase and found a pair of dry socks for him. It was easy. We'd traveled together enough that I knew Sanders packed his suitcase methodically. I wished I could find anything as quickly in the suitcases I packed. However, I'd promised myself years ago not to be as methodical and organized in my personal life, which included packing suitcases, as I was forced to be in my scientific career. "Well, that means the leaders at NORAD appreciate your efforts to introduce them to a scientist who may be a potentially useful contractor."

"Hmm. Do I have time for a shower before dinner is delivered?"

"Yes, your medium rare porterhouse steak and my seared scallops from MacKenzie's Chop House should be delivered here in thirty minutes. They said they could deliver on time because their all-wheel drive truck could get through almost any amount of snow. I picked up a bottle of one of your favorite red wines last night. We're set for a relaxing evening."

He gave me a weary smile as he stripped. "I guess that means you had a good day and tied up most of your investigation at the weird food company. *Or* it was hopeless, and you left in disgust?"

I have to admit for a man in his early fifties who wasn't a fitness nut, Sanders looked good. He still had a waist and his abs were flat. "Neither—the Fort Collins police didn't want me around when the suspects were cornered, but they may call if technical issues arise." I followed him into the bathroom. "By the way, I have a surprise for you. It's a book called *Games for Couples*."

***

Sanders paged through *Games for Couples* as we waited for dinner to be delivered. He groaned several times as he read aloud the text on how to make certain board games sexier, but he read the questions silently in "Questions for Private People." After dinner, he said, "If we keep sipping at this wine, your quiz might be amusing."

There were few surprises as we answered the questions to the quiz questions because we both could have correctly guessed each other's responses. Sanders had smiled when I read aloud the question, "When you were young, did you want to be rich, famous, or powerful?"

"That's easy for me because my family has been wealthy for generations and my uncle was a well-known TV sports commentator, who drank too much and died young. Thus, I knew by the time I entered college, wealth and fame didn't bring happiness. And most power was based on illusions." Sanders swirled the wine in his glass. "What amazes me is that despite our different backgrounds, you reached the same conclusions."

I noted he'd been tactful and had not mentioned my parents were sharecroppers. "You're partially right. I realized by the time I was in college that a career in science wouldn't make me rich or famous, but I believed my views would be respected because I had knowledge, even though I was a woman. I didn't think of it in terms of power, per se."

"You were more idealistic than me then and now." He looked at the quiz. "I think my answer to the next question—What was the longest moment of your life?—will surprise you. It occurred in New Mexico when I was tracking that woman and using you as bait to draw her out."

I noted that he didn't admit the woman was Maria, the Cuban embassy attaché who was also a contract killer for mob leaders in Miami.

Nor had Sanders admitted that he had been her lover and that he had betrayed my trust, but he *had* admitted he'd put me in danger. "There were a lot of pretty long minutes for me then, too."

Sanders closed his eyes and seemed to be concentrating. "After the initial volley of shots. I knew both Maria and I were wounded. I had no idea of your condition. You didn't make a sound. Although Maria was on the floor, I suspected her wound was less serious than mine. I also knew her task was easier. Mine was to bring her in alive for questioning, which was essential to clear my name and to break up the drug cabal. Hers was just to eliminate you and me. Realistically I thought I would die disgraced and probably not save you. However, I knew help was on the way if I could buy time."

He opened his eyes and put his hand on my shoulder. "Up to that point I'd never seen your ruthless side. You didn't shoot to kill Maria but shot at point blank range to destroy her right hand so she couldn't shoot anyone ever again."

I shrugged. "I knew it was important to bring her in alive but she was still deadly. I had no choice because you were wounded and help hadn't arrived yet."

Sanders leaned over and kissed me slowly and deeply. "I never thanked you adequately for saving me and my career." He kissed me again and then pulled away. "First, I want to hear about *your* longest moment."

I sighed. "I seldom speak of it. I was an assistant professor at Michigan State and up for tenure. My department head called me at five and ordered me to come to his office at five-thirty. When I arrived, the main office was empty and dark. There was only a desk light on in his attached office." I closed my eyes and remembered. "My department head was standing in front of the big arched window in his office watering his fig tree, which was at least five feet tall. He turned to me and said, 'The campus tenure committee doesn't think you are ready for tenure unless I provide more details. I don't want to bow to their whims.'"

Sanders was silent but he put his hand on my shoulder.

"I remember I was angry. I blurted out, 'I have twenty publications in scientific journals—more than enough to win tenure.' My department head said, 'They agreed but doubted your teaching credentials.' I was even angrier as I pointed out that I'd received a small teaching award and had favorable reviews from my classes. He said, 'Yes, but I didn't include that info in your file because I didn't think those details were necessary. Now I'm too busy to bother.'"

Sanders grip tightened on my shoulder.

My department head stepped toward me and said, "There's an easy way... to gain my cooperation." His brown eyes stared expectantly at me as his right hand reached toward me. The next minute was my longest one. Each second felt like an hour. I saw a pair of shears on his desk and suddenly remembered a scene in *Dial M for Murder*. It was weird."

Sanders snorted. "The scene where Grace Kelly stabs her attacker with a pair of shears left on a desk?"

I nodded. "Anyway, I studied the shears. Maybe my department head noticed. I don't know. I realized he was bigger than me but not by a lot. All I was sure of was I wasn't going to submit to him, even though I might be injured or killed in the process. I decided if he moved any closer, I would grab the shears and try to sink them in his back like Grace Kelly had done in the movie."

Sanders whispered, "What happened?"

"My department head suddenly pulled away from me. I stammered that he'd better take the time to answer the campus tenure committee's questions on my teaching. Then I slammed out of his office and ran down the street to my husband's office." I looked at Sanders. "You remember my then-husband was an assistant professor in history and had failed to get tenure the year before. At that point, he was pretty distant from me and preoccupied with his plans to enter law school and finish his last semester of teaching."

"Yes, you've told me it was a rough time for you before your divorce."

"My husband agreed with me but noted my situation wasn't unusual and no one would believe me. Even if university leaders believed me, they would not embarrass a well-known faculty member, like my department head. I wasn't important enough. Then he muttered that situations like this made him glad he was going to become a lawyer."

Sanders pushed me away to study my face. "Didn't the university have policies on sexual harassment?"

"Not then. They came later as more women complained. Anyway, I don't remember anything more of our conversation, but I know I cried steadily for the next four hours. The next morning I called the head of the statistics department at Cornell University."

"Why him?"

"I knew they had an open position and he liked my work. Then I went to see the dean to report the incident."

Sanders pulled me toward him. "I always figured there was an incident like that in your past. It was the only way to explain the steely determination with which you face hostility. Only one thing puzzles me—

                                              J. L. Greger

as I've watched you over the last two years, you've always avoided physical violence. Why did you consider it then?"

My eyes were wet with tears. "It was the first time I'd ever been threatened so directly." I wiped away my tears. "I forgave that department head years ago. What I couldn't forget was what I learned about myself. After that long minute, I knew I was capable of killing someone if threatened sufficiently." I paused. "I realized when faced with threats in the future, my flight instinct would flee and my fight instinct would rise. Thus, I've approached all subsequent emergencies thoughtfully, trying never to act spontaneously. That minute changed me."

Sanders placed *Games for Couples* on the table. "We've had enough questions. Time for something more physical." He pulled me to the bed, sending heat waves through my body as he started kissing my neck and working downward.

CHAPTER 22: Sara on Friday

Sanders and I overslept. When he awoke a little after six, he had only thirty minutes to get dressed and get to a breakfast meeting with a general from NORAD. The good news was the meeting was in Colorado Springs and not at the NORAD headquarters itself.

The bad news was I was awake, and so was Bug. We tramped through the snow until we located a bagel shop. The owner allowed us to step inside while I placed an order. Although Bug didn't eat bagels, I knew he'd enjoy a bit of cream cheese on his dog biscuits.

As I munched on a bagel and swigged a diet cola, I scanned my emails. The emails Scofield sent me the night before jolted my brain more than the caffeine in the cola. The first provided a name for the homeless man in the morgue—Herb Parson. The second email indicated Scofield had not only found the missing receipts from the *CT-food* file in Leslie's briefcase but also the packing slip for three cases of Cook's canned tuna. Scofield didn't know how Leslie had acquired the packing slip for the canned tuna but noted that Leslie had circled in red the purchase order number. As proof, Scofield had sent me a photo of the packing slip.

Scofield and I already had noted the seemingly complete list of foods purchased for the clinical trial had not included any mention of a small order of Cook's canned tuna. Nevertheless, I rechecked the list and noticed the purchase orders had been mainly in sequence. The purchase order number that Leslie had circled on the slip for the Cook's tuna didn't appear to be from the same sequence as the purchase orders issued by Miracle Foods. Then I noted the shipper wasn't Cook's Foods, Inc., but rather was Future Proteins, Inc., which was located in Denver.

I googled "Future Proteins, Inc." It was a small company specializing in plant-based meat substitutes. Its website was typical for a start-up company with the picture of its CEO and his history prominently displayed. I sent Scofield an email titled *OPEN IMMEDIATELY*:

> *The Cook's canned tuna was shipped from Denver by Future Proteins, Inc. Surprise! The CEO of the company was Herb Parson. I've attached the photo of him on the company's website. Note he has no beard in this photo. I think we now have a motive for his murder.*
>
> *If Leslie figured out the source of bad tuna shipped to the meal site, did Viola or Mendel also know?*
>
> *I will call FDA at eight when their offices open to learn whether they've ever recalled any of Cook's brand canned tuna. Maybe Parson knew of the recall. Although recalled foods are supposed to be incinerated or put in a landfill, I've heard rumors that does not always occur.*

***

"Good morning, Sara." I saw on my computer screen Scofield typing on a laptop in the interrogation room of the Fort Collins police station as she spoke. "It looks like we're finally making progress. Let's hope we can get Viola to talk. Western is now convincing Viola to come to the station." She coughed. "You know how persuasive he can be."

"I'm confused why you want to question Viola. It's obvious she didn't order the Cook's brand canned tuna."

"We learned a few thing yesterday about Viola after you left. Pitkin claims Leslie told him over a week ago to call Viola Sanchez if the police tried to question him and she—Leslie—wasn't available. That was when she hired him to stage the break-in at Miracle Foods. A note found in Leslie's home suggests he's telling the truth."

"So, Leslie was afraid even then, and she trusted Viola?"

"Seems so. Here's how else Viola is involved. When Pitkin called her yesterday, Viola told him to go to the library. About an hour later, an unidentified woman delivered a threatening note to him. The note was typed. The lab found fingerprints on it, but we have no fingerprints on file for Viola or the woman who delivered the note."

"What am I supposed to do?",

"You know more about Miracle Foods than either Western or I. You may be able to suggest the best way to questions Viola."

"I'm not good on video conferences. Just look at me on the screen. I may not be young, but my face isn't that red."

"Don't worry. We don't plan to inform Viola that you're monitoring this interview unless necessary. I'll be able to see you on my computer screen and you can type messages to me that will appear at the side of the screen. However, I won't be plugged in to hear you through an earbud because I find it's too distracting. But Western will be able hear all your comments through his earbud. Thus, you can prompt him with questions and comments." Scofield coughed. "You can even tell him to shut up while I'm speaking. He'll also be able to see you on his computer screen and read your notes, but to be honest he seldom looks at the screen during an interview."

"So, how do we improve my image? I don't want to provide gist for Western's comments."

"Welcome to my world. Pile books under your laptop so you're not looking down at the screen and turn on all the lights."

I looked at my screen and thought I looked better.

Scofield said, "Now check your view of the interrogation room. We'll have Viola at the head of the table with me on one side and Western on the side by the door. Can you see all three positions?"

"No, I don't think I'll be able to see Western."

Scofield adjusted the camera slightly. "Better now?"

"Yes." I decided to overstep my role as bystander and prompter. "Viola likes gossip. She told me several times that she was a good listener. So, share one piece of new info with her at the start, but don't reveal the identity of the man in the morgue at first. A womanizer such as Herb Parson could have bothered her or someone she knew."

Scofield nodded and typed on her phone for a minute before Western swung open the door to the interrogation room. It was obvious that Viola had not come willingly. Her steps were hesitant as Western guided her to the chair at the head of the table.

"That's perfect. I can see her face well." Then I realized I might have given away Scofield's scheme but neither she nor Viola reacted. However, Western nodded. I decided the systems were working as planned.

Scofield thanked Viola for coming before Western was seated. "We know now that someone from Future Proteins, Inc. sent three cases of Cook's brand canned tuna to the meal site. You

                                    J. L. Greger

know—the cans that were stolen on Wednesday night?" Scofield leaned toward Viola. "When did you figure that out?

Western flinched at Scofield's opening comment, but Viola's face didn't register surprise until the question. Maybe I was imagining what I wanted to see.

Viola leaned back in her chair. "What makes you think I did?"

"Leslie figured it out last week before the break-in."

Viola didn't bat an eyelash.

"It's also obvious Leslie trusted you. She told Troy Pitkin to contact you if she wasn't available. When did Leslie tell you about the source of the Cook's canned tuna? Or did you figure it out for yourself?"

After his initial show of surprise at the start of the interview, Western had hunched over his phone. Scofield had posted a note on the screen instructing him to read his emails to learn of my findings and her intentions during this interview. Suddenly, he flashed a grin. "Viola, there's no need to remain silent. We're not charging you with anything. We're asking for your help. If you want Mendel Lopez to save Miracle Foods, you need to tell us what you know. He certainly can't do it alone."

I thought Western's comments had worked when I saw Viola's shoulders sag.

"Leslie and I talked about two weeks ago. It was late on a Wednesday afternoon. Leslie had found a partially empty bucket of our company's fish product at the meal site."

"When?" Scofield said softly as if she didn't want to interrupt Viola's thoughts.

"She didn't say. Sometime after the first outbreak of hives and rashes. She'd also studied our laboratory records and believed a stupid mistake had been made. The homeless at the meal site had been fed a bad batch of our product."

"Did she explain what made the batch bad?"

"Yes, high levels of certain chemicals in our fish product sometimes made it taste less than fresh. One of those chemicals probably caused the rashes. She wanted to know who made the mistake. I told her that I thought another mistake had been made because I'd found three cases of canned tuna that I hadn't ordered at the site. I gave her the packing slip I'd found taped to one of the boxes."

I typed a message:

Scofield nodded and played with her phone. "Does this look like the packing slip you gave Leslie?"

Viola squinted at the small screen. "Yes. Look at the PO number. It couldn't be one of ours."

"What did Leslie say?"

"That's when I got scared because Leslie said, 'These aren't mistakes.' After that, strange things kept happening."

"What do you mean by strange things?"

Viola shrugged and stared at the ceiling. "The church woman getting sick, the man dying at the site, and subjects getting rashes again. Those were serious but the break-in last Sunday was laughable. It was an inside job."

"What makes you say that?"

Viola looked between Scofield and Western. "I'm not stupid. The doors weren't jimmied. The money in Leslie's desk drawer wasn't taken. I told Leslie that Monday afternoon. She immediately announced she was taking all the financial and personnel records home. I argued with her. We've always agreed no company records should leave the building, but she was hysterical on Monday."

Western squinted and a vertical wrinkle appeared on his forehead. He looked as bad as I did on the video screen. My attention returned to the important issues when he said, "I thought Leslie was hysterical most of the time. At least that's what Jim and you seemed to indicate."

"She's always high strung, but she's been out of control ever since the poor homeless man died. And I've been afraid, very afraid." Tears dripped down Viola's cheeks.

Scofield handed Viola a box of tissues. "We're afraid what will happen next, too. That's why we have to ask you more questions. Are you up to it?"

Viola nodded.

"Did you ever talk to the homeless man who died?"

Viola frowned. "Of course not. I didn't talk to any of the diners at the site."

Scofield tinkered with the keyboard for her laptop and the picture of Herb Parson from the website at Future Proteins, Inc. appeared on the wall. "Do you know this man?"

I thought Viola emitted a slight squeak. Western who had been circling the room, stopped behind Viola's chair. "Show his most recent photo."

The morgue photo of Herb Parson appeared on the wall.

"He's dead, too?" Viola seemed to shrink in her chair, but that might have been my imagination.

Western spoke first. "Yes. For your own safety, answer our questions. Do you know the man in these photos?"

Viola dabbed a tissue under her right eye. "He called me at home last June and said he had a business proposition for me. When I met him for lunch a couple of days later, he claimed the Lopezes wanted to sell Miracle Foods and he wanted my help in scoping out the company's financial state."

"What did you say?"

"I was pretty sure Leslie didn't want to sell Miracle Foods and had convinced Mendel to not consider any sales offers until the clinical trial was completed. She calculated by then Jim should have solved the major problem of off-flavors in the fish product and the worse textural problems in the beef and turkey." Viola shook her head and pointed at the image on the wall. "I thought this character was lying, but I didn't want to annoy him. If he was right, he could be my boss in the future."

"What did you do?"

"I told him I needed a day or two to think and asked for his business card. He hesitated and wrote his name and phone number on a slip of paper."

"Do you remember the name he gave?"

Viola quickly pulled a slip of paper all curled around the edges from a zippered compartment in her purse. "I saved the slip of paper. The area code suggested a Denver address but I couldn't trace the phone number to any business or home in Colorado. The name he gave was Herb Peterson. I couldn't locate any Herb Peterson in Colorado that fit his age and general appearance."

I typed a message:

Remember Jim's work habits changed last June. See if she knows whether Herb contacted Jim, too.

Scofield put her hand on Viola's shoulder. "He's the homeless man in our morgue."

Viola placed her flattened hands over her lower face. I couldn't decide if that was an act of surprise or a way to hide her emotions.

Scofield must have been disappointed, too, because she waited ten seconds before she continued. "His real name was Herb Parson. Leslie knew him. Did he mention contacting Jim last June?"

"No, Herb—whatever his last name is—said something like, 'Do not talk about our discussion today with anyone. If you do, I'll know.' I decided that I'd better be prepared to find a new job. The guy was creepy."

Western walked to the door. "I think we all need a cup of coffee before we continue."

Scofield scurried out after him.

I watched Viola. She tapped Scofield's laptop. I immediately ducked under the desk but I figured she saw a view of my motel room. I placed a book in front of my computer's camera. When I looked at the screen again, Viola was calmly maintaining a yoga warrior stance. She'd returned to her hunched over the table position by the time Scofield and Western returned.

I emailed Scofield:

Viola checked your computer as soon as you left the room and probably knows I've been watching the interview from a motel room. Then she calmly did a bit of yoga. She reassumed her worried look just before you returned. Her confession may have been an act.

Scofield scanned her phone as she sipped her coffee. "Viola, we have only a couple more questions for you? Do you know why Leslie told Troy Pitkin to contact you if he was threatened?"

Western frowned. "I wouldn't..."

Before he could say more I repeated out loud what I had emailed Scofield.

Western must have heard me through his earbud because he smirked and said, "Pitkin seems like a real wimp. What did you tell him?"

Viola closed her eyes. "I think I said to go to the library and calm down."

Western winked at her. "You've must have said more than that."

"I think... that's it."

Scofield coughed. "I can see you're tired." Scofield shoved an artist sketch toward Viola. "Do you recognize this woman?"

Viola gave an almost imperceptible gasp. "No. I don't think so. Can I go now?"

As soon as she'd left, Western's face turned red. "Why didn't you show me the sketch earlier?"

Scofield frowned. "I told you the artist had worked a long time with Pitkin and the sketch was on your computer." Her voice became louder. "As usual, you didn't check your messages."

"This is Jim Jackson's wife, Anne." Western studied the sketch. "He's got the body wrong, but the face is right. I'll get a search warrant. If we find a tan jacket with a ripped brown corduroy collar like the sketch, we've got her." He shook his head. "Boy, I hope the artist is wrong. Anne is a sweet grade-school teacher."

After he left the room, Scofield cursed a bit, and then turned on the sound so we could talk normally. "Do you realize we didn't use our best clue effectively with Viola because he didn't bother to look at the sketch?"

I thought a few seconds because I didn't want to become enmeshed in their spats. "You did learn something—Viola lied. I'm sure she has met Jim's wife. That makes me wonder how much of Viola's story was true. She's not only smart but also a good actress."

"No kidding. She had me convinced most of time."

"One thing I should tell you before you take on more pressing matters—I filed the preliminary reports with the FDA and USDA yesterday."

Scofield was obviously distracted. "What reports?"

"The agencies gave Mendel a deadline to file a preliminary report on the adverse events Jim reported during the clinical trial. A lawyer at FDA emailed me during the video conference. I think an FDA official from Denver may contact you today."

CHAPTER 23: Western in Action

Anne acquiesced immediately when Western showed her the search warrant and let him enter her home, but she refused to answer his questions. As uniformed officers searched through closets and drawers in her home for a tan woman's jacket, Anne called Jim who was at work at Miracle Foods.

Western knew Scofield was avoiding him as she busied herself printing out a message from the family's computer printer. She planned to have the lab compare the print-out to the print in note the mystery woman gave to Pitkin. Western couldn't blame Scofield for being miffed at him. He should have looked at the sketch when she first mentioned it.

Western was left to pace about a home he'd visited several times for church potlucks. He quickly noticed most of Anne's clothes in the closets were black or in shades of blue. Come to think of it, he couldn't remember ever seeing Anne wearing brown or tan. He wandered into the garage. Maybe she wore an old tan jacket to work in the yard. He found a man's tan work jacket with a corduroy collar on a hook by the door, but no jacket in a woman's size. He decided to collect the man's jacket anyway. Maybe Anne had worn it? That could explain why Pitkin thought she was overweight.

He sorted through the trash in the garbage can for a jacket. Although he found a torn blouse of Anne's, he didn't locate a jacket. He claimed the blouse just in case Jim had torn it during an argument with Anne.

Disappointed, he checked to see whether Anne had received any calls this morning. One had been transmitted from a tower not far from the police station. The call had lasted under fifteen seconds and had been received about twenty minutes before he and Scofield had arrived at the Jackson home. He assumed Viola had alerted Anne. That meant Anne had time to hide the jacket. If it was in the house, the officers doing the search would find it. He realized another possibility when he remembered how rutted the snow in the yard looked.

Western kept a pair of old-style galoshes in his car to wear over his shoes, but in all the excitement he had forgotten to transfer the galoshes to the squad car. He looked sadly at his new—well, they were new three months ago—shoes and plunged into the snow, probably about a foot over most of the yard. Dents in the snow indicated someone had circled the house several times. He also noted snow had been swept off the bushes and the loose snow around each bush was higher than in the yard in general. The snow around one bush was unusually high while the snow around another nearby bush was gone. He scraped away the deep snow by the one bush and found a worn, tan woman's jacket.

When he brought it inside, Scofield greeted him with her usual line. "You are so lucky." His cold, wet feet didn't feel lucky.

Anne turned ashen when she saw the jacket and did not resist when Western suggested she accompany him to the police station.

***

Western let Scofield take the lead in interrogating Anne at the station because he was uncomfortable questioning the woman who had taught his son in Sunday school. Besides, he thought he'd be better at noticing slight changes in her demeanor.

"You obviously tried to hide the jacket. We know you got a short call to your home twenty minutes before we arrived. Troy Pitkin described the woman who gave him the threatening note as middle-aged and wearing a tan jacket." Scofield sat down next to Anne and pushed the sketch toward her.

Anne glanced at it and gasped.

"Unfortunately for you, Troy Pitkin has a good memory for faces." Scofield lowered her voice. "Your husband must be a real heel to get you involved. Don't try to protect him. If you cooperate, we may not have to charge you with abetting murder and attempted murder."

Anne bit her lip and pulled a card from her purse. "This lawyer said yesterday that he'd come if Jim or I called."

Scofield handed her a phone. "Would you like water, coffee, or soda as you wait?"

"Coffee, please."

Western brought a cup of coffee with a packet of saccharin to Anne. He knew she liked her coffee black and sweetened with a non-caloric sweetener. He figured it couldn't be easy for her to stay so slim.

He sat down by Anne. "One thing puzzles me. Pitkin said you were overweight. He claimed you could barely button your jacket. How did you make yourself look heavier?"

She sipped her coffee. "It was cold. I wore several sweaters."

He winked at Scofield. In essence, Anne had admitted to delivering the note to Pitkin.

***

The lawyer who appeared at the police station quickly advised Anne not to make a deal with the police to gain immunity from prosecution and not to answer questions until the police formally charged her. He also reiterated several times she couldn't be forced to testify against Jim.

Scofield coughed. Western knew she was signaling him to stay quiet. He spoke anyway. "Anne, this lawyer may be acting in your husband's, but not your, best interest. You need to determine whether he considers you or your husband his client. I doubt he can effectively defend both of you in this situation."

Scofield stood and pulled Western toward the door. "We'll let you talk in private, but we will allow you make a call to get another lawyer if you wish."

As soon as the door closed, Scofield stormed down the hall. "If Anne keeps that dolt of a lawyer hired by her husband, she can claim in the future she had ineffective counsel and her testimony will be thrown out by a judge. I'm calling an assistant DA for advice."

Western hadn't thought about the legal consequences because he'd been too busy thinking about Jim Jackson. He wouldn't have described Jim's actions as those of a heel but rather those of a coward, but that was a small point. Jim appeared to be willing to sacrifice his wife in a futile attempt to save himself. Western sauntered slowly to their shared office and announced, "I think it's time to arrest Jim for his minor crimes—the break-in, vandalism, and theft of foods from the meal site. It will be a way to keep him from seeing Anne for the rest of the day. Give her time to think alone."

Scofield seemed rapt in her conversation with the DA as she scribbled a note. Western was surprised when she handed him the note:

***

For the rest of the morning, Western felt as if he and Scofield were shoveling an inch of snow from an endless path. None of the tasks required heavy lifting, but the list of things to do seemed endless.

By noon, a new lawyer counseled Anne to accept the DA's offer of immunity from prosecution. Anne ignored her lawyer's advice and refused to answer any questions remotely related to her husband. The resulting interview lasted more than an hour and yielded nothing except a lingering question: Which woman—Viola or Anne—had lied? Western hoped it wasn't Anne but knew Scofield was inclined to believe Viola rather than Anne.

***

Western was saddened by Jim Jackson appearance when he entered the interview room. Jim looked haggard with dark circles under his eyes as his lawyer, the one Anne had rejected, began the session by complaining that the theft of "a few cans of food" from the meal site amounted to petty theft.

Scofield countered that the value of the theft and the damages resulting from the break-in far exceeded Colorado's definition of petty theft. She proceeded to play the video tape of the break-in and noted two witnesses had seen a man park a blue 1990 Corvette at the meal site around the time of the break-in.

Jim remained apathetic in his chair as his lawyer said, "Your tape proves a Caucasian male, about six-feet tall, wearing a black jacket and cap caused the vandalism. That description would fit hundreds of men. Blue 1990 Corvettes aren't rare. For example, Wendell Lopez drives one."

Western shook his head. "The fingerprints we found on a top shelf of the emptied rack weren't those of Wendell Lopez."

Jim perked up a bit. "I delivered products from Miracle Foods several times to that meal site. I'm not surprised you found my prints. Besides, I've not been in the military or ever been arrested, you don't have my prints on file."

"Give it up." Western stood and stretched to his full height. "We lifted your fingerprints from your toothbrush this morning. We have a tape showing the thief touching an upper shelf in the storage area of the meal site, the exact spot where we found your fingerprints." He walked to the door. "Do you want me to bring you a soda or water? I don't want you to be thirsty as you confess to the break-in and explain your reasons."

The attorney answered. "Will you and your partner please leave for five minutes? My client and I need to talk."

The attorney smiled when Western and Scofield returned. "My client wants immunity from prosecution in return for him providing information about Viola Sanchez. She's already told my client's wife that you suspected her of an unnamed crime but you didn't hold her because you had no evidence against her."

Now it was Western's turn to smile. He and Scofield had anticipated this offer and had discussed the possibility with an assistant DA this morning. "It depends on what you give us, and the DA will only grant immunity from prosecution for the break-in."

"We're leaving." The attorney pulled Jim to his feet.

Western opened the door for two women and a man in gray suits. "These FDA and USDA officials and this lawyer from the U.S. Justice Department want to talk to you now."

Both Jim Jackson and his lawyer looked stunned.

Western knew he shouldn't, but he winked at Jim. "I didn't understand all of Sara's comments about the high histamine levels in several batches of Miracle Foods's fish product, but I think these federal employees did. They seem to think you misled the FDA with your reports of adverse events during the clinical trial. Did you know individuals, as well as companies, can be fined over a hundred thousand dollars for seemingly minor lies?"

Scofield began to cough violently as she grabbed Western's arm and pulled him to the door.

Once in the hall with the door closed, Western whispered to Scofield. "I think I scared Jim thoroughly. After an hour of grilling by the Feds, Jim should give us what we need to arrest Viola. If not, I'll charge him for the break-in and vandalism."

Scofield pushed him forward, hissing, "Don't talk about cases in the hall."

He thought that was funny because she had had voiced a more sensitive point earlier today in the hall, but he was smart enough to remain silent.

When the door to their office was closed, she said, "This wouldn't have happened if Sara hadn't filed reports to FDA and

J. L. Greger

USDA officials earlier this week. We owe her a big thank you. Evidently, she also talked to someone yesterday and told them we needed help encouraging suspects to talk before another attempt was made on Leslie Lopez's life."

Western nodded. "I bet she told her FBI friends that she'd be the next person killed if they didn't act."

"I doubt Sara would phrase it that way." Scofield looked at her empty coffee cup. "I'm not up to listening to Jim's answers to the FDA officials. Besides, we're recording the interview. Let's get a late lunch at the coffee shop down the street."

Western was pleased because Scofield never suggested doing anything slightly social with him, but he didn't want to seem too eager. "We probably should get back here in time to monitor the end of the interview from the observation room."

CHAPTER 24: Sara's Thoughts

I'll admit I was glad Sanders was busy at NORAD. As soon as I finished the video conference, I called the FDA official who had found my preliminary report alarming.

The call turned into a conference call with a scientist and a lawyer from FDA's base office in Maryland and two officials in the FDA regional office in Denver. They all agreed with my conclusion that Jim had intentionally made several batches of the fish product with dangerously high levels of histamine. That wasn't illegal, but he had allowed these contaminated products be fed to human subjects in the clinical trial at the meal site. That meant he'd knowingly endangered human subjects and lied to—or at least intentionally misled—FDA officials.

The lawyers also wanted to know who else in the management of Miracle Foods had allowed this to occur. They noted the fines would be in the range of a hundred thousand dollars against Jim and each of his co-conspirators. I emailed them the organizational chart for Miracle Foods and referred them to Western and Scofield because I thought they would be interviewing Jim Jackson later today.

An official from the Denver FDA office stayed on the phone after the others logged off. "A friend in the Boulder Office of the Colorado Bureau of Investigation asked me yesterday about the best way to analyze for peanut proteins in samples that the Fort Collins police sent him. He wanted my help because this is not a routine analysis for a forensic lab. He mentioned a Sergeant Western in the Fort Collins Police Department told him any questions about the samples should be forwarded to you as well as to Officer Scofield. Are these analyses for peanut proteins related to our previous discussion about Miracle Foods?"

"If you're asking whether I think all the mayhem at Miracle Foods is interrelated, the answer is yes. However, I suspect it's not all caused by the same person."

Ten minutes after I finished talking to the FDA official, I received an email from the Colorado Bureau of Investigation. Actually, the email had been sent to Officer Scofield and Deputy Medical Examiner Sam Drake, and I received a copy.

The lab had found peanut proteins in Parson's stomach contents but not in the meal samples made with either the Miracle Foods's tuna product or with real tuna. There could be little doubt that Parson had been targeted.

I figured someone at the meal site had somehow added peanuts to the meal fed Herb Parson. Everyone at the meal site had told Western that they'd never seen Mendel, Wendell, or Pitkin at the site. That meant those three didn't do it.

The diners at the site had also told Western that they'd never seen Jim or Viola, even though both were in the kitchen at the meal site regularly. That cast doubt on the validity of comments by the diners, but it didn't matter because I couldn't imagine how Jim or Viola could have gotten the peanuts in just Parson's meal.

That left Leslie as the individual most likely to have added the ground peanuts to Parson's food. I was shocked at this conclusion. Leslie certainly had reason to hate Parson, but I'd thought of her—at least since her accident—as a victim, not a villain.

There was a problem with my hypothesis. Logically Herb Parson would have avoided Leslie. On the other hand, there was one more detail that supported my conclusion. If she had dated Herb Parson or at least socialized with him, Leslie could have known of his allergy to peanuts.

Then I realized two other possibilities. Another diner at the site could have had a grudge against Parson. The indigents frequently got into shoving matches. Western had told me one had been stabbed by another at the meal site last year. Somehow, I found it difficult to imagine any of the indigents I'd seen at the site would be organized enough to buy peanuts, grind them, and add them to someone's meal—even to the meal of someone he or she hated.

A third possibility seemed more likely. Mendel, Viola, Jim, or even Leslie could have given the ground peanuts to another diner, the cook, or Mike to add to Parson's meal. It wouldn't take much of a bribe to gain cooperation from the homeless, Mike, or the cook. All of them were destitute. After Parson died, the "accomplice" would have been too terrified to admit to the police what he or she had done.

It was a nice hypothesis, but there were several problems. I was at a loss as to how a homeless diner could add ground peanuts to another diner's food without inducing a fist fight. It was easier to imagine the cook or Mike adding the ground peanuts to the food.

Even that was problematic. Mike and the cook seldom looked at the diners as they shoveled food onto plates at the kitchen service window. The diners grabbed the plates somewhat randomly. It would have been difficult for the cook or Mike to deliver the peanuts to the plate that Parson selected. Of course, the cook or Mike could have sprinkled ground peanuts on several plates after they saw Parson in line, knowing Parson would grab one of them.

Then it hit me. Scofield had mentioned that Mike appeared to "redistribute" more than just leftover food from the meal site. What had she said? "The meal site director complained red plastic salt and pepper shakers with the Miracle Foods insignia had disappeared."

As I thought about the red plastic shakers, I realized anyone could have added finely ground peanuts to a salt shaker and handed the shaker to Parson. That ruined my hypothesis that Leslie was the most logical suspect in Herb Parson's murder.

I felt a headache coming on. My scenarios were becoming more and more contrived, but I was arrogant enough to summarize my musings and email them to Sam Drake and Scofield. I titled the email: *What do you think?*

I looked up and realized Bug was staring at me. I wondered for how long. Bug never barks when he wants my attention; he just stares. If he'd been staring a long time, the stare is steely and he runs to me when I stand. Bug definitely looked annoyed and he raced to me when I walked to the window.

Bug was right. We needed a break. The motel must have cleared snow from the lot about an hour or so before. There was a high ridge of snow and ice behind my car left by the plow and additional two inches of snow over the lot in general.

***

Two hours later, Bug and I dragged ourselves back into our motel room. We were wet but satisfied because we'd gotten lots of exercise before we drove to a deli. Bug had enjoyed a bit of beef brisket. Who am I kidding? He ate over an ounce of meat, and I got the rest of the sandwich. At least the rye bread and fresh slaw were good.

I scanned my emails. Sam Drake had copied me on an email he sent Scofield:

> *Parson's widow called me to inquire about Parson's gold jewelry, specifically an 18K medical alert bracelet saying "peanut allergy." She claimed he'd left his wedding ring and Rolex watch at home when he left a month ago but had worn his bracelet. She wanted the medical examiner to return the bracelet to her immediately because it was worth seven thousand dollars. I attached her photo of it. I didn't ask why she had such a photo.*
>
> *I buy Sara's theory that Leslie killed Parson, except the bracelet introduces reasonable doubt. Most of the men and women on the street could get pretty creative if they thought they could get such a bracelet.*
>
> *I can add the widow wasn't unhappy about losing Herb. She said, "Dispose of the body when the police are through but find the bracelet."*

I read Scofield's reply:

> *Denver police will question the widow and search Herb Parson's office at Future Proteins, Inc., ASAP.*
>
> *Pawnbrokers throughout the state have been alerted to be on the lookout for the bracelet.*
>
> *Western and I are watching federal officials finish up their talk with Jim and his lawyer. Looks like he will face several hundred thousand dollars in fines from FDA. Western thinks Jim will give us evidence against Viola in return for immunity from prosecution for the break-in at the meal site. I think it more likely his wife will remember a few more details when she realizes the federal fines will bankrupt the family.*
>
> *Looks like Mendel owes Sara big time. Miracle Foods may face no fines if Mendel continues to cooperate and can show Jim acted alone.*
>
> *Do you have any ideas on how to get answers from Viola and Mendel?*

I reread the last sentence of Scofield's email several times. I thought I did know how to leverage more information from Viola and maybe Mendel. All Western had to do was "stretch the truth" and intimate in his less than subtle way to both Mendel and Viola that federal officials would probably levy large fines against them on Monday. Of course, Western needed to wait until five to deliver his message. Then neither Mendel nor Viola could reach federal officials until Monday morning. Sixty hours of stewing might make one of them more talkative.

***

Sanders emailed me that one of the officers he'd been working with at NORAD had invited us to dinner. He gave me an address and said he'd expect me to get there by six-thirty with a bottle of wine. He said he'd warned them that I might bring Bug.

This was a simple request, except I always got lost in the winding streets of modern subdivisions. The street signs are hard to read at night. No, that wasn't exactly true. The GPS in my car didn't allow me to be lost but I often missed turns and had to backtrack. The net result was that a supposed twenty-minute drive often lasted forty minutes.

It was almost five and the sun was setting. I decided Bug and I would leave right away, find the location, park a few blocks away, and wait. I couldn't believe my eyes. when I opened the door to my motel room. A man in a black jacket and knit cap was lying on the icy ground next to my car, which was parked only a few yards from my door. He was reaching under my car. I pulled Bug back into the motel room and dialed 9-1-1.

I don't remember screaming, but I may have. Anyway, as I looked out my window I saw the man run across the lot. Then I saw a blue Corvette.

I knew the license plate number was essential to distinguish between Jim Jackson's car and Wendell Lopez's car, but the sun was glaring in my eyes as it approached the horizon. There was no choice. I threw open the door to my room and ran toward the blue Corvette. I tried to stay between parked cars so I couldn't be rammed directly. I wasn't fast enough. The driver backed out of a parking place and roared away. I'd only seen the first four letters on the back license plate.

The local police arrived while I was explaining the situation to Scofield. We all agreed the local police should tow away my car and have it checked. I also needed to get a room in a motel down the street. First, I had to call Sanders. I'd goofed up his plans again.

                                                    J. L. Greger

CHAPTER 25: Western's Dreams

Western awoke suddenly. He was sitting in his recliner in front of the television. The program on the screen was certainly not the local news he'd sat down to watch. The phone wasn't ringing. The house was quiet—too quiet. He staggered to his son's room.

"When did you get home?"

The young man looked away from his computer and stopped chewing the slice of pizza in his hand. "A half-hour ago. I told you then that I was leaving two slices in the refrigerator for you." He bit into his slice. "You must not have heard me."

Western rubbed his eyes. All he was sure of was his back ached. The darn recliner wasn't as comfortable as it used to be. "Did you hear a loud noise a minute or so ago?"

"Dad, you must have had a hard day. The only loud noises in the house since I got home were from the TV. I keep telling you that you need to get your hearing checked."

"Yeah, I know my hearing is going but I don't want to bother with a hearing aid. They never work."

His son chuckled. "You don't want to be kidded by your partner about getting old. Why don't you just ask her for a date?"

Western involuntarily found himself standing straighter as he thought of Scofield. He didn't think his interest in her was that obvious. "Son, you've got our roles reversed. I give the advice, not you." He paused. "Is it that obvious that I've noticed her?"

His son turned back to his computer. "Only to someone who remembers how you looked at Mom."

Western gasped. He recalled his conversation with Scofield before he left the station. They'd both agreed everyone—but Sara—had lied to them today. Scofield was convinced Mendel was the mastermind behind the attempt on Leslie's life and the sabotage of Miracle Foods. But she agreed with Western when he suggested Herb Parson had been the original mastermind with Mendel as his chief henchman. Jim was just a loyal follower.

Then he remembered how Mendel looked at Leslie in her hospital bed. He doubted Mendel would intentionally hurt Leslie. Scofield was wrong because her divorce had been too bitter and she'd forgotten the look of love. That meant Viola was the chief henchman. God knows, she was tough enough. "Son, you've known the Sanchez kids ever since grade school. Do they ever talk about their mother?"

"You're back to being Sergeant Western, the crime solver again." His son sighed. "We don't talk much, but Elena and her brother have complained that Miracle Foods had taken up all their mother's thoughts during the last year." He chewed on another piece of pizza for almost a minute. "I asked Elena why she lived at home last semester. When we went off to college, she'd bragged the best part of college was getting out from under his mother's thumb. I…"

"Dorms are expensive. That's why you live here. I couldn't…"

His son interrupted. "It's okay Dad." His face became contorted like it did when he was little boy being naughty. "Do you interrupt everyone like you do me? I was about to tell you something odd. Seems Mrs. Sanchez was afraid for her children's safety. Her son claimed she'd become real paranoid. That's odd because Mrs. Sanchez had a reputation when we were in high school of taking on all comers. Remember the time she forced a school board member to resign after he called Hispanics *wetbacks* at a board meeting."

Western did remember, but he wasn't going to allow his son distract him. "Did he give examples of Viola being frightened?"

"No, and I didn't ask." His son turned to his computer and began to type.

Western whistled as he walked down the hall. He'd just spoken to a wise man. He was sure Viola had been Herb Parson's henchman. He suspected Parson had threatened her kids because nothing else would frighten her. He thought a bit more as he turned off the television. "Nah, she cooperated with Herb Parson because she wanted to turn the tables on the uppity Lopezes."

He decided to call Scofield to tell her his thoughts and plot one last interview for tomorrow morning before they took the rest of weekend off. It was also a way to check on Scofield's social life.

***

"Did you review your emails?" were the first words out of Scofield's mouth.

"Why would I? You take care of all those details." Western decided his plan for tomorrow was looking shaky. "What happened?"

                                   J. L. Greger

"Colorado State Patrol stopped to help a motorist who was in the ditch along I-25 about forty miles north of Denver. The driver claimed she'd lost control of the car when a blue Corvette almost sideswiped her. Having received our alert for a blue Corvette, the officers alerted us around seven."

"How long had the driver been in the ditch?"

"The woman thought she'd waited at least a half-hour for help. The Colorado State Patrol estimated the near accident had occurred only ten or fifteen minutes before they found her. They didn't issue a citation for reckless driving because her passengers all confirmed her story about the blue Corvette."

"Sara was threatened about five. The timing is consistent. However, the driver made good time getting around Denver considering the rush hour and slick roads."

Scofield replied, "That's what I thought and immediately had uniformed officers determine whether Anne Jackson and her son were at home and learn the location of Wendell Lopez during that time."

"Why did you check on Wendell? The four letters Sara gave matched the license plate number for the Jackson's car." He paused, "Oh, you wanted to scare Mendel and Wendell. Good idea."

"I was being thorough." Scofield coughed. "Mendel told uniformed officers that he hadn't seen Wendell since he left the house around noon. He suggested Wendell was with Seth Evers on campus. However, campus police talked to Seth's roommate and couldn't locate Wendell or Seth."

"And the Jacksons?"

"No one was home when the police checked at seven-thirty. Anne and her son drove up to the Jackson home ten minutes later."

"Sara was threatened around five. They could have gotten back by a little after seven. They must have made a stop." He sighed. "Where are you?"

"At the station."

"I'll meet you in ten minutes."

"Did you read the other email?" Scofield coughed. "Think about this as you drive. A pawnbroker here in town purchased a gold med alert bracelet last week. The catch was broken."

"Could he describe the person who brought in the bracelet?"

"Better than that, he recognized the seller. The broker said, 'The scrawny kitchen assistant with the long gray ponytail at the meal site for the homeless brings an item in every month or two. The man always says, 'The items were left at the site and no one claimed them.'"

***

"Anne, it's time to stop playing games. You can't save your husband, and now you face jail time if you don't cooperate. Someone shoved explosives into the tailpipe of Sara Almquist's car. Sara saw a man in a black jacket and cap drive away from the scene in Jim's blue Corvette. We know Jim didn't do it because his lawyer didn't get him released from jail until after five." Western debated whether to make the next comment because it might be considered inappropriate. "Think of all the kids, including your son, you taught in Sunday school. At least respect them enough to be honest." He was surprised Scofield didn't cough.

Anne bit her lip. "Tom and I never left Fort Collins yesterday. We ran errands all afternoon."

"That's a lot of errands. You didn't get home until after seven-thirty. You'd better hope someone remembers seeing you. Start naming where you went." He said more slowly to add emphasis, "Perhaps you don't realize the charges against you could include abetting a murder attempt. That can carry a life sentence."

Western thought he finally gotten through to Anne. Her eyes widened and she gasped, but she remained silent.

"Well, what will it be? And don't forget we can also charge your son Tom because he was with you." He hated to say the next sentence. "Somehow I don't think he'll stand up well to tough questioning. And don't fool yourself—officers will be tough with him. We can charge him as an adult in Colorado."

Tears trickled down Anne's cheeks. "We're safer here than at home."

After Western alternately pleaded with and stormed at Anne for another five minutes, Scofield stomped to the door. "I'm not wasting any more time on you."

Western hated to admit it but Anne was proving harder to question than most experienced criminals. "Why don't you call your lawyer? Maybe he can convince you to be sensible and cop a plea." He reached over and patted Anne's hand. "It's time to save your son, if not yourself."

***

"About one this afternoon, Mom pulled me out of school because of a family emergency. "When I asked for an explanation, she started harping at me. She wouldn't stop lecturing me about acting like an adult. I'm so tired of hearing, 'You don't realize how much your Dad and I love you.' I know..."

                                        J. L. Greger

Western interrupted the boy's complaints. "What was she lecturing you about?"

Tom blinked. "I've told you. It was the same thing I've heard every day for the last two weeks. I have to 'grow up,' whatever that means."

Western felt sorry for the boy. He thought Anne was so used to teaching first graders at school and second graders in Sunday school that most of her conversations with adult church members were also at that level. "I guess your mother doesn't understand you're almost a man now. What happened next?"

"Mom said we were going shopping but first she had to pick up Dad's black jacket and cap. When we pulled into the garage, a blue Corvette was parked there, but it wasn't Dad's car. I told Mom we had to report Dad's car missing to the police. She said she'd let someone borrow it." He shook his head. "That's typical of Mom. She never explains her actions."

Scofield looked up from her phone, "Give me a list of the places where you went shopping. I need to check to see if anyone can confirm your story."

Tom named at least ten stores. In each case, he explained his mother or he had tried on clothes but she hadn't bought anything except a tee shirt for him. "Not one I wanted. It's red and says *My Mom Loves Me*. What guy wears a shirt like that?"

Western had started to pace as soon as he glanced over Scofield's shoulders at her phone. "Son, what did you two talk about as you did all this shopping?"

"We didn't talk. I asked questions and she ignored me, even when we stopped at McDonald's for supper. About a block from our house, she told me if I was brought to the police station, I should ask for your help. That's why I told you everything. I've no place to go if you arrest Mom and Dad." The boy wiped his eyes.

Western wanted to hug the boy but thought that wasn't appropriate. "You'll be fine. I'll bet our minister will be happy to have another man in the house tonight. Living with a wife and three daughters is a bit tough for him at times."

***

Western turned to look at the blank wall when Scofield rushed into their shared office. He didn't want her to see the tears in his eyes. He didn't need to worry.

Scofield was in a dither. "After the lab didn't find any traces of brake fluid or explosives on Anne's or Tom's hands or gloves, Anne argued with her lawyer for ten minutes and chose to remain in the lock up tonight against her lawyer's advice."

Western didn't turn to face Scofield. "Anne obviously doesn't feel safe in her home. Don't forget the only time she talked freely was when she thanked me profusely after I suggested our minister could house Tom tonight."

"Her husband Jim must be a real bully."

"I doubt it. Jim didn't have an opportunity to threaten her today because he was here being questioned at the station." He wiped his eyes. "Only a threat to Tom's safety would make her behave so illogically."

"Tom is a nice kid. The DA will agree with you that he shouldn't be charged with abetting a crime."

"Of course, he told the truth. Tomorrow we'll check out the stores for anyone who remembers seeing Anne and Tom. I bet the clerk at Six Dog T-Shirt Company will remember the woman who bought a shirt for her son, which he hated. My son would have put up a fight if I threatened to buy such a shirt." Western turned to watch Scofield because his tears had dried.

Scofield stopped pecking at her phone. "If I understand you right, we should warn the minister that he should tell no one he's housing the boy."

"Already done."

"We should have police check out the Jackson house and take Jim into protective custody. No one is safe in that house tonight."

"I've taken care of those items, too. I don't think we'll have to wait long enough to warrant your half-hour or longer drive home in the snow and another drive back. Why don't you come over to my house? We can enjoy coffee or even hot cocoa. I'll make a fire in the fireplace. I reckon we'll get a call in an hour or two from the officers watching the Jackson house. I just can't guess what Viola or Wendell will do, and I'm not up to questioning either of them without more evidence."

"You've not mentioned Mendel."

"He loved his wife." A tear dripped down his cheek. "The hospital called—Leslie died ten minutes ago."

CHAPTER 26: Sara at a Dinner Party

Sanders thrust a small bouquet of yellow baby roses at me as I opened the door to our new motel room. "I'm glad you called. I was tired of listening to a discussion about maximizing the potential of LIDAR systems." He seemed to stifle a smile as he looked me up and down. "You seem to be no worse for wear, but I thought you might enjoy the yellow roses." Then he wrapped his arms around me and kissed me. We ended the embrace when Bug tried to sit on our feet.

"You'd better check your case. I didn't have much time to clear out of our other room."

As I put the roses into a water glass, he checked the compartment in his case where he often hid a gun. It was one of those points we never discussed, but I guessed one reason he often hopped on military transport planes was it eliminated his need to get special clearance on commercial planes to carry firearms. "Did you salvage anything from your trip to NORAD?"

He shrugged. "Fostering interactions between scientists and engineers in agencies like NOAA and NORAD is always good." He paused. "I also saw an old friend. She's eager to meet you tonight."

"Any special reason?"

He ignored my question and rushed Bug and me to his car.

***

I'd expected the dinner party would be a buffet for all the people Sanders had been interacting with at NORAD and their significant others. Thus, I hadn't been concerned that we were arriving at seven not six-thirty. Boy, was I wrong. Only one other couple was seated at the dining table when the host, a NORAD officer, welcomed us to the party. Nora and Ben were both lawyers and worked in a firm headed by the hostess, Andrea.

Although Andrea was about my age, I suspected Nora, a smashing younger woman with black hair and an ivory complexion, was Sanders's "old" friend. Sanders had a history of dating young socialites in the Washington, D.C., area. I slapped myself internally. Jealousy was never attractive. Besides everyone over twenty has a romantic past. I flashed my biggest smile and hoped that it hid the worry lines that I was sure were deeper than usual after a trying day. Then I settled Bug near my feet.

The conversation began with comments on the weather and road conditions, but as soon as everyone had taken a couple mouthfuls of salad, Andrea said, "I—actually all three of us in my law firm—wanted to talk to you because a client approached us with her concerns about Miracle Foods. We have a couple of questions for you."

I gulped. "As you probably know I've been investigating problems in a clinical trial conducted by Miracle Foods. FDA and USDA required this scientific review because several adverse events occurred."

Ben chuckled. "I guess you could call *death* an adverse event."

I hoped that their client wasn't Herb Parson's wife or someone who ate at the meal site. I doubted the latter. The homeless generally don't have the funds to sue, but then again one of their relatives might have spotted a window of opportunity. I looked at Sanders. He usually avoided speaking to lawyers and wouldn't have intentionally introduced me to someone planning a lawsuit. His brow was wrinkled. He must have been a very good friend with one of these women and trusted her implicitly.

"It isn't appropriate for me to discuss details because the death is part of a continuing police investigation. However, I'm curious. Who is your client?" I expected Andrea or one of her associates to say they couldn't divulge his or her name and we'd spend the rest of the meal talking about the weather and other safe topics.

"We think we're acting in our client's best interest. She sought our help because she knew Nora and wanted no one to know her plans until she gathered certain evidence." Andrea nodded to Nora.

Nora swallowed hard. "Leslie Lopez planned to divorce Mendel Lopez but didn't want to proceed until she determined if he was involved in a hostile takeover of Miracle Foods."

Andrea frowned. "Technically the term—hostile takeover—is legally incorrect because Leslie and Mendel owned Miracle Foods without any stockholders." Andrea's rather snobbish voice softened but still sounded condescending. "But *hostile* is the correct word for the actions of the owner of the larger firm Future Proteins, Inc., in Denver—Herb Parson."

Nora nodded. "Leslie and I both encountered Herb Parson when we took a course from him nine years ago."

Her husband Ben covered her right hand with his left hand. "Tell her everything. I suspect she knows the truth already."

"Well, yes." Nora looked at her lap. "I was only twenty-three at the time and was flattered when Herb asked me to come to his condo for drinks. He was sophisticated and charming. He flattered me and said, 'I had the most potential of all the students in his class.' I willingly had sex with him." She raised her head and stared at me with confidence. "I believed him and continued to see him a couple of times a week until Leslie told me a story. It seems Herb had an active social life nine years ago. While he'd been seeing me, he'd also met Leslie several times for dinner. They'd gotten into an argument after dinner one night in his condo. She'd rushed to her apartment, and they got into a scuffle on the back stairs of her apartment building."

I wanted to say *I know about the stairs incident* but thought it was wise to reveal as little as possible. "What did you do after you heard Leslie's story?"

"I confronted Herb. He laughed at me. I dropped out of his class and never saw him again."

Ben had his left arm around her shoulders. "She applied to law school and moved to Boulder. That's where we met."

"Did you have contact with Leslie afterward?"

"Not really. That's why I was surprised when Leslie called me last October. She said she couldn't contact a lawyer in Fort Collins or Denver because either Mendel or Herb would find out."

Sanders nudged my knee with his hand. "Well this certainly is more exciting than listening to details about LIDAR technology but let's change the topic for a while. I'm hungry."

I was relieved that Sanders had given me time to think. I shifted my legs and used my right foot to stroke his leg. "I'm hungry, too."

The hostess rushed to the kitchen and several minutes later brought out a large pan of lasagna. The host tried to refill wine glasses but only Sanders and he wanted a refill.

I felt sorry for Sanders. He'd been drawn into one of my messes again. As usual, he proved his diplomatic skills as he refocused the discussion with questions about the Fine Arts Center and Pioneer Museum in Colorado Springs. I assumed he'd been exploring the internet for things to do this weekend while he was supposedly listening to discussions on LIDAR. That didn't surprise me. His interest in scientific topics was limited to gleaning useful tools to gather data on the motives and actions of others. I stopped feeling sorry for him and continued to stroke his leg with my foot and hoped no one noticed—except Sanders.

After Andrea served a fruit compote dessert, I decided to learn how much Leslie had shared with the lawyers and how often they had communicated. Nora noted Leslie was nervous about anyone overhearing her conversations and generally called from her car. "Weren't you concerned for Leslie's safety when she seemed so distrustful of everyone?"

Andrea stiffened and lifted her chin. Her voice was cold. "Leslie wasn't unusual. Many of our clients pursuing divorces are frightened. We try not to augment their emotions by acting overly concerned. Hysterical clients don't get large divorce settlements. Besides, she couldn't have been that nervous, she emailed several long documents from her home office."

I admit I was finding it hard to like Andrea. She seemed to lack much empathy, but maybe her comments were like the jokes that surgeons made during tense operations. Andrea was hiding her emotions so she could concentrate on aiding her client. I tried to refocus my question. "Was there anyone Leslie could trust or turn to besides her lawyers?"

Andrea turned to Nora. "Didn't you tell me that she named someone we could contact if we couldn't reach her for twenty-four hours? Wasn't that how you learned of Leslie's accident?"

Nora nodded. "Viola at Miracle Foods was her emergency contact, but Leslie insisted we not email or call Viola at work. Viola called me the day of Leslie's accident—probably two or three hours after the accident."

I stood. "If you don't mind, I'd like to contact two detectives in Fort Collins. May I use your living room while you finish your dessert? Sorry to be rude, but I think I can save them and you a lot of time and stress."

I texted and then called Scofield but got no response. I figured she must still be in the middle of an interview at nine. That was a bad sign. Maybe the info that I'd gained could influence her questions. I called Western. His phone rang several times.

"Sara—is this call necessary? Scofield and I were just sitting down by the fire for hot cocoa. It's been a long day."

I wished I could say no because it appeared that Western had finally gotten up his nerve to—dare I say it—be romantic with Scofield. It had been obvious he was interested in Scofield but had received little encouragement from her. "I'm so sorry. But I'm having dinner with the lawyers who Leslie contacted about a divorce from Mendel. They also know a lot about Herb Parson. I've tried to not give them any info, but I think you need to talk to them and not rely on secondhand statements from me."

He must have covered the phone receiver with his hand because I could hear muffled voices but nothing distinct. Then Scofield spoke, "We've got you on speaker phone. Recap the main points."

"Three lawyers here at dinner claim Leslie contacted them because she wanted a divorce. She gave them ways to contact Viola if they couldn't reach her."

"You didn't mention the last point earlier," growled Western. "Any other surprises?"

"One of these lawyers took a class from Herb Parson. She confirmed Leslie's claim that Herb pushed Leslie down a set of stairs." I paused and waited for either Scofield or Western to give me instructions. All I heard was whispers. "Look, I could botch this case if I say or do something wrong. I should also warn you I don't much about these three lawyers, except Sanders has known one of the women for quite a while." I waited for a reply.

Scofield coughed. "Can you put them on a speaker phone now? Try not to react to what we say but watch them and email comments to us."

***

The lawyers, particularly Andrea, were reluctant to speak directly to Western and Scofield but finally consented. The lawyers' reticence, the slowness of Scofield's responses due to apparent weariness, and Western's long absences from the discussion resulted in the next two hours being a slow-paced game of cat and mouse.

However, Scofield's emails indicated that the slow responses by Western and Scofield were ruses. Scofield and Western were reassessing the victims and villains in the case and confirming the lawyers' statements as they spoke. Scofield seemed to believe the lawyers would not respond readily to her calls after the audio conference.

Around ten, I emailed Scofield and asked whether it was time to end the conference. Western—who generally let Scofield do all their electronic communications—replied:

The best broths are made when the meat is stewed slowly.

That's when I asked the host for a diet soda.

About ten minutes later, Nora and Ben started to whisper. Ben then moved closer to Andrea and whispered in her ear. She glared at him as he said, "I see no reason to hide the documents that Leslie gave us. She had asked us to not share them with anyone, but they in no way incriminate her. Thus, even though our senior partner disagrees, I don't think my actions would constitute malpractice."

Ben transmitted a series of documents to Scofield. The first were documents supporting a lawsuit against Herb Parson from nine years before that Leslie had never filed. Ben explained, "It didn't make sense to me why Leslie hadn't pursued this suit. The trauma induced by his physical attack and his description of her as a 'flighty temptress' to several entrepreneurs had reduced her ability to raise funds to establish Miracle Foods."

Andrea gave a thin smile. "She wisely decided such a lawsuit would be bad publicity for her after she secured funding another way."

Scofield had coughed. "You mean after she married Mendel Lopez?"

Andrea raised her chin. "Yes, the suit would have potentially caused her husband to lose confidence in her ability to run a start-up company and put their marriage at risk. Even now, Mendel could use these documents in court to affect a divorce settlement."

Ben transmitted another set of documents to Scofield. "These are reports from a psychiatrist who treated Wendell. Again, I don't think we're breaking Leslie's expectations of confidentiality because they prove Wendell had threatened her life and...."

"However, the reports were sent to Mendel." Andrea voiced trilled as she continued, "Leslie admitted to Nora that she had copied them without Mendel's permission. Again these details in Mendel's hands could affect a divorce settlement."

Nora said nothing but began to hiccup uncontrollably. I emailed Scofield:

> *Nora has shrunken in her seat and is hiccuping violently. I'd guess she was Leslie's actual lawyer and knows both her husband and Andrea are right. She failed her friend morally by not forcing her to move out of the house and contact police, and she is now lessening her friend's divorce settlement.*

Scofield replied:

> *It's a moot point. We don't want them to know that Leslie died tonight. They might try to destroy evidence.*

I gulped my diet cola to hide my surprise at Scofield's comment.

J. L. Greger

At eleven, it was apparent Ben was ready to resign from Andrea's law firm but Nora was too terrified to act. She kept whimpering, "I'll be debarred."

Scofield kept grilling them on whether Leslie had any evidence of collusion between Mendel or Wendell with Herb Parson.

Nora finally sobbed. "Give them the recording."

Ben played a long, rambling recording of a phone conversation between Nora and Leslie in mid-January. Near the end of the recording Leslie said, "You really can't give me any good legal options. I'll have to eliminate Herb on my own."

In the recording, Nora had quickly said, "I'll pretend I didn't hear that comment. I will again advise you to talk honestly with your husband."

Western whistled. "One murder solved. Sara, you called it right."

Scofield repeated the comments she'd made at the start of the interview, including the statement that parts of the recording might be used in a trial. She added, "You three should not leave the state. I will get back to you after I speak to the DA on Monday."

It was almost midnight when Sanders, Bug, and I left the dinner party. Ben shoved a note into my hand as we left.

As soon as he pulled the car away from the curb, Sanders sighed. "I would have never accepted this invitation if I'd known this was a law team seeking to grill you for information." He reached over and patted my knee. "I must compliment you on how well you revealed little but got them to talk."

I tried not to sound agitated. "As soon as you're out of sight of the house, pull over. I need to read the note Ben gave me." I flipped on the light and read the note.

He parked the car in the well-lit lot of a branch bank and snapped the lock on the car doors as I called Western. "Ben, the young male lawyer, just advised me that a young man called their law office around noon today and asked how to reach Sanders at his hotel. I think that's how someone located me and my car." I listened carefully to Western's response.

Sanders was silent during my phone conversation. His voice was professional—deeper and slower—when I concluded the call. "What did the Fort Collins police advise you to do?" His worried voice reminded me that I should never play poker with him. He read my expressions too well.

"Be on the alert for Wendell Lopez in a blue 1990 Corvette but recognize Seth Evers or Troy Pitkin could be operating under his orders. The police can't find any of these men. Western gave me a local police number to call if I see any of the suspects."

"Anything else I should know?"

"It seems Wendell's psychiatrist thinks Leslie and her lawyers were foolish not to recognize that Wendell was a real threat to Leslie and to any other woman who annoyed him. Western plans to ask DA to consider charges against our dinner partners on Monday."

Sanders pulled onto the street. "Why don't you keep your phone handy and be ready to call the number Western gave you."

I petted Bug who was slowly licking my hands. "What puzzles me is how did your lawyer friend even know I was working at Miracle Foods and would be in Colorado Springs today?"

"That's my fault. I'm proud of you. It was no secret that one reason for my visit to NORAD was I wanted to be with you this weekend. However, I'm disappointed Andrea runs such a sloppy—and greedy—law practice. I should have realized the truth when she replied to your question about Leslie's safety."

"Really? Andrea said their clients were often nervous."

"Andrea was too cool, and she jerked her chin up like any good matron from Rittenhouse Square in Philadelphia would when offended. Remember that's my background, too. I didn't hear all the conversation in the living room, but I suspect Andrea was more worried about protecting Leslie's potential divorce settlement and the law firm's percentage than about Leslie herself."

I would have whistled if I could have. "So, you've known Andrea for a long time?"

"She was the girl next-door when I was growing up."

I must have sighed because he coughed. "Oh, you thought the good-looking one was one of my past flames?"

"Only until she spoke. Her voice was too little girlish for your taste."

He chuckled. "I think that's a compliment—and Andrea was never my type."

I glanced to my right and instinctively tightened my grip on Bug. "Blue streak on my right." I tried to stop screaming. The car was one block away moving in our direction.

CHAPTER 27: Western on Saturday

Western woke at seven feeling great, even though he'd gotten only five hours of sleep. Scofield had reluctantly admitted at one in the morning that she was too tired to drive to her home thirty-minutes away from Fort Collins and wanted to use his spare bedroom. He thought that was a good first step.

Now he smelled coffee and was flooded with happy memories because he hadn't awakened to that aroma since his wife died ten years ago. He strolled into his kitchen and saw his son and Scofield bent over the Saturday paper. Scofield was sipping coffee and reading the front section of the paper. His son was swigging a cola and studying the sports pages. His son stood as soon as he saw his father, high-fived him, and hurried out.

Scofield looked up. "No one has spotted Wendell or his two potential victims or accomplices—Seth Evers and Troy Pitkin—yet."

"Wish we understood the power Wendell exerted over those two young men." Western poured a cup of coffee. "Hell, I'd like to understood why the Jacksons, Viola and her children, and even Mendel were too frightened to talk."

Scofield fiddled with her phone. "It's one of three things. Each of them is guilty of something and doesn't want to reveal his or her own secrets. They're afraid because they know Wendell is crazy and don't think we'll be able to catch and convict Wendell. Or they don't know anything."

Western pulled out the entertainment section of the paper. Maybe he could interest Scofield in a movie this afternoon. On second thought, he realized that wasn't a realistic goal. They'd still be mired in this case at five. Besides, she'd want to go home—not spend more time with him.

He thought of Sara. She had the perfect situation. As a consultant she could work on cases that were interesting and walk away if they got too dangerous. Last night that blue car sure spooked her. Colorado Springs police, who had been circling the neighborhoods near Andrea's home, had located the blue car only minutes after Sara's call. However, the blue car was not a Corvette and the driver was a scared teenager. Western thought it would be fun to tease Sara about her panic the next time he saw her.

He felt his good mood evaporating, and he knew the real reason. It wasn't this case, per se. He was tired of working on murder investigations—the gristly scenes, the unlikeable characters, the long hours, the pressure.

He pulled a carton of eggs out of the refrigerator and a loaf of bread. "How about scrambled eggs and toast?"

Scofield didn't respond.

"You know a good breakfast is the basis of a good day. And I'm a master at scrambling eggs."

Scofield bit her lip before she smiled. "I usually skip breakfast, but I'm not eager to go into the department either. You know we have no reason to feel sorry for ourselves. Your calls to the DA last night wore him down. He doesn't usually authorize us to offer immunity from prosecution to witnesses without checking with him first."

Western stopped whipping the eggs. "His decision had nothing to do with me. His son's birthday is today and he didn't want to be bothered by our calls."

Scofield shrugged. "Look at the bright side. We can offer immunity to Viola's children and Anne Jackson if they provide useful information and we believe they're telling us everything they know about the Lopezes."

Western adjusted the heat and poured the eggs into the frypan. "That really isn't much. I bet the Sanchez kids listened to their mother and avoided the Lopezes. They have nothing useful to share. Anne won't talk out of loyalty to her husband." He looked up from stirring the eggs. "I tried to tip the scales and talked to Anne's—also my—minister last night. I reminded him that Anne's greatest loyalty has to be to her son and to justice. Not sure he bought my argument."

Scofield stood. "I'll set the table."

Western opened the cabinet door where the plates were stacked. "The DA's offer to give Viola immunity for state crimes won't fool her. She'll know that won't protect her from federal charges brought forward by FDA and maybe USDA. It's a waste of time to talk to her until we have more leverage."

"Let's start this morning by leaning on Mike. Both Sara and I noticed he knows more about what goes on at the meal site than the director and the cook."

Western brought the toast and eggs to the table. "You mean he's the shadiest character at the site. I checked last night—he's been arrested several times, but charges were always dropped because he supplied evidence against others. Besides, anything would be more rewarding than interviewing Viola."

***

Mike's one-room apartment looked so bad it was difficult to imagine he'd gotten the bed, chair, coat rack, and table from Goodwill and not from a dumpster. However, Western was pleased by what he saw. A box of red plastic salt and pepper shakers was on the table.

Mike watched Western examining a shaker that had a seal with the Miracle Foods insignia. "Knew I should have finished removing the seals last night." He cocked his head, "The director was going to pitch them. She seems to think there should be no reminders of Miracle Foods at the meal site. Don't know why." He gave a twisted grin "Certainly improved conversation at the site and on the streets."

Scofield opened the only door, which led to what could be described as a half-bath and sat down on the only chair. "Weren't you afraid after Herb—I mean Herman Preuter—died?"

"Nah. We all knew he didn't belong on the street. His problems weren't our problems."

"What do you mean?"

Mike flopped on the bed. "He only pretended to be homeless. I followed him one day from the site." His grin revealed he was missing several teeth. "He didn't see me, but I saw him go into a motel room. He stayed there a long time. Made me curious so I followed him another day. He went to the same room."

Western growled, "Mike, I'll bite. What's the hotel and room number?"

"First you need to forget about these pretty red containers."

"You've got to complete your story before I start forgetting certain points." Western leaned over Mike. "I think your story should include a gold bracelet.... and what you did with at least one of these pretty red containers."

Mike looked up at Western with watery blue eyes. "A man can't live on what they pay me at the meal site. I have to pick up odd jobs."

Western pushed Mike and sat down by him on the bed. He hoped bed bugs and fleas couldn't hop from Mike's bed and burrow into his coat but he needed to intimidate Mike into talking more. "Let's start with how you picked up the gold medical alert bracelet."

Mike rubbed his chin. "First time I saw it was the day I followed Herman to his room at the Best Western near the campus. It was when he reached for his plate of food at the window. You know the serving window between the kitchen and the diners? Anyway, I saw a flash of gold on his wrist. Now *that* was interesting." Mike smacked his lips. "Knew old Herman was either a thief or didn't belong." He paused as if to think. "I'd already figured something was strange about Herman. He didn't act right. Even wondered if he was an undercover cop." Mike sat for almost a minute staring at his hands.

Western bumped his elbow into Mike's ribs. "Why did you follow him?"

"A man in my situation has got to be on the lookout for… *opportunities*. An undercover cop would pay me twenty dollars to keep my mouth shut. A thief would either pay me or I'd collect a reward for turning him in. A man hiding out could be dangerous or could be—let's say— grateful. I had to be smart."

"The bracelet?"

"Yep. Had it on that day. The day he died."

"How did you get it?"

"Wasn't easy. When they started screaming that he was gasping for air in front of the building, I ran out." Mike shrugged. "Everyone was looking at his face. No one at his hands. I pretended to be pulling his coat off and grabbed the bracelet." He shook his head. "Problem was the little chain on it broke. Cheap pawn broker gave me a lot less for it—only three hundred dollars."

Western almost felt sorry for Mike. "Do you realize the bracelet was worth five to seven thousand dollars?"

Mike uttered a string of curses. "Like I said—a man in my situation has to be careful." He hung his head. When he looked up he was smiling. "I might have info that would interest you enough to make you forget the bracelet."

Western looked over at Scofield. She was smiling as if she enjoyed listening to this wily, old con man. He gripped Mike's bony arm. "It better be good."

"I liked having Miracle Foods people at the site. Miss Leslie was pretty. She gave me little gifts. Like a bottle of beer or five bucks most days when she came to lunch. In return, she asked me questions about the diners."

"Anyone in particular?"

"No."

Scofield coughed.

"About Herman," Mike admitted

"Was that why you noticed the bracelet?"

"No, but it made me watch him more."

Western didn't want Mike to clam up or start negotiating as they reached critical questions. This was the time for a bluff. He doubted that Mike had seen the obits in the Saturday paper yet. "Now Mike, think hard. Did you tell Leslie that you'd followed Herman? You know we'll ask her, too?"

Mike winced. "Sure. She gave me a Jackson."

"What did she say?"

"Nothing. Well, 'Thanks.'"

"What else did she ask you to do?"

Mike blinked his eyes.

"Did she ask you to hand one of those shakers to Herman on the day he died?'

Mike frowned. "No, she didn't ask me to do anything."

Scofield looked like she was ready to cry as their leading explanation of the crime slipped away.

Mike blinked again. "But she pulled a new red salt shaker out of that purple purse of hers and put it in the middle of the table near the door."

"Didn't you think that was odd?"

"Not at the time. Miss Leslie liked the tables to look pretty and sometimes put red or green napkins or little baskets of candy on the table." Mike shook his head. "When Herman died, I got to thinking. A man in my situation *has* to think. I took the two salt shakers off the table by the door. That's the table Herman always sat at."

Western was confused. "Why two?"

Mike straightened and looked annoyed. "I couldn't tell which the one was the one Leslie put there."

Scofield pulled her chair closer to the bed. "Was anyone with Leslie that day? Do you recognize this man?" She showed him a picture of Jim Jackson.

"He helps deliver stuff from Miracle Foods."

"Was he there with Leslie?"

"No. She came alone."

Western suspected that Mike was still hiding something. "Did she talk to anyone that day? Or leave with anyone?"

"I was busy serving the food, so I don't know. But she usually walked around the tables and talked to people during the meal. The only thing I remember was... " Mike grinned. "If I wasn't worried about the bracelet, I'd remember more."

Western didn't care what the DA thought, Mike's testimony looked like it might solve the murder of the man at the meal site. "I think I've almost forgotten the bracelet. Help me erase my memory completely."

Mike sighed. "She took two shakers off the table and put them in her purse."

"I thought you took the shakers off the table?"

"I did, but I replaced them with two from another table. Those are the ones Miss Leslie took. I thought Miss Leslie or police, like you, might be generous with me if I kept them."

"Where are they?"

"In a box under the bed. I figured they were more valuable than the other shakers. I don't see much TV, but I know you police can do DNA analyses. I picked them up with a napkin.

Western didn't have the heart to tell Mike that so many people had probably handled the shakers that no usable DNA would be found. He put his left hand on Mike's bony shoulder. "Scofield here has recorded what you've said. She'd like to show you a few more pictures now that your memory is improved. See if you've spotted any of these men in the last couple of weeks."

***

Scofield slammed the car door shut. "No one should have to live like that." She paused. "His identification of Wendell doesn't prove much because as he said, 'A kid with his hair in spikes is easy to spot. No one else is dumb enough not to wear a cap in winter.' But it appears Wendell was lurking around the meal site on Wednesday afternoon—the day of the break-in."

Western stopped at a stop sign and winked at Scofield. "That suggests Jim was just following orders when he stole the tuna on Wednesday night. Only this time Wendell was the boss."

Scofield sighed. "I don't see how we'll get any useful comments from anyone else until we locate Wendell. I'm so tired of running in circles."

"Calm down. While you were finishing up with Mike, I told the captain we needed help. He's already sent a technician, and two uniformed officers to the Best Western University Inn where Parson was staying. The lab will check out Mike's salt shakers right away. The captain will inform

   J. L. Greger

Mendel that he'll be charged with abetting his wife's murder and any other murders that Wendell commits *if* he doesn't cooperate with police and help us locate Wendell."

Scofield gasped. "That's a risky bluff. Mendel's lawyers..."

"That can't be helped. While you interview the Sanchez kids, I'll round up Mendel. Then I'll let him stew while we talk to Anne Jackson. After a night in jail, I suspect she'll will have lost her loyalty to her husband."

"I've got an idea." Scofield flashed a rare smile. "Why don't we put everyone involved in this case in a big room with several loaded guns and see what happens? It would be like Agatha Christie's novel *And Then There Were None* and would save us a lot of work."

Western coughed this time. He hadn't realized this case was depressing Scofield, too.

CHAPTER 28: Scofield near Lory State Park

Scofield was surprised that Viola's children had a lot more to say about Wendell during the new set of interviews. She wondered what had changed. She assumed Western would say that Viola had finally given them permission to talk.

The son thought Wendell "only acted dumb" to annoy adults, especially his father. Elena was more analytical about Wendell's bad behavior. She thought Wendell resented Leslie because Mendel spent less time with him after he met Leslie. Both siblings had agreed on one point. Wendell and Mendel were into cars and had a well-equipped garage. That amused Scofield because it disproved Western's previous conclusion that Wendell was too dumb to sabotage Leslie's car.

Scofield was about to wrap up her conversation with Elena when someone tapped on the window of the interview room. She figured Western wanted to remind her about an unanswered question. She rushed out.

The captain was waiting. "A Larimer County Sheriff's deputy spotted Wendell's blue Corvette at Mendel's ranch near Lory State Park this morning, but he didn't approach because he wanted back up. Meanwhile, Western found the front door open and evidence of violence at the Lopez home in Fort Collins." The captain chuckled, "In his typical fashion, Western reported that he couldn't decide whether the disarray in the son's room was evidence of a fight or a typical teen's room." Western had uniformed officers seal the home and rushed to the cabin at the Lopez ranch.

The captain shook his head. "The Larimer County Sheriff just notified me they found a badly injured man inside the cabin and a body in the snow behind the cabin. I need someone who'll keep me updated while Western gathers clues. You might as well ride with the second ambulance crew. They'll be here in a minute or two."

***

The first ambulance with its siren blaring whizzed past the second ambulance in which Scofield rode at the edge of Fort Collins. Scofield hoped that meant the passenger was still alive. She had texted Western as she left the police building, but she didn't expect a reply when he was absorbed in looking for clues. She checked anyway.

Ten minutes later, she trudged up the pathway of gray packed snow to the cabin's front door. She noted only one set of footprints around the cabin to the back and decided Western would not want anyone to contaminate his murder scene by following those steps. She yelled to the ambulance crew to follow her into the cabin through the front door.

She gasped as she entered the so-called cabin. It was gorgeous with its walls, balcony, and rafter ceiling of polished pine and a huge fireplace of field stones. A sheriff's deputy looked up from the outline of a body taped on the wood floor. "Your partner Western is in back. The ambulance took away the man who fell from the balcony. The evidence suggests he was pushed by the man Western found in back. The older man is also in back with Western. He shouldn't be out there, but he was uncontrollable"

That meant Mendel was alive. "Who was your victim? What's his prognosis?"

"We found no identification, but Western said it was Seth Evers. The EMTs feared Seth had a spinal injury because he couldn't move his legs. My partner jumped into the ambulance to take his statement. I'm waiting for the crime lab crew to take measurements." He pointed to a break in the wood banister on the balcony. "Otherwise, I'm almost through here. The older man has already answered my questions as much as he can."

Scofield looked around the room and saw multiple doors. "Which door leads to the back?"

"The one behind the fireplace. I'll tell the morgue crew you're in back. They don't rush in cases like this and do their paperwork before they retrieve the body. Besides, they've already removed two bodies from an accident scene this morning. Icy roads in the Rockies keep them busy in winter."

She wasn't prepared for what she saw in the backyard. A man in a black jacket had swallowed his gun. The snow drifts were spattered red behind his head. Mendel was kneeling by the body and stoking the sleeve of his son's jacket. Western was hovering over him.

Western didn't turn to her. "Is the second ambulance crew here?"

"Yes."

"Mendel, you've said your goodbyes to Wendell. It's time for you to come inside." He lifted Mendel to his feet and pushed him forward as Scofield motioned to the ambulance crew to wait. They both helped

Mendel sit on a sofa near the sheriff's deputy and then returned to the backyard to watch the removal of the body.

"Wendell's death is a suicide, most likely." Western frowned. "The question is: what caused him to do it? Mendel was present and claimed Wendell and Seth had fought—more of a shoving match—on the balcony after they awakened around ten. Seems they drank too much last night. Seth fell. After Mendel called an ambulance, Wendell went to the backyard."

"Did you record Mendel's comments?"

"Of course, but I don't think they're complete or accurate. The timeline doesn't seem right to me."

"What do you mean?"

"Seth's comments were hard to interpret. He was hysterical because he couldn't move his legs, but he seemed to feel pain when I touched his legs."

"That's a good sign."

"Yes, but Seth claimed he laid on the floor a long time after he fell."

"In his state a couple of minutes could seem like a long time."

"True." Western turned to give instructions to the ambulance crew. "Tell Sam Drake in the medical examiner's office to look for bruises indicating fighting before the fall and check the blood alcohol level immediately. I've already sent photos to Sam. Try not to touch the gun. The lab crew will check it for fingerprints." He turned back to Scofield. "Seth claimed Mendel and Wendell fought and Wendell stormed out of the cabin before Mendel called for help. The deputy riding in the ambulance is going to try to clarify Seth's comments."

"Did Seth say whether he was pushed through the railing on the balcony or lost his footing and fell?" Scofield was typing on her phone rapidly.

"Another unclear point. Seth admitted yelling at Wendell but never mentioned throwing a punch or receiving one. I couldn't see any cuts or swelling on Seth's or Wendell's face. Seems strange to me." He shook his head. "I'll never get used to suicides." He stood. "Why don't you see how Mendel answers your questions? I want to check out the loft for signs of fighting."

Scofield stepped into the great room. Mendel was still hunched on the sofa where they'd seated him. She decided acting motherly was the best way to approach Mendel and went to the kitchen to see if any beverages were available. The only beverage in the refrigerator was beer.

                                                        J. L. Greger

However, a pot of lukewarm coffee sat on the counter. She wondered who had prepared the coffee and microwaved a cup.

She handed the heated coffee to Mendel. "Drink this. You'll feel better if you talk."

"Doubt it." He took a sip and then another.

She kept her voice low and soft. "It easy to have lots of regrets at a time like this. What do you most regret doing or saying during the last twelve hours?"

He took another sip. "I... I regret telling Wendell he was a screw up."

She was glad she had turned on the recorder when she left the kitchen. "When?"

"As soon as he got here last night."

"Is that all you said or did?"

"No, I let him—really both guys—have it last night. They blew me off and started drinking and playing their music loud. I went to bed." He looked at her and shook his head. "Couldn't sleep in our—my and Leslie's—bedroom at home. That's why I came here."

"What about this morning?"

"I found them passed out in the loft, made coffee, and took them some." She leaned closer to Mendel to encourage intimacy. "What did they say or do?"

He gulped. "They told me to go away, especially after I complained that the loft smelled like a barn. One or both of them had vomited in a wastebasket."

"What happened next?"

Mendel stared at his coffee mug. "I said unkind—but true— words. They yelled at me and then at each other. To get away from the noise, I went to the garage. I also wanted to check to see whether there were any drugs in the Corvette."

He paused and she thought Mendel was probably thinking about editing his story to protect himself. She lied. "You were being a good father. What did you find? Is that why you went back into the cabin?"

"I found weed and empty beer cans in the car. That did it. I stormed back into the house and up the stairs, and..."

"Go ahead. It's not a crime to yell at your kids. The jails aren't large enough for everyone who's ever done that." She secretly thought *but some things should never be said.*

"I said, 'I don't know which of you two jackasses is the bigger fool. You could have killed yourself driving on winter roads while smoking and drinking.' Then I grabbed Wendell's arm. Seth pushed me away from Wendell. I fell backward down several steps but managed to grasp the railing and keep myself from tumbling farther down the stairs."

"Keep going. Let it all out."

"I don't know what happened exactly. I heard Wendell scream and then Seth yell. They started shoving each other hard, not playfully. I heard wood cracking. I think it was the banister. I looked down. Seth lay on the floor. All I could think was *Wendell's finally done it.* Mendel sobbed violently."

"What did you say or do?"

"I... I said, 'You numbskull—you killed your best friend!'" Mendel looked up at me. "Maybe I also said I was tired of cleaning up his messes. I certainly thought it."

"Wendell shrieked and ran past me down the stairs. I heard doors slamming. My leg ached. So did my wrist. I just sat there... I don't know how long before I grabbed the railing and pulled myself up. I was coming down the stairs when I heard Seth moan. Then I heard a gunshot." Mendel sobbed so loudly that Western must have heard him and came down from the loft.

Scofield ignored Western and rubbed Mendel's shoulder. "What did you do?"

"I rushed to the back door hoping I wasn't too late, but I was. I don't know how long I stood by Wendell before I called 9-1-1." Mendel looked up cautiously. "What happens next?"

Scofield thought for several seconds. "I'm going to try to confirm your story. Western needs to check your legs for bruises and your wrist for signs of a sprain. I'll look for the two coffee mugs in the loft. The lab crew will check for fingerprints at odd angles on the railings."

Western said, "The lab crew has already checked the gun case by the back door." He sat down on the other side of Mendel. "There was no place in the gun case for handguns only shotguns and rifles. Where did Wendell get the handgun he used?"

"It's mine. Wendell knew I always carried it in my briefcase. He must have taken it."

"Are you sure?"

Mendel knit his brow. "I heard lots of doors slamming. He must have gone to my room before he went out back."

"We'll check for his prints on the doorknob of your room and on your case." Western spoke more loudly so Scofield, who was already at the stairs to the loft, could hear. "The lab crew already fingerprinted two coffee mugs in the loft. Have one of them come down and take the photos of Mendel and check out his room. You'd also better update the sheriff's deputy and see if his partner got anything more out of Seth on the way to the hospital."

CHAPTER 29: Sara's Change in Plans

I meant to sleep in Saturday morning but awoke at six out of habit and because I was tense. I crawled out of bed trying not disturb the covers so Sanders wouldn't awaken. In the process, I stumbled over Bug's food dish. Unfortunately, he hadn't eaten all his kibbles last night. Pieces of dog food flew all over the carpet. Sanders awoke amidst my cursing.

He pulled me back under the covers. "I've been thinking about how to spend today and tomorrow." He kissed my ear and then worked down my neck. "We don't have to rush out of here. I bet your Fort Collins police friends—what are their names?—solve both murders today. After what they learned last night from the three lawyers it won't take much to pin the death of the homeless man..."

To save him from saying *What is his name?,* I said, "Herb Parson."

"Yes, they'll pin his death on..."

"Leslie Lopez. But there's still the question of who cut Leslie's brake lines and put explosives in my car's tail pipe."

"I bet they'll get a confession today, and that means we might as well stick around and enjoy the sites in Colorado this weekend." He kissed my shoulder. "Then on Monday you can finish up your inquiries on who sabotaged the clinical trial, file your final report, and drive home."

"That would be better than driving to Albuquerque today and driving all the way back on Monday or Tuesday."

"Exactly, and I know how to start our Colorado adventure." His tongue parted my lips and he kissed me deeply.

***

Three hours later, I felt much more relaxed as we finished an order of Tuscan Eggs Benedict and an order of chicken and waffle that we had picked up at the Urban Egg restaurant. Bug preferred the chicken with a bit of the waffle, but Sanders and I couldn't decide which dish we liked most.

As Sanders read the entertainment section of the *Colorado Springs Gazette*, I said, "I've never seen the Air Force Academy. Maybe after we pick up my car from the Colorado Springs police garage, we can tour the campus."

"Hmm." Sanders stalled as he usually did when he was going to disagree with me. "I checked. The police garage opens at one on Sunday. That means we can pick up your car before I fly out on a military transport tomorrow. Today we'd be less recognizable in my rental car. Why don't you tell your police friends in Fort Collins of our plans as I extend our stay in this room?"

Sanders hurried off on his errand, while I contacted Scofield. She texted back:

> *Mike from the meal site confirmed your theory. Leslie placed a salt shaker presumably with ground peanuts on the table where Parson ate on the day he died. If the lab finds peanut protein in that shaker we can close that investigation.*
>
> *I'm curious how Leslie ground the nuts without creating a paste. That's what I get when I put peanuts into my food processor. Do you know how she did it?*
>
> *I'm about to interview Viola's children again.*
>
> *We still haven't found Wendell. So, stay alert.*

I knew the answer to her question because I frequently ground nuts for baking. I emailed her:

> *It's best to pulse nuts for less than five seconds in a blender. Probably twice. If you allow heat to build up, the fat in the nuts melts, and you get a paste.*

***

The austere aluminum spires of the chapel at the U.S. Air Force Academy were impressive. They made the A-frame building look like it was covered with a series of praying hands. At least that was my interpretation of the modern structure. After we strolled around the campus with Bug, Sanders studied the Web for our next options. I checked for messages from Scofield.

> *Wendell is dead. Seth Evers is critically injured. The physical evidence support Mendel's claim that Wendell committed suicide after fighting with Seth, but Mendel's role is still unclear.*

***

The drive to Garden of the Gods was breathtaking. The peaks seemed redder and the pines greener than usual, probably because of the snow. However, the wind cut though my clothes when we began to hike. Bug bounced through several piles of snow and then whined because he wanted to be carried. Sanders after half of a mile complained his muscles were aching from tramping through snow during the last two days. I shouldn't admit it, but I was delighted and suggested we enjoy the area from a comfortably heated car. We found a safe spot with a great view and turned on the radio to soft background music.

I'd taken only one swig of a diet cola when Sanders said, "I was thinking about our conversation two nights ago. What happened after your encounter with the department head?"

"Not much. I went to see the dean the next day. He asked a few noncommittal questions but gave me no sympathy or encouragement. I remember thinking I'd probably get tenure and be promoted to associate professor because he wanted to protect himself and the university from a law suit, but I'd be ignored for the rest of my time at Michigan State."

"What happened to the department head?"

"About a week later we had a department meeting. Everyone was surprised when our department head was a half-hour late. He didn't apologize but noted he'd just met with the dean. After a boring two-hour meeting, our department head announced he was stepping down. During the next week, the dean interviewed two of the three male professors in the department—but neither of two female full professors—and appointed one of the men as head of the department."

"Did the old department head leave the university?"

"You can't be that naive. Everything went on as if nothing had happened." I shrugged. "I continued to team-teach two courses a year with him for the next five years. Several times he suggested that he'd be more cooperative if I wore sheer black hose when I met with him. I didn't resist and wore the stockings."

"Really? I've never seen you wear sheer dark hose."

J. L. Greger

"Of course not. When he retired, I pitched all my sheer dark stockings." I stopped and decided it was all right to let Sanders see my petty side. "However, when I was asked to organize his retirement party, I didn't think twice. I said, 'Get someone who doesn't know the truth about the bastard.'"

Sanders kissed my nose.

"You know what was funny. His retirement party was the one of the splashiest parties I've ever attended."

"Did that bother you?"

I hated to admit the truth. "Let's just say I bought a new dress for the event. Something I rarely did. I wanted to appear confident because a month later the professors interested in epidemiology in the Statistic Department voted to create a separate department. The new Epidemiology Department included most of the women and minority faculty members who had been in the Statistics Department."

"Didn't you become the department head in the new department?"

"Yes, but not until three years later. By then I didn't care about my career in the same way. I did my best for the Department of Epidemiology and developed research projects all over the world, mainly because they gave me an excuse to travel. As soon as I completed twenty years at the university and my retirement accounts were secure, I quit and moved to New Mexico."

"How many..."

I put my finger on his lips. "Let's not talk about my history anymore. I think my career would have been easier and perhaps more satisfying if I were a white male but I know I was luckier than most minority members and women in academia. Mainly I wish my department head hadn't forced me to recognize my real self. I guess I should thank him, but I won't."

"As white male, it's hard..."

I decided the best defense against more questions was a good offense. "Why don't you tell me how the new modifications in LIDAR technology will improve the patrol of coastal. areas. I never bought your snow story."

He shifted about in his seat for at least a minute. "I should have known you'd see through my cover story. Most people don't realize NORAD is responsible for monitoring potential maritime as well as aerospace threats to the U.S. and Canada. We really did test the technology on snow on Thursday but my main discussions were on Friday." He paused and slowly exhaled. "You made your point. You don't want to talk more about the sexual harassment in your past." He put the car in gear and drove toward Colorado Springs. "I've been talking to my boss."

I managed not to sigh and tried to keep my face nonchalant.

"A deputy assistant secretary of state position will open up in probably three to four months. She thought I'd be a shoo-in if I solved one little problem in Brazil in the next couple of months while I served as the deputy chief of mission."

I feared she'd asked him to do the impossible but didn't want to burst his bubble. "Brazil has several pretty big problems—deforestation of the Amazon, child gangs, drugs, poverty, and the anti-science attitudes of its leadership. What specifically does she, or perhaps I should say the State Department, expect you to accomplish in a couple of months?"

He turned and winked. "You know I can't answer that question, but I'm glad you'll understand why I won't see you much during the next couple of months." He returned his focus to the road. "We haven't seen a movie in a while. When I scanned the entertainment section of the paper this morning, I noticed one of the theaters is showing a new mystery. We can see who guesses the bad guy first."

CHAPTER 30: Sara in Fort Collins on Monday

"The Denver police—really Herb Parson's widow—gave us a pleasant surprise this morning."

I took one look at Scofield on Monday morning and knew she must have enjoyed her weekend. The dark circles under her eyes had disappeared and her voice had lost its usual nasal sound. She also wasn't coughing, but then again Western wasn't in sight. "What happened?'

"The ledgers of Future Proteins, Inc., show Herb Parson cashed a check for thirty thousand dollars last June and labeled it in the ledger and on the check as 'cash payments to Miracle Foods employees for services.' Note the plural. The ledgers also show cash payments of five thousand dollars a month for the next six months." Scofield smiled broadly. "I've just ascertained Jim Jackson bought his 2000 Corvette and paid off his credit cards debts in June. I'm now subpoenaing the financial records of Wendell Lopez and Viola Sanchez."

"Why Wendell's?"

"Although Wendell wasn't an employee of Miracle Foods, he would have overheard Mendel's and Leslie's discussions. And we have another new source of information on Wendell."

I waited to speak thinking she'd say more. She didn't. That puzzled me but I figured she was busy and settled Bug and his paraphernalia in a corner of her and Western's shared office. Finally, I asked, "Where's Western?"

He should be back from the hospital momentarily. He thought Seth Evers might be talkative today. Western won't admit it, but I think he went as much to give Seth a pep talk as to question him. Doctors say Seth will walk again but it will take considerable rehab." She looked around her office. "We also have a problem. It seems Mendel lied—a lot—on Saturday. Seth's doctors think Seth wasn't hallucinating. He really did lie on the floor for a long time after his fall—probably for an hour — before Mendel called 9-1-1. Seth insists the father and son argued much of that time."

"Does he know why?"

"Not exactly. Seth says it sounded like the same argument they'd had for the last year. It seems Wendell expected Mendel to give him a business—probably a bar—to manage when he graduated. Mendel claimed he couldn't until he sold a property, perhaps Miracle Foods."

"We should have realized the real beef between Leslie and Wendell was money."

"Yes, and story gets better. Last summer, Seth claims Wendell started bragging he'd found a way to force his dad to sell Miracle Foods. But Seth didn't know any details, except he waited outside the Best Western Inn near the campus several times in January while Wendell met with someone."

"So, when Leslie killed Herb Parson, she also killed Wendell's source of income and dreams. Do you think Wendell or Jim knew who killed Herb Parson?"

She shook her head. "Doubt it but I suspect Viola and perhaps Mendel guessed."

"Do you think either of them will admit their suspicions?"

"Of course not, but Seth made one more interesting comment. Seems Mendel hoped you would show that Miracle Foods was—in his words—a flop."

"What?"

"Seth says that Wendell claimed his dad had decided that Leslie's plans for Miracle Foods weren't what he wanted, and he was tired of arguing with her."

"Hmm. So, you're guessing Mendel...?"

"Decided to end the argument, but Western insists Mendel loved Leslie." Scofield stretched. "Unfortunately, the first thing on the agenda today is to sort out the charges against the Jacksons. Justice and FDA officials are ready to act, if we can't. That means we have to talk to Viola." She looked at her watch. "No wonder Western is taking so much time with Seth. Viola is one of those rare witnesses he can't frighten."

***

Western slowly circled the table in the interview room after Viola was seated. After his second lap, he sat down by her. "Viola, my instincts say you're hiding something."

From my viewpoint in the observation room, I noticed Western behaved differently around Viola than around the college students. He didn't lean over her or put his hand on her shoulder. Even when he sat down by her, he stayed an arm's length away.

Scofield didn't cough as I expected while Western did his routine. For a second, I wondered whether Western and Scofield had signed a

                                        J. L. Greger

truce this weekend after seeing a movie and doing who know what else together.

Western brought me back to the matter at hand. "Let's start with something simple. Why did you warn Anne after you saw our composite drawing on Friday?"

Viola shrugged. "I felt sorry for Anne. I knew you'd use her as a pawn to trap Jim, just as you were trying to use me to trap Mendel. Such a waste of time. You should have spent your time questioning Jim and Wendell."

I didn't know whether I believed Viola, but I realized her anger was real. Scofield must have felt the same way. She said her noncommittal "Okay" and asked, "Why did you have Anne Jackson deliver the threatening note to Troy Pitkin in the library?"

Viola's nostrils flared. "What are you talking about? When Troy called me on Thursday, I was at work. I told him to stay in the library until five-thirty. I planned to talk to him then, but you picked him up before I arrived."

"That's all? Didn't you remind him of Leslie's accident and tell him to get a lawyer?" Scofield didn't look at Viola as she punched numbers on her phone.

"Of course not. He didn't need a lawyer. He'd done nothing wrong."

Scofield pushed her phone in front of Viola. "This is the note Anne delivered to Troy. She claimed you dictated the content."

I thought that was an overstatement, but police were allowed that privilege.

Viola read it silently. "This doesn't make sense, but it explains several of your questions on Friday." She rubbed her temples as she leaned over the table. "Let me think. Oh, no... it can't be. I think that was the day." She gulped. "Wendell and Seth were lolling around the office for a while on Thursday at midday. I told them Mendel would not be in until later, but they stayed anyway. A little after one, Wendell left. I remember because I thought he'd be late to class. Seth stayed for a while. One of them might have heard my conversation with Troy." She shook her head. "I don't know."

Western pointed at Viola. "Did you receive payments from Herb Parson?"

Viola lips puckered as if she was ready to spit at him. "I'm no fool. My financial future depended on Miracle Foods succeeding. Go ahead and check my financial accounts. Maybe then you'll get over your obsession with my secrets."

Scofield nodded. "I doubt you did anything stupid. That's not your style, but I agree with Western. You know an important detail about someone else's actions." Scofield studied her phone. "Why would Jim Jackson take a bribe?"

Viola looked like a fish coming up for food floating on the surface of a pond. Her mouth formed an "O" several times as she gulped and looked toward the ceiling. "Jim is not a good food scientist. Leslie was the one who suggested he should read the literature on fish spoilage to find an answer for the off-taste in our fish product last May. Then she began to meet regularly with a prof in biotech—a Dr. Earl Shrago."

Viola had finally mentioned something important. I emailed Scofield:

> *Is Dr. Shrago the man with the gray beard who Pitkin and
> Wendell saw Leslie meet with at the Lory Student Center?*

Scofield glanced at my note but let Viola continue.

"About six months ago, Leslie began to nag Mendel that they should fire Jim. By October, she was convinced Jim was hiding something."

"Why didn't she act?"

Viola face turned red, and she straightened in her chair. "I'm not a mind reader."

Scofield leaned forward. "But you're a good listener. You can guess."

Viola flinched. "I don't think Dr. Shrago would take the job of director of research at Miracle Foods until the clinical trial was completed. Dr. Shrago also didn't want a long-term position. He and Leslie felt they needed to groom the next scientific director or directors at Miracle Foods immediately."

I emailed again:

> *Strange Viola knows so much about Leslie's plans. Odd they
> considered multiple scientific directors. I wonder if Mendel knew
> her plans.*

"Okay. How did you learn of Leslie's plans?"

"Since Leslie no longer trusted Jim, she needed my help to plan the clinical trial and monitor the student interns. She also provided a small grant to Dr. Shrago to study fibril formation in cell cultures. I don't understand the project, but he hired my Elena to work it."

"Hmm. One of the student interns was Troy Pitkin. What did you think of him?"

"Nice, smart kid." She paused. "I met with him in October—no, it was earlier—because Jim had complained that Troy was being difficult. Troy in response to my questions had mumbled, 'Tell Mrs. Lopez to check the histamine levels in the fish.' I didn't know what histamine was, but I told her. That's when she started sharing more with me. You remember what I told you last Friday?"

I texted Scofield:

Maybe she knows where Troy Pitkin is.

Scofield leaned forward and touched Viola's hand. "One of our biggest concerns now is finding Troy Pitkin. He's disappeared. We know he didn't like Wendell and didn't trust Jim."

Viola gave a broad smile. "I was wondering when you were going to think of him. Last Thursday night after Western bullied him, I decided you weren't concerned about Troy's safety and I arranged for him to stay with my sister and brother-in-law on their small farm about five miles from Fort Collins."

Scofield was furiously typing on her phone. "Why with them?"

"That's the brother-in-law who works at the police garage. He knows how to protect his farm. I also sent my daughter to stay with my sister on Friday. I thought she'd be safer there than at my house and it would give her a chance to get to know Troy."

I thought that was a strange statement. Scofield must have thought the same. She blinked. "I'm not following your thoughts. Why did you want Troy and your daughter to talk?"

"Your questions on Friday made me think. If Leslie died, Mendel would sell Miracle Foods." She shook her head. "That would ruin my... Leslie's plans for Dr. Shrago to lead the research at Miracle Foods with the help of my Elena and Troy Pitkin."

I texted Scofield:

You finally learned her secret, but how much of it was Leslie's idea?

"Why would Mendel consider your plan to restructure Miracle Foods?"

"It wasn't my plan. It was Leslie's plan."

"Oh, really?" Scofield's voice was icy. I figured she was about to discard most of Viola's earlier comments as fiction.

Viola answered quickly. "Well, why do you think Leslie was meeting regularly with Dr. Shrago? Why do you think he hired my Elena? And why do you think Leslie was so interested in Troy Pitkin?"

Scofield just stared at Viola.

Viola must have sensed Scofield's skepticism. "Leslie gave Mendel her plan in early January. He must he have read it because he made a funny comment when he asked me to book his and Jim's flight to see Sara Almquist in Albuquerque" She frowned. "What was it? Something like, 'Since this is Jim's last rodeo.'"

Scofield's voice was warmer, but still cautious. "Did Jim or Wendell know of her plans? For example, would Mendel have told Jim of Leslie's plans on that trip? You know—out of pity for a fellow male?"

"I've wondered that, too, but I don't think so. Mendel always thought of the bottom line. He knew Jim had to go. As for Wendell, all I know is he was becoming more and more angry in January. Constantly making threats to Leslie and even Mendel."

"Did your daughter and Troy Pitkin know of Leslie's and your plans?"

"It's obvious you don't have children. You have to let your kids think they make their own choices." She smiled.

CHAPTER 31: The Case against the Jacksons

I noted Western and Scofield followed their usual pattern of behavior. They whittled away all the easy tasks before they tackled the real problem. I suspected it was a way to reduce the time spent talking to the real culprits—an unpleasant task to say the least.

Troy Pitkin's and Earl Shrago's comments were consistent with Viola's statements. Shrago had a written offer from Leslie and Mendel. Troy had only a verbal promise from Leslie that she would "find a good job" for him at Miracle Foods. The only problem was Viola couldn't provide a copy of the plans Leslie gave Mendel.

A conference call with FDA and USDA officials, a U.S. Justice Department lawyer, and the DAs for Larimer and Denver Counties had resulted in a prioritization of potential charges against Jim Jackson. That was a polite way of saying federal officials and the Denver DA would let Western and Scofield spar with Jim today. Then they would act.

The DA for Denver County thought the records at Future Proteins, Inc., built a case for industrial espionage and the stealing of trade secrets from Miracle Foods. The obvious culprit was Herb Parson with the help of Jim Jackson. As this was new evidence, the DA for Larimer County was undecided on how to proceed. He thought a civil suit by Miracle Foods against Future Proteins Inc., might be the best avenue to achieve justice.

The U.S. Justice Department lawyer noted he would charge Jim Jackson and perhaps someone at Future Proteins under the Economic Espionage Act but first he wanted to address the FDA's concerns. FDA officials explained a charge of adulteration of food could yield a maximum of several years in jail, but probably much less. However, they felt they could charge Jim Jackson with tampering with drugs because Jim had intentionally allowed a contaminated *experimental* food to be fed in a clinical trial. There was one more detail they needed to check before they could make that charge. However, if they decided to go that route they could claim a hundred counts because the histamine-rich fish product had been fed twice to fifty people each time. One FDA official's final comment amazed me. She hoped she didn't have to use her power because it might damage the emerging cultured meat industry *but* she would if the Larimer County DA couldn't prove their cases against Jim Jackson.

I was confused by that comment and asked, "What do you think the case is?" Scofield mouthed *thanks* to me immediately.

The official replied. "That's what I hope you find out today, but I perceive local police will have a hard time making a case for a major crime. Three key players are dead, one primary witness is a wife who doesn't have to testify against her husband, and a key witness, Mendel Lopez, who will turn off all potential jurors if he testifies."

Western's face turned stony, and Scofield coughed.

***

I was back in the observation room when Anne Jackson and her lawyer entered the interrogation room. She looked old enough to be Jim's mother and wore a mismatched old sweatshirt and baggy pants.

The lawyer immediately said, "My client is willing to cooperate because she no longer has to fear Wendell Lopez."

"Let's start simply." Scofield scanned her phone. "Did Viola call and order you to deliver a note to Troy Pitkin?"

"No."

"Who did? What did he or she say?"

"I don't know who he was. He said he had a message from Wendell and dictated what I should write on the note and how I should deliver it to Troy."

The police would have to determine whether Seth Evers would admit to making the call, but I decided it wasn't worth bothering Scofield with a text message. She was on a roll.

"Why did you follow his orders?"

"Wendell barged into my house on Thursday morning. He called my son Tom into the kitchen, showed him a handful of pills, and asked, 'Do you know what these are?' When Tom nodded yes, Wendell laughed and told Tom to leave the room. Then Wendell said, 'You can see how easy it would be to kill Tom and make it look like an unintentional overdose.'" Anne began to sob. "I knew why Jim had..."

The lawyer put his arm around Anne's shoulder. "My client does not want to incriminate her husband. I think she has provided sufficient proof that all her actions were forced responses to physical threats."

The muscles on Scofield's face tightened and her eyes narrowed. It was obvious she was annoyed that Anne had decided to protect her

J. L. Greger

husband. "Your car was used by Wendell Lopez in Colorado Springs to escape after he tampered with Sara Almquist's vehicle."

Anne whispered in her lawyer's ear.

Western didn't wait for Scofield to speak. "Before you object, Sara Almquist reported the license plate number."

The lawyer whispered in Anne's ear.

"I let Wendell borrow Jim's car because of his threats to my son."

"You did more than that. You let Wendell park his car in your garage while he borrowed yours. That means you were abetting his crimes." Scofield was so annoyed with Anne that she didn't wait for Anne to speak. "We can bring your son in. He has already told us a blue Corvette other than his father's was in your garage when you took him on your shopping trip, but Jim's Corvette was in the garage when police stopped by your house at seven-thirty."

Anne stared at the table.

Scofield started a series of questions to determine Jim's whereabouts on Tuesday night. Each time Anne's lawyer objected. Finally, Scofield said, "Anne, I know you were under duress but you threatened a witness, lied to police about the source of the note, and abetted a murder attempt. That means prison time. We have no reason to ask the DA to reduce the charges against you because you have not cooperated." She stood. "You should realize if we can't convict your husband, federal courts will for his part in potentially poisoning fifty people at the meal site." She opened the door. "In other words, your sacrifice will not save him."

Anne shrieked. The lawyer asked Western and Scofield to leave and to turn off the microphone to the observation room while he talked to his client.

Five minutes later, the lawyer called them back into the room. "Anne will answer all your questions on condition that all charges against her be dropped."

Scofield noted no promises could be made until the DA reviewed Anne's statement. I knew that was moot point. The DA had already decided as long as Anne told the truth and answered all questions, she was free. He wanted Jim, not his family, punished. Scofield droned on and on with questions pinpointing phone calls that Jim received and made while at home and the timing of his absences.

The first point Scofield scored was Jim had received a call from Wendell on Wednesday evening. Anne had taken the call on the family phone and recognized his voice. Jim had left immediately saying he was going to the lab. Anne had called the lab phone later and no one answered.

This confirmed Western's suspicions that Wendell and Jim were in collusion and trying to confuse police after Troy Pitkin had attempted to deliver flowers to Leslie. I wasn't sure it was worth the effort, but Scofield must have felt it proved that Wendell was prepared to make a second attempt on Leslie's life. Thus, Jim could be charged with abetting a murder attempt. I thought that case was shaky, but I speculated Scofield and Western were trying to cover all their bases.

The second point Scofield scored was Jim had pickle juice on his coat and slacks when he came home on Tuesday night at about two in the morning. Anne knew because she did his laundry the next morning and his clothes stunk. She also admitted she'd delivered two and half cases of cans with red labels to the city dump on Wednesday at noon time because Jim had begged for her help. I thought—and judging by Western's snorts, he agreed—Jim was not a good husband. However, the break-in and theft would only get Jim at most six months in jail because the damage and losses were probably less than five thousand dollars.

Scofield wasn't able to score a third point. Anne didn't know how Jim got the money to purchase a 2000 Corvette or the cash for Tom's college fund. She said Jim had talked of working for Future Proteins, but in January he admitted the owner of the company had called him "a loser who couldn't even sabotage a clinical trial successfully" Evidently Herb Parson had purchased the tainted canned tuna as a backup plan because he thought Jim hadn't produced enough contaminated cultured tuna to ruin the clinical trial. The only concrete evidence Anne provided was the bank account in her son's name containing twenty thousand dollars.

The scene in the interview room was a sad one. Anne was moaning, "Jim, forgive me." Scofield and Western looked disappointed. The only person smiling was Anne's lawyer. He murmured, "Now, now Anne. If you've told them everything, you're a free woman."

***

Scofield started the interview with Jim aggressively. "As you know, you will be arraigned today for the break-in and vandalism at the meal site last Wednesday, as well as the theft of canned tuna. We have your fingerprints, eyewitness accounts of your car at the site, video footage of the theft and vandalism, and your wife's account of the sequelae. It's a sure-fire conviction."

Jim stared at the table as his lawyer said, "Those are minor crimes. Your next point?"

I could see Scofield was trying to keep a confident look on her face as she smiled at Jim. "Okay. We know Wendell ordered you to drive around on Wednesday night in an effort to provide an alibi for himself.

                                              J. L. Greger

Your wife will testify on that point. He planned to kill Leslie in her hospital room. If he had succeeded, you would have abetted murder. What did he have over you to force you to cover for him?"

Jim looked at his lawyer who replied. "He doesn't want to incriminate himself."

Scofield texted me:

Call the FDA official and the Justice Department lawyer. See whether they've determined if they can fulfill their threat of charging Jim with a hundred counts of drug tampering. You can answer their questions better than Western.

"Okay. Let's try these charges. You like tinkering with cars—why else would you have bought a 2000 Corvette? We can build charges against you for murdering Leslie Lopez and the pedestrian she hit after you cut the brake lines on her car. You had a motive and means. She was about to fire you and prove you had accepted bribes for industrial espionage. Did you do it?"

Jim looked at Scofield with tears in his eyes. "No."

"That's enough," said the lawyer. "Cutting a metal brake line takes time and requires special equipment. Obviously, my client couldn't do it in a parking lot without being seen."

Scofield didn't bother to look up from her computer. "A lawyer in the U.S. Justice Department has just informed me today she will be filing a hundred counts of tampering with drugs against your client. When Miracle Foods registered their clinical trial with the FDA, they mentioned the eventual health benefits of cultured meat, such as having low cholesterol levels. That means the food product can be considered a drug in the clinical trial. Your client in his role as research director of Miracle Foods signed all clinical trial documents submitted to the FDA."

Scofield stood and motioned to Western. "The Justice Department will contact you later today or tomorrow."

CHAPTER 32: The Answer?

Western was convinced Wendell killed Leslie; Scofield suspected Mendel had committed the murder. That meant the investigators needed to interview Mendel again but neither officer thought they could distinguish the truth from lies in Mendel's story without more evidence.

Accordingly, Western went to the hospital to see whether Seth Evers could confirm details in Viola's story or provide more insight into Wendell's actions. Scofield talked to the DA and went to Jim's arraignment for vandalism and theft.

Bug and I stayed in the police conference room while I made sure FDA officials and Justice Department lawyers had all the records they need to convict Jim Jackson for a hundred counts of drug tampering. One FDA official sighed as I completed my work. "Last week, we figured we could use all these data to pursue drug tampering charges against Mendel and Leslie Lopez, Miracle Foods, *and* Jim Jackson. However, if the Justice Department arraigns Future Proteins for industrial espionage, we can't win a case against Mendel Lopez and Miracle Foods for drug tampering. The documents Elena Sanchez delivered to me an hour ago further weaken our case against Mendel."

"What documents?"

"Elena delivered a packet of documents around one. She said her mother had retrieved them from Mendel's home office. Evidently as soon as she left the Fort Collins police station, Viola Sanchez went to the Mendel Lopez's home and forced him to find the records. I assumed someone had also delivered a copy of the documents to Scofield or Western."

"I doubt it. This morning Scofield asked for a copy of Leslie's plan for Miracle Foods, but Viola claimed she didn't have it. Please transmit a copy electronically to Scofield. I think she'll be happy to interrupt her conversation with the DA to talk to you."

***

Scofield tore into the conference room thirty minutes later and announced, "Viola has had us chasing our tails for more than a week." She placed a pile of documents in front of me. "You might as well look at them while we wait. Uniformed officers are picking up Viola, her daughter Elena, and Troy Pitkin. Western is executing a search warrant of Mendel's home office and then bringing him in."

Leslie had signed the first page of a three-page report and dated it on January 1. Underneath, Mendel had added his initials to the page on January 2. Scofield had written a large red question mark on a detachable note by the date. I wondered why but decided she wanted me to read quickly and not ask questions.

There were three other sections of the first page of the report. Each stated one of Leslie's goals for Miracle Foods followed by a paragraph of explanation which cited other documents in the pile in front of me. The first three goals were consistent with Viola's comments that Leslie wanted to replace Jim Jackson as the director of research with Dr. Earl Shrago. She also planned to hire Elena Sanchez and Troy Pitkin as researchers with the intention one or both would replace Dr. Shrago upon his retirement in a couple of years.

I choked as I read the next point which was on a separate page. Leslie wanted Mendel to disinherit Wendell unless Wendell accepted psychiatric treatment in a certified facility. Then his inheritance would be placed in a trust administered by a psychiatrist or a clinical psychologist.

Scofield pulled documents from the pile. "They appear to be similar to the ones the divorce lawyers in Colorado Springs supplied. The DA has already begun discussions with the Colorado Bar Association about disbarring or censoring the three lawyers you spoke to on Saturday night. He thinks the psychiatric reports made it clear Wendell was a threat to himself and others and they hadn't advised Leslie in a responsible manner."

I noticed that Mendel had also initialed and dated this page. The date was January 20. "Don't you think it's odd this was dated almost three weeks later than the front page?"

Scofield frowned. "That's why I put the question mark on the first page. Just wait until you see the next page."

I turned the page. "Well, now we know Viola's big secret!" The fifth point was that Mendel would recognize Elena Sanchez as his biological daughter.

Scofield coughed. "This proves Western was right when he called Mendel a Don Juan. This also explains a comment Mendel made about Viola holding the past over him. Note that Mendel initialed and dated it on January 20, too." She pulled another document from the pile. "Here's the result of a paternity test from a year ago. There's no doubt that Elena is Mendel's daughter, but it's unclear how long Mendel has known."

When her phone beeped, Scofield pulled the report away from me before I could look at the last page. The worry lines on her face deepened as she listened to the caller. When she disconnected, she said, "Western has found nothing of interest in Mendel's home office..." she smirked. "...except lots of women's phone numbers. When he charged Mendel with Leslie's murder, Mendel said, 'Ask Viola.'"

I must have looked surprised.

"You're wondering what the basis of the charge was?" She laughed. "That's Western's way of blowing off steam. He figures Mendel can't sue him for a false arrest because Western can claim this document..." She pointed to the one we'd been studying. "...suggests Leslie was blackmailing him. Mostly, Western's trying to scare Mendel."

"Obviously that tactic didn't work," I said.

Scofield smirked. "Yes, but I admire Western's guts."

I figured Scofield had become more tolerant of Western over the weekend or at least finally admitted her feelings. I said nothing and waited.

"Western also said Seth Evers confirmed all Viola's comments including that Wendell had become angrier at both his father and stepmother during the last month."

I decided to try to provoke a candid comment from Scofield. "So although Viola had misled you, she's not lied, per se."

"We'll see."

***

While Scofield and Western interviewed Viola and Mendel, I chatted with Elena Lopez and Troy Pitkin. Both commented more than once that they no longer had to apply for jobs or sweat job interviews during their last semester in college. I thought they faced a much more daunting task of trying to save a faltering company but thought it unkind to state the truth to the young hopeful couple.

I realized they were less naive than I thought when Elena said, "Mom talked to a lawyer about suing Future Proteins for the

J. L. Greger

loss of trade secrets. She wants their payment to be shares in Future Proteins."

Troy nodded. "Dr. Shrago thinks we'd be better off with cash to support our research during the next year, but Mrs. Sanchez seems confident that Mr. Lopez can supply the needed cash in the short-term."

That statement seemed strange. "What did Mendel say about Viola's decision?"

Elena's dark brown eyes seemed to grow bigger as she stared at me. "I thought you saw Leslie's plan. Mom's the CEO of Miracle Foods since Leslie is no longer alive. Mendel relinquished day-to-day management of Miracle Foods to Leslie in January and is only chairman of the board."

I gasped. That must have been the points discussed on the last page of the report. No wonder Scofield hadn't let me see that page. Leslie's death had allowed Viola to move from being the financial officer to being the CEO of Miracle Foods. That was a motive for murder!

I found it hard to concentrate on interviewing Elena and Troy more and was glad when Scofield texted me that they weren't needed for further questioning.

***

An hour later, Viola strutted out of the police station with Mendel following her like a dog on a leash. Scofield and Western waved me into the interview room.

"Let's start with the little stuff. The DA is happy. He agreed with me that Seth Evers could be charged with abetting Wendell's crimes, but the next six months of rehab will be a much harsher punishment than jail time for his foolishness." Western winked at Scofield. "Your turn now."

"Okay. Jim pled guilty at the arraignment because the DA had agreed to not charge him with abetting Leslie's attempted murder while she was in the hospital." She shook her head. "The DA would have dropped the latter charge no matter what. He was eager to close the cases against the Jacksons and let the Feds put Jim away for years with no more work on our part." She sighed. "The sad part is Jim Jackson is not a bad man. Just a weak one struggling to survive in the competitive field of biotechnology."

I couldn't wait any longer. "Enough details. What about Viola and Mendel? Why didn't Viola give you a copy of Leslie's report at the start of the investigation?"

"She didn't have a signed copy." Western winked at me. "Remember how you thought Viola was looking for something besides the personnel reports in those three boxes Leslie took home?"

"Oh, she was looking for Leslie's signed report?"

Scofield cleared her throat without coughing. "The copy Viola had contained only the first five points. Evidently Leslie had hinted there would be a sixth point—the one which appointed Viola CEO of Miracle Foods if Leslie died—but hadn't shown it to Viola."

Western whistled. "I'm surprised. You haven't asked the key question—was it Mendel or Wendell who cut the brake lines on Leslie's car?"

"Well?"

"We'll never know for sure but Viola provided Mendel with an alibi. She claimed that Mendel arrived at her house last Monday at supper time. Leslie had just forced him to initial the sixth point on her report." Scofield pushed the page toward me. "Evidently Leslie had told him she wanted complete control of Miracle Foods. She reasoned that Miracle Foods had morphed from the brew pub she owned when they married and..."

Western stood and walked around the table slowly. "We think she also told him she was filing for a divorce, but neither Viola or Mendel would admit that, even after a lot of questioning."

Scofield didn't cough during the interruption. "Okay. The important point is Mendel claims he stayed Monday night at Viola's house. They both claimed he left for Reno at seven Tuesday morning—the day you arrived at Miracle Foods. Viola's son confirmed that Mendel ate supper with him and his mother on Monday night but couldn't say whether Mendel stayed all night."

I was trying to soak in all the details. "So, they're claiming Wendell was the only one at the Lopez house Monday night and hence had to be the one who cut the brake lines?" I studied the page with the sixth point that now made Viola the CEO of Miracle Foods and Mendel the chairman of the board. "Although Mendel initialed this, I don't think this document would withstand a court challenge."

"Yes, but he insisted he wouldn't challenge any part of the document. That's not consistent with what Seth claimed Wendell told him, but today Mendel said that giving Viola responsibility for Miracle Foods was a relief." Scofield sighed. "Makes you think."

Western sat down and hunched over the table. "The biggest screw up in all of this was Mendel and he faces no legal charges."

Scofield shook her head. "But he suffered the biggest losses. He lost both his wife and son because he didn't listen to them over a period of years."

Western snickered. "But he's listening to Viola now."

I couldn't resist. "I wonder if Viola will check her brakes every time she gets in her car?"

Western guffawed so loudly, tears ran down his face. "Justice has been served." He put his hand on Scofield's shoulder. "I told the captain today that I'd accepted a position in the Colorado Patrol. This case made me realize I'm tired of investigating murder cases. Then Scofield can get the promotion she deserves when she becomes the sergeant heading the violent crimes division."

Scofield gave him a quick peck on his cheek. "He's being modest. His new job is a step-up. He'll be in charge of the executive security unit, which protects the governor and legislators. It's logical because he knows most of them." I saw a sparkle in her eyes that I'd not noticed before. "That means he won't be my supervisor and we can discover if we have a future together."

"I've decided I like working with smart women—like you, hired gun." Western pointed at me. "Now it's your choice of where we celebrate the end of this case. Just remember I don't eat fake meat."

***

I called Sanders when Bug and I stopped for a break on our way back to Albuquerque. He listened to my summation of the case and said, "How soon can you and Bug get to Washington? My boss wants to talk to you because you'll be my liaison when I need to transmit certain classified information from Brazil." He didn't pause long enough for me to answer. "Most of all, we need to plan our future together after Brazil."

It wasn't the most romantic offer I'd heard, but it indicated he'd accepted my limitations. *Let the games begin.*

THE END

THE SCIENCE BEHIND THE STORY

This murder mystery involves a new or at least expanding industry—the production of alternative meat products. These products are unappealing to some, the hope of the future for others, and a bit mysterious to everyone. Here are a few facts that may help you sort through the hype.

The ecological benefits of consuming less meat and obtaining proteins from alternate sources has been widely publicized (Center for Sustainable Systems, University of Michigan. 2020. *Carbon Footprint Factsheet*. Pub. No CSS09h-05). For example, the production of a pound of most meat alternatives creates a smaller carbon footprints (i.e., releases less greenhouse gases, including carbon dioxide and methane) and requires less water and energy than the production of a pound of beef. Note that the carbon footprint of producing cultured meat alternative during the experimental stage is much larger than what results from manufacturing the anticipated final products.

There are hundreds alternative meat products appearing on the market now. No one statement is true for all of them. Here are summaries of three types of these products.

Plant-based alternate meat products are designed for those who want to reduce meat consumption but crave the flavor, mouthfeel, and satiety produced by meat. Generally, the plant-based meat alternatives are highly processed and usually contain soy protein and/or pea protein with wheat gluten and other isolated proteins added to give the product meat-like chewiness and flavor. For example, leghemoglobin—a heme protein originally from soybean root nodules but now usually produced by yeast cultures—is added to give meat alternatives a bloody appearance when raw and a brown cooked appearance when heated (How safe are plant-base meat alternatives? *Food Technology* [Feb. 2021] pp. 50-3).

The combination of proteins in most plant-based meat products provides a complete array of amino acids similar to those that occur naturally in meat. The products are higher in beneficial fiber and generally lower in saturated fats than meat. The primary problem with these products is the allergenic nature of the soy, wheat, peanut, and tree nut proteins that compose meat alternatives. This makes labeling of these products important. However, a number of consumers find the complicated formulations of these products and the long list of ingredients confusing.

Fermented proteins (e.g. tempeh, yogurts) have been used for thousands of years. Scientists discovered in the 1960s that certain fungi, which could be grown in huge vats, would produce fibrous strands of mycoproteins that could be arranged like muscle fibrils (Tiny organisms, huge potential. *Food Technology* [January 2021] pp. 51-7). Currently the most popular meat alternative made with mycoproteins is sold under the Quorn trademark.

Mycoprotein products have been found in clinical trials to be a good source of protein with a high satiety rating and the added benefits of being higher in fiber and lower in saturated fat than meat. The incidence of allergies to the protein produced by fungi appears to be low (Mycoprotein: Nutritional and health properties. *Nutrition Today* [January/February 2019] vol. 54, pp. 7-15). However, many of the mycoprotein products have an egg white binder and thus don't meet the criteria of vegans who eat no animal-based foods (Mimicking meat, seafood, and diary. *Food Technology* [February 2018] pp. 23-35).

Cultured meat, sometimes called "clean" or "cell-based" meat, is grown in a laboratory from cultured animal cells. This breakthrough in the application of biotechnology was first announced in 2013 but continues to be mainly experimental because of problems in the production of a juicy meat alternative with an acceptable mouth feel (Lab burger adds sizzle to bid for research funds. *Science* [9 August 2013] vol. 341, pp. 602-3).

This novel accurately depicts the production of cultured meat cells in large, closed, sterile vats and the formation of meat-like structures by using biological scaffolds (Is the future of meat animal-free? *Food Technology* [January 2018] pp 17-21). Unfortunately, many technical problems impacting the production of a meat-like texture at a reasonable cost remain. These products would have the same nutritional and allergenic properties as regular meat, although the fat content would depend on the additives used.

In the U.S., the United State Department of Agriculture (USDA) will be in charge of the manufacturing and labeling of cultured meat, but the Food and Drug Administration (FDA) will be responsible for ensuring cultured meat undergoes premarket safety tests (https://www.fda.gov/food/food-ingredients-packaging/food-made-cultured-animal-cells). The Singapore Food Agency approved the sale of cultured chicken bites in 2020 (Cell culture meat wins approval. *Science* [11 December 2020] vol. 370, pp. 1253).

I want to add a disclaimer. **Histamine intolerance** (called scombroid poisoning when due to ingestion of spoiled fish) is a real health problem (https://www.ncbi.nlm.nih.gov/pmc/articles/PMC3314039). However, problems with histamine build up in cultured fish cells have not been reported in the scientific literature and is a problem solely for Miracle Foods in this novel.

ABOUT THE AUTHOR

J. L. Greger is a biology professor and research administrator from the University of Wisconsin-Madison turned novelist. She lives in New Mexico with her dog. The pet therapy dog Bug in her mystery/thriller novels is based on her own Japanese Chin. She includes tidbits about science, the American Southwest, and her international travel experiences in her Science Traveler Series.

The Flu Is Coming. In the first book in the series, a woman scientist traces the spread of a deadly new flu virus among the frantic residents of a quarantined New Mexico community. (New Mexico/ Arizona Book Award Finalist)

Murder…A Way to Lose Weight. A dean in a medical school helps police discover whether an ambitious young "diet doctor," disgruntled patients, or old-timers with buried secrets are killers. (Winner of the 2016 Public Safety Writers Association contest and New Mexico/Arizona Book Award Finalist)

Ignore the Pain. A woman scientist learns too much about the coca trade and too little about a sexy new colleague while on a public health assignment in Bolivia.

Malignancy. A woman tries to escape the clutches of a drug lord and accepts a risky assignment as a science consultant in Cuba. (Winner of the 2015 Public Safety Writers Association contest)

I Saw You in Beirut. A woman's past provides clues for the extraction of a nuclear scientist from Iran. The author's experiences as a science and education consultant in the United Arab Emirates and Lebanon are featured.

Riddled with Clues. A homeless man and a woman scientist are targeted by drug gangs after she listens to the strange tale of an undercover drug agent about his war experiences. The memories of an actual CIA agent in Laos during the Vietnam War are featured. (New Mexico/Arizona Book Award Finalist)

A Pound of Flesh, Sorta. The police and a woman scientist can't decide whether a package contaminated with the bacteria that causes the bubonic plague is a plea for help by a whistleblower or a threat from gang leaders awaiting trial. (New Mexico/Arizona Book Award Finalist)

Dirty Holy Water. A woman who usually serves as a science consultant for the FBI learns there is a thin line between being a victim and being a villain when she becomes the chief suspect in a bizarre murder case.

Games for Couples. Did lethal compounds in a cultured meat product—meat made in a test tube—kill a man in a clinical trial? Or did the toxic competition between biotechnology companies and spite of battling couples cause his death?

http://www.jlgreger.com

J. L. Greger